To Kick

1066
KNIGHT
HARALDE

May it intrigue

you

John Wright

ISBN: 145362127X

ISBN-13: 9781453621271

1066
Knight
Haralde

JOHN WRIGHT

To Elaine my wife without whom
This book would not be written

FOREWORD

THOUGH THIS 1066 saga about two men of horse who cross over an historic barrier from the enlightened Silk Road to Dark Age Europe in 1066 of William the Conqueror's seems a romantic saga, it also touches on the themes of the myth of history, the mythology of heroes, arms and the man, religion, the science and medicine of the day and the birth of the code of chivalry.

In the previous novel *1066 The Healer*, Riennes de Montford arrives in Normandy and England from the East a trained surgeon at a time when the best medicine in Europe used bleeding, leeches and magic potions to cure the sick. He and his brother, an Eastern-trained trader and agriculturalist, trek across Britannia using their Eastern knowledge to help people and to aid them in their quest to recover a Longshield fiefdom in Wales.

In *1066 Knight Haralde*, the two have regained their family fiefdom but now face the task of winning the support of the serfs who traditionally shun foreigners. Rhys of Gwent, the best longbow man in northern Wales, refuses as a free man to even pay any taxes or fealty to Lord Haralde.

Thanks goes to Chris Lewis, editor of the Victoria County of Sussex and reader in history at the Institute of Historical Research, University of London; John Clark, curator at the Museum of London for an insight into the cunning of William the Conqueror, and Prof. Frederick Suppe of Ball State University, Indiana, for his background about Welsh lords and family life.

1066
KNIGHT
HARALDE

BY
JOHN WRIGHT

chapter 1

Something foreign is but only something new.

A LARGE BLACK BIRD ruffled the scarce cover of leaves to land on the upper branches of a tree. So shiny black was the raven, the tips of his feathers flashed silver in the sun.

The bird bounced to a roost, danced sideways then cast stark eyes downward to the ground, looking for a morsel, and if not that, anything that might be a curiosity. For a raven, known as a thief and trickster by the Welsh, loves curiosities.

He had landed at this particular spot because of the small spring and stream that leaked from it. Always, life came to this spot to drink and sometimes death followed that life, and what was left he would partake of.

The curiosity first came as a sound. He cocked his head sideways as he heard the heavy grunting of some animal and the heavy clump, clump of its feet. Then he saw an indiscernible shadow coming down through a passageway cast in darkness by the heavy forest canopy.

It was a humped six legged, bent over, breathing heavily, tripping sometimes over forest twig traps. The bird cocked his head the other way, as if to use a better eye, and the shape materialized into the light of the clearing as two creatures.

A man it was, barefoot, dressed in a patchwork of browns, greens and wine colors. He seemed to materialize in such terra cotta cloth out of the background of the forest. On a belt at his side bumped a quiver full of arrows. The man was staggering a bit under the weight of another creature on its back; a dead deer whose head and feet flopped back and forth, its throat cut so that blood ran down the man's back. The man also carried a straight staff, no, a stave, an unstrung bow.

The bird danced to one side, then to the other as the man came fully into the bright clearing to drop his burden by the stream, and to drop himself to drink.

The raven cawed once, then twice.

Rhys, the wild forester from Gwent, raised his dripping head out of the spring and jumped to his feet. In a flurry, he strung his bow, made it taut.

The longbow man looked around for the disturbance, then looked up at a movement. The raven cackled.

Rhys smiled slyly, then put finger to lips: "Shhhh!"

When the bird cacked again, Rhys picked up a stone and flung it. The bird leaped skyward, turned and flew off in a series of raucous 'caws'.

"And say naught to no one," Rhys shouted his merriment, laughing at the bird not to bear witness to anyone over his nefarious poaching activities.

Everyone knew ravens spread mischief in communities by telling tales of what they saw. Folklore belief in these things was embedded deep in him.

He dunked hands into a small stream pool to wash away the blood.

He must hurry with his kill to feed his two children now hidden away in a shepherd's abandoned lean-to on the slate slope of a nearby mountain.

Rhys lived off the bounty of forests, did so as a free man. He was regarded the best archer and hunter with a long bow in northern Cymru. The forest provided all he needed for him and his children.

He had fled to the forests after a tragedy befell him early in life at the hand of a ruthless Welsh lord. He refused to pay any loyalty, tax or geld to any lord or manor.

He could find no other way to live, although he worried deeply about long absences away from his children. He feared sudden illness befalling one or both while he was away.

He stood up, looked at his kill, a young deer, and was disturbed.

He looked skyward at the retreating black flapping bird as it jigged towards the horizon.

And whisper naught into the ears of those foreigners, he mused. They will have at me now that their troubles are over.

Recently, two young lords had appeared to claim the Longshield fiefdom where Rhys poached. Held by Lady Saran Longshield these many years after the political murder of her husband Steorm, one of the young lords turned out to be her long lost son, believed drowned off a south Wales beach ten years ago.

Haralde Longshield and his brother Riennes de Montford had arrived out of the far East, out of the mists of time and place. They had caught him poaching the king's deer on their arrival just two weeks ago.

Instead of punishing him, they had stood aside, allowed him to take his stolen game when they learned it was to feed his children. They petitioned him for any of his surplus venison be dropped off at the Longshield stronghold.

They disputed his claim of that of a free man. They chided, calling him the Fremen, a plural state that just could not exist in all Britannia. However, they let him pass. No uchelwyr, no overbearing Welsh lords of power had ever allowed him this before.

In the weeks to follow, he found himself supplying wild game to the Longshield palisade impounded under siege by a Saxon bandit army. Aelfgar the Wild had declared he would overrun the wooden fortress, take Lady Saran to his bed and become the new lord of the land.

Under cover of night, he had visited the Longshields and was struck by the strength of character of the two young lords. Over the wall, he had bantered with them, joked how he was a free man on the outside while they chose to be prisoners inside. And they in turned chided him for being on the outside, and missing all the fun they were having inside.

In time, the two turned the fortunes of war around, killed Aelfgar and brought order to the upland mountain fiefdom.

How was it that these two foreigners who first unsettled him and the local peasantry in the fiefdoms of Neury and Wym now played upon his mind, his curiosity?

Rhys heard laughter way down the valley beyond the wooden wall of his forest. It was the sound of children running in and out through the heavy open gate of the stronghold. They were enjoying their freedom from fear and the near siege starvation they had suffered.

Rhys glowed inwardly over how the two lords had made light of their imprisonment, joking with him over the wall in an attempt to keep everyone's spirits up.

He had come to like from a respectful distance Haralde and his brother Riennes. How was it a Norman was Haralde's brother and what was he doing way up here a long way from his homeland? He had some kind of magical way of easing peoples' ills. They called him a healer, a mysterious myrdin. There was talk of his skill as a trained Eastern physician. Rhys had no idea of just where was this mysterious East.

Rhys heard heavy hoof beats and the huff, huff of rider and mount coming towards him. He unstrung his bow, heaved up his game and was about to flee back into the dark of the wood, when the horse stopped and stomped.

He pulled a bush aside. There immediately below Haralde had just ridden up on a hill on one of those heavy dark destriers he and his brother had ridden into Wales.

Rather than try Haralde's temper with another king's poached deer, Rhys let the cover fall back into place and he melted back into the safety of the greenery.

The Frisian spun on the spot, throwing up clods of earth, sticks and stones; round and round until it staggered, then squealed in protest and fatigue. Haralde Longshield, riding with his hands pointed skyward, guided his black horse through the manoeuvre only with his knees. The boy-man inside laughed with joy as he brought the animal to a halt.

He vaulted out of his saddle, landed both feet together and took up the beast's head. The black whinnied shrilly.

"Yes, yes my beauty," soothed Haralde, leaning his head against the horse's jaw and comforting him with a smoothing hand. "Rest. Rest. No more. A barrel of grain for thee this night."

Today, he was happy, light of heart. He had come to stop on a hill to look down at his family's fortress. People were out on the field in front, packing their belongings into wagons and drays, preparing to return home to begin spring plantings. Children shouted and played, dogs barked, mothers called out and men bellowed gruffly to bring order to all the confusion. He was aglow for the first time in his adult life. These were his people. This was his fiefdom. His soul swelled, the inheritance of land enriched his merchant mind. The going-home dream he suppressed as a boy kidnapped by Vikings and sold as a slave into a land beyond the Eastern sun had come into full bloom as a young man, at this moment, at the top of this hill.

Almost a year ago, he and his brother Riennes de Montford, a Norman also kidnapped with him as a boy, had escaped the bonds of their enslaved youth in servitude to the Ger Khan on the other side of the world to finally as young men reach this his home and family. Both were exhausted and tainted by the violence of their lives as experienced horse warriors. They sought only peace and the quiet resumption of their lost lives as boys. However, violence again awaited them in Wales. He returned here to find his father dead, yea but his mother alive and a rebel army hammering at the gate of the family redoubt to carry her off. Even during the emotional embrace of a mother re-united with a son thought long dead, a usurper attempted to burn down the wooden gate and seize the Longshield fiefdom of Neury and Wym for himself.

Verily, no time was there for his mother Saran to cleave to her son. From boy to man, the role of thegn of this land was pressed upon him immediately. Within days of his arrival, he had to fight to save his mother and his dream.

Now, for a moment atop this hill with this big animal, he had a chance to breathe freely, to revel in his arrival home, to savour the memories of his childhood here, to grieve over the loss of his father.

There. There was his Riennes coming out the gate with a group of men bearing stretchers of two final enemy bodies bound for burial in the killing field in front of the fortress. His people called him The Healer. He was a great physician, probably unbeknownst to all of Wales and Britannia. His brother Riennes had attended to stitching up open battle wounds, setting broken bones and attending to general siege sicknesses. They had their own leech, one with the healing touch so powerful they spoke of him in open admiration.

Unbeknownst to them however, he had also spent nights opening and probing into the bodies of the brigand dead in his morbid interest into the internal workings of the human curiosity. So superstitious, so ignorant were his people that if they ever discovered this, they would burn him at the stake for a warlock.

Oh, how much he loved that man here and now, not a brother by blood but by the bond of suffering, surviving and even prospering together for 10 years in a far Silk Road kingdom near the Hindu Kush mountains. Having journeyed for almost a year across deserts and seas, Riennes had traveled with him across Britannia in support of his claim as the thegn of Neury and Wym in the wild upland March frontier between Wales and Britannia.

The horse rumbled. "There, there my lovely. We will get thee to your grain and grass. Just one moment more," murmured Haralde to the restless beast.

The Frisian, a heavy war horse, had been without grain for awhile, and only these last two days turned out to graze. Without proper feed, the horse's stamina was not what it should be. Haralde felt the high-spirited war horse needed a run none the less.

Haralde knew and loved horses. In fact, he had an affinity for the husbandry of all agricultural animals; sheep, goats, camels. He had been raised with horse from a boy to manhood. He knew them as a desert herd boy, a horse fighter, then as an owner of a herd of fine horses under the auspices of the Ger Khan, their desert king, ruler and master.

He had ridden through the night on horses in raiding forays, feeling even as he slept hunched over in the saddle every breath and step of the beast between his legs, had eaten horse, had drunk mare's milk and even their blood in times of thirst. As a boy raised on small desert horses, Haralde had acquired riding and fighting skills. He with his brother were taught to shoot under the horse's neck, to hide on one side with one foot hooked over a saddle pad, and at full speed, to strike the ground, bounce back up to the saddle again to end up backwards to loose arrows from short horn bows.

He could do none of these things with the heavier Frisian. These were not fast, nimble, shifty, quick-footed as desert horses. Yet, he needed to train this mount to accept sudden movements and turns needed in the hot work of battle. He had moved suddenly from one side to the other and hung way down to get his black to maintain balance with sudden weight shifts by him, the rider.

Haralde sighed, relinquished this moment to the pressing demands of his principa: duty, honour, service. He mounted up and thundered down the hill to join the commotion before the Longshield wooden stronghold, now his and Lady Saran's.

He hauled up at the bottom of the hill and beside a number of pits that had been dug into the slope. Days ago these pits succeeded as a major ruse to defeat a brigand army led by Aelfgar, an exiled Saxon rebel lord.

On a strategy, he and Riennes hid Munch, a farmer and a prime longbow man along with a host of the sons of farmers, themselves skilled archers, in these pits under wooden wattle doors covered in dirt, sticks and stones. Aelfgar's army swung past this slope and lined up in front of the stronghold, presenting unbeknownst its rear ranks to these hidden archers. On a signal, Munch and his young men erupted from their holes and launched a buzz of arrows upon the brigand rear while he, Riennes and Tyne of Cumraugh, his fortress commander, charged on horses out through the gate and crashed against Aelfgar's front ranks. Caught between the two forces, the brigand army broke and ran only to be ridden down by the stronghold's few horse soldiers. Haralde rode Aelfgar down and beheaded the rebel leader with his sharp, curved, Chinois kandos sword.

Haralde clicked his battle horse forward and the two ran at a crowd at the base of the hill. To flaunt his speed and skill, both pounded across the front gate and the watchers on the wall raised their hands and shouted their admiration.

However, his mount without his feed of grain had no bottom, no sand and began to falter. Haralde felt it through his knees.

People were moving around outside the gate, loading things on carts. Godfroi, the monk who had walked with them across Britannia on the bench of his dray, sat upon it again even though having swore an oath never to drive that machine again. The monk had stuffed the goods of a poor family into the back of his dray because they had no means to transport them back to their hovel.

An ox that Haralde pulled behind the very same cart across Britannia was in the traces. A cow he also brought grazed with his own farm animals on the plain before the wooden walls. Everywhere, there was the bright bark of laughter.

Haralde and Riennes had walked days before over the killing ground to check on the dead corps, amazed to find most had fallen to the longbow. Haralde was very impressed; armed men brought down by lowly serfs. Both bowmen themselves, they remarked how deadly these big Welsh bows were. Haralde saw something of significance in these weapons. He had ordered all brigand weapons gathered and stacked in a room, the beginnings of his private armory.

They found three brigands moaning, still alive. Haralde had made to pull out his dirk and put them down, but Riennes had put a staying hand on his arm. No, he said. This they had left behind in the kingdom of the Khan. Now was the time for mercy, here in their own lands amongst their own people. Thus, Riennes and the women of the village had nursed them. Two died, one made it. Tyne had said he would turn the survivor into one of his stronghold soldiers, or dead he would be anyway if he refused.

Haralde collected all the wattle coverings and nailed them to the outside fortress wall as war trophies. The farm boys were seen at times standing out there admiring them, their eyes full of their own death-dealing, manly deeds. Farmer boys they were no longer.

Owain, one of them but of a softer nature, declined to join his fellows outside. Munch had told Riennes and Haralde later that Owain's bow proved to be the more deadly of all of them. Yet, the boy wanted no truck with the killing anymore. In fact, Riennes told him Owain was showing an aptitude for nurturing. His brother now was mentoring the youth in medicine.

After the fight, the days had been spent in talking to those in the fortress from Neury and Wym. Haralde and Riennes wanted to set awhile. But nay, said his mother. The land was in turmoil. Their lords must be about amongst their people. Talk to them, let people see them and be instructed on what they must do, and more important, to be reassured there was no longer any danger and to begin their spring plantings.

Riennes and he were physically weary and gaunt from almost a year of voyaging and traveling from the other side of the world. Seldom had they had a proper meal in all that time. However, they agreed they would get out down to the Neury village at the River Clee ford.

Also, it was agreed Riennes would escort those from Wym now within the stronghold. Made lord of those lands by Bishop Odo, Regent of England, he was obliged to show himself and prepare them for an oath of vassalage on a special occasion sometime in the future. In a couple of days he would rejoin Haralde at Neury.

There was a pause after both had agreed to split up for a few days. They looked at each other. Another day in the future haunted them; mayhaps a parting of some permanence. It went unspoken but both knew Riennes would have to return to Normandy and pull out the man and his family who illegally occupied the Montford manor. The brothers had clashed with this interloper and his family before crossing over from Normandy to Britannia to begin their trek to Wales. Haralde joked, and promised Riennes a food feast to burst his belly for Lady Saran and Tyne had announced they wished to join in marriage in the month to come.

A group of farmers and youths with long wooden staves, unstrung longbows, came out the gate to greet Haralde. They laughed and some smirked as they watched their lord acting up. They yelled at him as he attempted a show by leaning way out to see if he could pluck a wildflower off the ground. His Frisian staggered sideways and Haralde fell off in a cloud of dust. The crowd of young men howled, and then slapped hands over their mouths. Haralde regained his seat, set an authoritative demeanor, settled his dignity and came huffing up to Riennes.

Riennes greeted him with one hand over his eyes. As Haralde dismounted, he peeked through his finger, and then let out a whistle of relief.

"T'is true then that sometimes an old man will act out the foolishness of youth," chided Riennes.

Haralde walked over to him and with both hands shoved him gently backwards and chided: "Give me one month here on our own ground and not even a fuzzy-cheeked lad will be able to keep up with me."

They half wrestled for a moment to knock the other off balance, then turned arms around each other's shoulder and looked at the stronghold and the spectacle of the people preparing to leave in a day.

"Now begins another road, do thee think?" asked Haralde in what his people regarded as their odd, foreign way of speaking.

"My dear, deeply do I believe thee are right," agreed Riennes. "And this time, by our own efforts, it will be a road of our making."

"Well said. And a smooth road it will be," agreed Haralde clapping him on the back.

"But first, something else brother."

"What Ren?"

"Harry. Your filth, it is an arrogance upon my sensibilities."

Haralde stared for a moment, incomprehensive. Riennes's parlance did that to him sometimes.

"Thee stink, my lord."

"Aaaah! And thee dare insult while upwind of me thusly Lord de Montford."

"I recommend a baptism, a cleansing."

They grinned at each other, Then Haralde: "The aqueduct!"

Riennes broke first, Haralde in pursuit, both laughing on the run towards an ancient broken Roman aqueduct that still partially delivered a stream of pure mountain water to the fortress.

Saran spun around, watching the blue cloth float about her, a gossamer flutterby. Blue silk it was called. Such a deep colour. And such a smooth, light, sexual feel to it.

She held a roll of it, enough to make a dress, no, a gown. She never knew such material existed. The only non-woolen clothing she had was of a kind of linen and it was the only long dress she wore. Her late husband Stoerm had brought it to her from London after old King Edward had ordered him to court. It might have been her husband had mentioned the material called silk then. She just couldn't remember.

A wedding gift from Riennes. He had brought it all the way in the back of the dray from London. One moment she fretted how she was to find something to wear when she and Tyne were to join as man and wife; another moment he was presenting her with a roll of this blue, saying it was his wedding gift to her.

How did he know to present it her, before the day they announced their joining? Her Riennes was so sensitive. She had noticed this from the beginning. In a thousand little ways a woman observes a man, she had discovered this of him. There was about him something, an unexplainable foresight.

The day Haralde had climbed up the fortress wall and revealed he was her son long lost, Riennes was in the background. She fainted into her son's arms. He carried her into the family donjon, the only stone keep in northern Cymru, and told her of how Riennes had saved his life so many times in growing up together in Eastern lands. In a scene that was being told even now across their fiefdom, Saran had walked out of the keep, across the yard to where Riennes waited, took him into her arms, kissed him full on the mouth and declared to all Riennes for all time was her second son.

Anyway, it was her's, and so much of it. No one would ever see a woman dressed like this again, not here. After years of projecting an outward male coldness as her armor, this soft, warm silk had uncovered the femaleness buried deep.

She turned on children's laughter coming through the arrow slit opening in her room high in the keep. She smiled at that wonderful sound. Yet, when it became a shriek and many more little voices joined in, she went to the opening and peered out.

Up on the wall catwalk, dirty-faced children were laughing, squealing, pointing. She glanced over to where they were pointing, then gasped, shocked. She stepped back, regained herself, stepped forward and took in the sight of her Haralde and Riennes.

The two young men were cavorting under the water streaming down from an aqueduct; a broken, leaking artifice left over from Roman times that fed water to what was then a one-storey officer's stone barrack, but which the Longshield family had improved to a three-storey keep. They were naked under where it leaked in spots along its length as it closed with the stronghold. The two were enjoying, bathing, splashing each other, pushing, yelling, grabbing in jest each for the other's maleness. It was the enjoying, the pleasure on their faces that disturbed her.

She turned to yell at the children to get off the wall when Tyne popped up beside the little ones. Her Hibernian lover took one look at his two lords, grabbed the children and turned them away from the wall. He yelled down and mothers came running. He handed them down one at a time. They were not supposed to be on the wall in the first place.

She turned back, then turned her face away for a moment as Haralde and Riennes showed the full moon of their white asses. They walked a short distance up the grassy slope to a small knoll open to the sun, sat down naked, crossed their legs, put their hands on their knees and sat immobile for a good while.

She had seen them do this disturbing thing before, sit like this for a long time, quiet, reflective, as if praying. For everyone in the fortress motte and bailey, unsettling it was, foreign. As one, they acted as proper protective and strong lords, but as two, they performed oddities that did not conform to local customs.

Another foreign thing: the first night they ate together, they thanked her for their food by briefly bobbing their heads with prayer hands brought to their foreheads. It disturbed everyone. The people went round the common, whispered to each other about these foreign new lords. They did not like it. Yet, after awhile, she did. It began to touch her as a sacred thing. She felt the act appreciated the nature of food as something more than just sustenance.

But this? "My God!" she exhorted.

She heard Tyne come clattering up the stairs. Her door banged open and he barged in.

"Woman! Something terrible!" It spluttered from him like spit. "My Lord Haralde, your son, Lord Riennes! They are . . . . not like men! They are . . . . !"

"Quiet! Quiet! Do not shout." She took his hands in hers and led him to their large straw pallet bed and sat down. "I know. I saw them just now."

"I swore an oath of loyalty to them, to that pair of . . . . how must one say this . . . . I cannae stay here. You cannae stay here also. We must leave."

"Quiet. I know. There must be some reason for this."

"What? Skin naked. And dancing together like . . . . two wenches!"

She suddenly grinned, laughed and put her hand over her mouth.

"What!"

"So funny you looked when you said that."

He stood there, his mouth open over her odd reaction. Then it clapped shut, he put his fists on his hips and glared at her.

She put her hand up and got her laughter under control.

"You know it must not be," she said. "It was not such when you charged together and broke the brigand line. It was not such when we worked together and planned and were successful through their courage and their leadership. Did you see this when you all went, gathered up all the bodies, stripped them, and buried them?"

Tyne stood glaring at her, softened, then blinked his eyes and pondered what she said. Then: "No."

"I will talk with Haralde. A reason for this is simple, sure am I," she said leading him out of their chamber and directing him back down the stairs. He had many tasks yet to perform, as the common was all assembling baggage to return to farms and fields of home.

He left and she sat down to wait. Patience was her armor, one that had served her well. She spread the blue silk over her knees and began to sew.

In an hour, she heard her son downstairs, yelling for a woman, a wench, a maid to bring him food, water, more forthright, ale which he claimed all had been hiding from him, their lord who now thirsted and hungered.

"And if there be no food nor drink, I will settle for the wench," he roared. There was a titter of muffled laughter from the slave women who were fixing food in a room adjacent to the family room. Their mirth also came from his fractured Welsh, whereby he had demanded a woman on his food.

She went out to the top of the stairs and called his attention. "Stop yelling. Food and drink will be brought forth to my lord in good time. Haralde. Come and talk to me."

Haralde bounced up the stairs, taking them two at a time.

He followed her into her room, took note of the blue silk, and stroked the green silk shirt he himself wore tucked into a broad belt. His legs were bare. He carried his breeches and leg wrappings in his arm. She wondered if he was wearing anything under his shirt.

She stared at him a moment, so he stood still knowing she was going to be serious here.

"Uuhh . . . ."

He came over. "Thee are disturbed. What is it?"

"I saw you washing just now, you and Riennes. So did everyone here."

"Aaah," he said, as if understanding what she was intending, but then knitting his brow in doubt.

"Uh, think you not that it is unhealthy for a man to bath so?" she started. "Such exposes you to drafts and the ague . . . . you and Riennes. A Welsh lord does not do these things. And if he does, should he not do it alone?"

Haralde's hand pursed his chin. His eyes crinkled in puzzlement, tried to comprehend his mother's words.

When he didn't, she went on: "Who knows what spirits and dark forces are adrift out there. A wraith might catch you out, possess your sensibilities."

Haralde almost wanted to burst out laughing. His mama was lecturing him on his toilet habits, as if a little boy.

"Is there something I must know about you and Riennes?" she risked.

Comprehension lightened Haralde's face, and this time he did burst out laughing.

"I saw you two bathing, naked, pushing . . . . touching each other."

Haralde grinned, spread apart his strong, long legs and put his fists on his hips. With a glint of mirth in his eyes, he asked: "Mama. Having glimpsed what thee did, do thee not think your son a fine figure of a man?"

"Do not joke with me Harry. I have wiped the shit from your ass and the snot from your nose and vomit when sick. I nursed you as a child and know your body intimately. It is not what I asked."

Haralde nodded his head, gathered Saran up in arms, sat her down on a bench and set out to explain.

"Mama. I know what thee mean. It is not intimate, not in the way thee think. It is our way," he started.

"You have strange ways. We do not know if we agree with them. Your speech sometimes causes a confusion in our heads. I am learning mind you. You are improving each day when we talk."

Haralde kneeled down so that he could look level into his mama's eyes.

"First off, understand where we come from, people bathe, cleanse themselves, and even perfume themselves. It is an act of pleasure, and a necessity of good health, we believe."

"It is not healthy to bath often. Your father never . . . ."

"Second, Riennes and I share the water bond."

That stopped her. She blinked, puzzled.

"Mama. Riennes and I as two little boys with no sponsors, no one to protect us, almost died from thirst and from sickness many times. We survived out of necessity. We swore to each other to share water one with the other, even if there was only enough for one. In that way are we here today."

And Haralde began a discourse of their 10 years in exile, of being little boys, slaves, beaten, lost runaways, life in the desert, of harsh overseers, life amongst fighting men, living on little food.

"We are sand brothers. There were times we dug holes in the sand, covered ourselves with the sand against the coming cold of night, wrapped ourselves in each other's body to share our heat and shivered through the night to make it to another day. Always, we dreamed of finding water to moisten our swollen tongues."

He told her other stories, of stealing not coin but water from the prized livestock of a band of desert nomads they were slaves of.

As his years of kidnapped and exile unfolded, tears began to form in her eyes, and a mother's pain grew in her breast. She was not there for him when he needed her.

"We swore to share all, to protect each other or die trying. To this day . . . ." Haralde was cut short as his mama fell into his arms. His shoulder muffled her tears and crying.

"No more. Tell me your stories later, but no more of this," she said, pulling her head back and wiping away her tears. "I understand."

"We stink in here, behind these walls and being under siege," Haralde went on. "Then all morning over the dead bodies, stripping off their leathers, their weapons, and burying the dead. So soaked in sweat and things. The sound of water tumbling from the aqueduct . . . . it was too much. We just ran to it."

"As my boys that you still are. No more," she insisted taking his face in both her hands and kissing his cheeks.

"Mama. Listen to me and understand this. Riennes knows things; about cuts, wounds, fevers, hurts, even to the workings of the body inside. He feels we all here in the stronghold must bath more. He links it to healthy. Mama. If Riennes asks after thee, how thee are feeling or suggest things to make thee feel better, do such. He has taken instruction in such matters from a very great healer. And I have seen him do things thee would not believe mama."

She nodded her head. "Yes. Yes. Thus I will."

"And mama, if anyone so much as puts a bad tongue on Riennes in your company, thee must not tell me."

She shook her no, that she would not, but her expression asked why.

"Because I will fall upon him or her, without compunction, without regret, without anger. I will kill them. It will just simply be done."

chapter 2

A wica can only bewitch
A guilty soul of the beguiled.

"**N**ow gather your people. I will leave thee to them and will meet thee in Neury," agreed Riennes.

Haralde nodded yes, mounted up, swung away and plunged into the host of carts and animals and bawling livestock and children that were his.

Munch led his young men with him out in front of the host, a van to protect any errant attack by remnants of the rebel host. Their bow strings were taut notching arrows.

All were anxious for home, concerned for families and farms in Wym. Munch was a spinster with two sons. He had sent his two sons to hide with an uncle and aunt in Neury when the brigands struck. He had an obligation, made long ago to Haralde's father, Stoerm Longshield, to protect Lady Saran when the lord was away, so had gone to the stronghold to stand with her against the rabble. Grateful he was that Longshield had returned, albeit a younger unsettling version of Stoerm, he thought. A new kind of Longshield, odd, foreign, strange and with ideas that unsettled.

"How will your sons know to return?" Riennes asked as he mounted and walked beside the group. They wanted to stay together for the trek into neighboring Wym.

Riennes would stay one night with Munch as Wym had no stone or wooden manor motte nor bailey stronghold of its own. Wym was a much flatter country, more given over to farming.

"By the time we reach Neury, the word will have gone before us. They will hear and be home soon enough," smiled Munch. "I suspect Rhys may have already spread the word."

Rhys, the phantom Welsh Fremen, who with his longbow had supplied deer, fish and other meats to the stronghold during Aelfgar's siege, was known by every man as a forest spirit; a free man who no one dared to tame. Often Haralde and Riennes would see out of the corner of their eyes a sort of common silence by the local men whenever the two lords would ask why they would not bring Rhys in before them.

They talked with their people as they entered the forest and headed down the old Roman road. Riennes sidled up to his young men, and listened to their excited adventures about the fight. Owain said nothing of it. Killing was not a thing to talk about. Riennes liked Owain. It seemed the boy carried himself more a man now.

The host crossed the ford at Neury, carts bumping over rocks, spray flying from horses, small livestock heaved up bawling and snorting into the carts, children laughing and some swimming and parents holding onto them as they did, fearing they might be swept away.

Riennes, mid-stream, felt a sudden warming flood over him. Something important was about to happen, something that made him feel good inside. He leaned down, fished up a child splashing in one of the pools as the current began to carry it away. He hauled up a drenched duckling, a little girl soaking wet. "Well done wee one," he said of her swimming effort. "Thee swim as good as a duck." About to bawl, the little girl forgot her fear as Riennes's words made a game of her momentary terror.

He handed her to the concerned mother wading over to him against the heavy current. He wondered if it was the joy of the playing children that made him feel as he did.

Haralde splashed by him. "We need to pile these rocks up and rebuild a bridge once here," he shouted, already planning. Riennes nodded and pointed upstream. Men were leaving fish weirs, splashing their way towards them.

Men stood in front of a big stone house, some with cups in their hand, waving, some running to assist, and yelling: "Is it over? Are they gone?" As they grabbed harnesses and reins and unloaded livestock, they were told in whispers what had happened, and more important, pointed to the two giant young men approaching on heavy war horses.

"Who are thee?" demanded Haralde of these new men as he and Riennes came up to them.

Five of them snatched off their grease-stained caps, and bowed quickly. The fishers came crowding in and followed their example. Haralde leaned down, creaking in the saddle.

"Thee. Your name!" He pointed to one fellow, who started quaking.

"Aled, sir. And these are all men of Neury." His eyes darted around the crowd and the men all nodded their heads, confused.

"Do thee know me?" asked Haralde who dismounted and walked into them. They parted, heads down, bobbing and not knowing why they acted obedient.

Then: "Oh my God! He looks like . . . . ," someone blurted out. Haralde moved immediately in his direction and came to an old man.

"Yes. Thee are?"

"Geraint."

"Do thee know me? Do thee remember me?"

The old man's rheumy eyes went over his face. "You look like our . . . . Lord Longshield. Nay, but he is gone, yet . . . . and you speak as an outlander, foreign."

"Thee are right master Geraint. I am Lord Longshield."

Immediately, the men went down on their knees and bowed their heads, trembling. A ghost was amongst them?

Haralde laughed, put his hands on the old man and raised him up. "Up everyone. There will be time enough for this. Geraint. I am Haralde. I . . . ."

"The boy!" exclaimed Geraint. "The boy Haralde! You look like him. I remember. But you are to be dead these many more years!"

"Hear me." Haralde's voice was a command. "I am that boy. I am my father's son. Lady Saran is my mother. I did not drown many years ago. I was carried off. Thee will learn later of me. Listen. Aelfgar and his men are no more. We have killed them all."

Haralde walked around them, looking at each whose eyes slid off his and tried to hide. They were fearful.

"No. Look at me. I am your lord. Thee will look at me. Accept this. And there will be no fear here. Thee are mine, my vassals, but I will treat thee all as men. I will learn the names of each and every of thee as soon as I can. But I demand immediate obedience, do thee understand?"

They all bobbed their heads, mumbled, were tongue tied, but a gleam, a smile began to cross their faces. Their lord. Order was coming. Protection. Wait. Maybe he was a cruel one, a heavy rock to bear.

"And this is my brother." He introduced Riennes. And Riennes instinctively did the right thing. He dismounted and also walked amongst them, looking them directly in the eye, nodding here and there. He then went to Geraint, sensing this was a senior of the community. "Master Geraint. I also speak foreign. I am of the Frankland. Yet, I will soon speak well in your tongue. I am to be one among thee."

Haralde spoke in Welsh slowly, explaining Riennes was the overlord of Wym, and was on his way to meet the people there.

The men started smiling and bobbing their heads in understanding. They took note of how Haralde and Riennes treated them.

"In my absence, thee will obey Lord de Montford in all things of Neury and Wym," instructed Haralde as he took up the reins of his horse

The carts and the people with their livestock passed them and fanned out through the trees, down lane ways, over fields. Through the trees Haralde could see them heading to other vills and clusters of wooden huts.

It was quiet in the fields. There was no sound of tilling, no bawling of oxen, of babies, no barking of dogs, and no dust of activity in the air as in other villages they had seen.

He wanted to know why no one was afield working. They told him all had been hiding. He instructed the men to go out and tell all to come forth, to get to work, that all of Neury should be busy. The men nodded and started running towards those villages.

"Master Geraint. What is this house?" asked Haralde looking at the big, two-storied stone building. "I seem to remember this, only smaller?"

The house was only the second in the whole fiefdom built of stone. It had a foreign aspect to it.

As Haralde and Riennes approached with the horses at their back, they saw an open space on a stone verandah, cups on trestle tables and stools. The house had a stone outbuilding behind, a stone fence and a garden and a dovecote noisy with birds. Because wood was plentiful, it was unusual to see a stone building here.

Riennes felt his senses sharpen as he approached with Haralde, Geraint and a few other men. He sensed amongst the men a kind of discomfort, ambivalence and they hung back.

"Haralde!" Riennes whispered a low sharp warning, that he was feeling something. Haralde nodded slightly. Riennes looked about cautious, as if something or someone was lurking hereabouts. Then, an intake of breath from Haralde made him turn.

A woman stepped out the doorway holding the hand of a small boy.

"I am Magda, my lords. Welcome to my house and to your lands," She said in Welsh. She had heard Haralde and Riennes approaching with the men from the river.

She cast her eyes down, pulled her son to a kneeling position, and there, trembled. She was afraid.

To Riennes, it was as if the light had changed when she stepped out, or as the wind had ceased to whisper. He was turned about. He had expected an assailant, an ambush, but rather it was about her. She was the good feeling he had coming across the river. She was no peasant. She was a woman's woman. More than that, she was a presence. First, her beauty hit him. Her full body rounded through even her rough woolen dress. She had long black hair to the small of her back. He felt an instant sexual pull towards her. Then more. A powerful spirituality hit him. It was a strong feeling inside him, this important part of her. It emanated from her. His sensibilities were all thrown ahoo. No one had ever had this effect on him in all his life.

Haralde's senses were more carnal. He moved towards her, had to touch her, took her hand and lifted her up.

"Thank thee mistress Magda. Rise. Tremble not so. No harm is here. And who is this youngster? Your son?"

"Yes my Lord Longshield." She turned and pulled her son forward. "He is Orim ap Odard."

Haralde put his hand under the lad's jaw and turned his face up to appraise him better. Riennes noticed a slight movement of Magda's hand towards her bodice. He knew at that instance she had a dirk within the folds of her clout. He stepped up beside Haralde, hand moving slightly over his own dirk.

"How old are thee Orim?" Haralde asked calmly.

"Almost eight of years." . . . . Then mimicking his mother . . . . "my lord."

"Thee are not afraid, are thee boy?"

He glanced at his mother. Something passed between them.

He turned back to Haralde, a look of intelligence, and courage flaring in his eyes.

"No my lord," he challenged Haralde.

"Good. We will be friends then," he said putting his hand lightly on that of Riennes's which hovered over the dagger. "Do thee know how to ride horses?"

"No my lord."

"Then we will see that thee will," and in a sudden move, Haralde hauled the boy off his feet, carried him back and lifted him into the saddle of his black.

The boy stiffened, his breath caught in his throat but before he could cry out, he was settled into Haralde's saddle. The boy instantly felt the heat of the large animal between his legs, and was startled by that, then exhilarated.

Magda made as to intercede, hand plunging into her clothing.

Riennes gently placed a restraining hand on her arm. She jerked her eyes up to him. The dark eyes flared at him. They were terrified. Then, they connected, Riennes and Magda. The full beauty of her rounded face, of her dark eyes, black eyebrows, mouth, and rich lips captured him. Her long black hair to her waist shone black-blue like a raven's wing. Her skin was tawny from being out in the sun. Her beauty was her own, original, captivating. Eyes locked with eyes instantly soothed her fear for her son's safety. Riennes felt a slight faintness. She was as he. They knew instantly something of each other. Yet neither could plumb the depths of the other. It was as if they canceled out each other, and were normal one with the other.

Never in all the recent years could he not plumb a man or woman's character, or sense feelings. Riennes was known as a prescient only to his brother. He was one who had the gift of a seer, who sensed the moments or events to come that coalesced just beyond his senses. She too was of his cult. He knew that instantly. And because it was so, she denied him any access to her character, and just as important, to her future. She was one of the first he had ever met who denied him that. He was confused. Therefore, he was intrigued.

Her hand eased slowly out of her clothing, empty. Riennes took a step back.

"And my companion before thee is Lord Riennes de Montford," said Haralde from the horse as he gauged the boy's reaction over the quick lift from verandah to saddle. The boy was still frightened. Yet, his intelligence controlled his fear. Good.

"Mistress Magda, I greet thee," Riennes smiled lightly. He held out his hand to take hers, but she refused. He hungered to hold her hand, to make contact. Her head dropped again in stiff submission.

"Magda. Riennes is the new overseer of Wym. He is a Frank nobleman, and my companion," Haralde explained as he showed Orim the reins of the horse and what they did. "As he will be here now, I would be much pleased if thee speak in Saxon to him, a language he is more familiar with, until his tongue can better the Welsh."

Magda would not look up.

She said softly: *"Beal sire, seingnor de Montford, salu a Neury e Wym".*

If Riennes wondered why he and Haralde had been treating Magda with such deference compared to the others, they knew by that reply. A woman who knew three languages and maybe more, was a singular person for a churl here in Haralde's Neury.

Haralde's eyes brightened at her use of Norman. "I think Mistress Magda just welcomed thee, my lord."

"Thee speak Frankish?" Riennes inquired.

Magda refused to look up. "No my lord. My husband did. He was from across the northern seas, from near your country. I understand some of it, can speak a little of it." Haralde looked at beautiful Magda and then at Riennes, then it crossed his mind. He will want to come often and talk to her then. A sudden spark of jealousy shamed him.

He lifted Orim from the horse and put him to ground. Orim scrambled for his mother and fled into her arms.

"And Odard? That be your husband? Is he about?" asked Haralde casually.

"My husband has been dead these many years," she answered flatly, then raised her head, glared at them and in an accusatory tone, added: "Slain before my eyes right where you stand."

Riennes caught her eyes flick to the two kandos swords over their backs, to the daggers in their belts and knew that vindictive reply was leveled at both of them. Then she stared downward again.

"Thee need not tremble so Magda. Your lord holds no menace for thee or anyone in Neury," assured Haralde to smooth her fright so that he might better appraise her.

Riennes looked at the benches around her verandah and the hand-made wooden cups on the trestle table. He glanced back at the outbuilding behind her garden. There were chickens scratching around. He heard pigs and sheep behind in her fenced-off toft. His eyes settled immediately on bunches of herbs and roots and leaves drying on a rack.

"Did thee and your husband farm here? What rent or tax did thee pay to my father?" Haralde delved in trying to find out what rent or tax obligation he held Magda in thrall.

"Your father brought Odard here from Britanny and we were enfeofed to him not by tax but by an oath of special service to your family," she answered straight and honest.

"What kind of service?" asked Haralde.

"He was of the Old Religion. He was a renowned healer."

Haralde's eyes shot briefly to Riennes.

"Your house? It seems to me it was smaller, if I remember right?"

Magda nodded yes. "It was a stone building in ruins. My husband said it was of the long-ago design, that it must have been a manor or a house of a Roman military leader. He rebuilt it to our desires using local stone and timber," she explained.

He spoke to change the subject. "Without a husband, what do thee do here Magda?"

She was silent for a moment. Then: "I make things men want. I sell needs to people here."

Haralde and Riennes glanced at each other.

"And what do men want of thee?" asked Haralde. His merchant nature was up but he also as lord was trying to establish in his mind where Magda should be in the future order of things.

Magda turned to her son. A silent understanding passed between them. Orim turned, and darted as little boys do through the door and into the dark interior of their stone house.

Haralde slowly shook his head in wonder as he looked up to the second storey of the house and along its stone walls. Architect from the Middle Sea here? A Roman house here was one thing, but one of this size surprised Haralde.

Riennes was aware of a buzz behind him amongst the group of men. They were gossiping. Their tongues talked wicked. At that moment, Godfroi came up to them, and they pulled him into their midst, talked low, strong words, and pointed to Haralde, Riennes and Magda.

Orim came bounding out with an earthen jug and two wooden cups. He poured an amber fluid into the vessels and in agitation, offered each to Haralde and Riennes.

Haralde lifted and sniffed. His eyes widened. "By the Khan's grace! Ale?"

Riennes flicked a tongue lightly into it. He smiled. "And good too." And sipped.

Haralde sipped, then realized he had a thirst, drank deep, and enjoyed slaking that thirst.

"Riennes! What say thee?"

"Harry. The same as thee! The best I have ever tasted in this land!"

The two held out their cups for another sample. Orim poured them just half a cup this time. Haralde roared out at that, enjoying the boy's husbandry of his mother's offering.

They bumped cups and drank again.

"Aaaah!" Haralde wiped his lips with a finger and licked it. "Thee make this?"

She bobbed her head yes.

"And thee sell this?"

"Nay my lord. There is no money here. I trade things for it, eggs, meat, a hen, some wood, sometimes a man or woman's labour."

"Not this time," remarked Haralde, who dug into his clothing and pulled out a pence, and gave it to Orim. Riennes smiled, also found a coin and gave it to Orim.

The boy looked down into his hand with wonder, and with wide eyes looked up to Magda, then gave it up to her.

She looked at the coins, then at the two men.

For one moment, her face softened, turned beautiful, thought Riennes.

"However, if no one pays thee, I wish to know how thee will pay your tax or a rent for this house to your lord?" asked Haralde.

Magda shook her head. This was it. This was what she feared; she and her son turned out, to live in some nearby hovel. "I do not my lord. Not since your father's death have I been asked. Lady Saran has asked naught of me."

"Hmm." Haralde offered his cup to Orim again, was given a small draught again, sipped it, smacked his lips, and then gave to Magda his decree.

"From this day forth, a keg of your ale will be delivered to me, your lord, to my household each month as your due. Does that meet with your understanding Magda?"

"It will be a burden for my son and I, but I will abide it," she answered.

It was his right, and she knew it. Secretly, she was glad this would be all he demanded. It might at last establish her place in this male community that shunned her. She now would pay for her place here and no one could whisper different behind her back. Besides, she thought as she squeezed in her palm the first two pence she had seen naught for so long, there might be more coin to be had out of her new circumstances.

Riennes smiled over her insight. He felt a keg of ale would be nothing to her.

"And is this what thee mean by thee sell things men want," Riennes asked coyly.

"Yes my lord."

"And of the things people here need?" he went on.

"I sell them potions and curatives and charms," she answered.

Riennes head turned thusly again to the plants drying on the rack. Here was a thing of great interest to him.

"My lords. I would speak with you?" interrupted Godfroi who had come up from behind them. They turned to see the monk standing in front of the group of men. They all hung back, not wanting to come close to the house.

Haralde and Riennes went to their spiritual advisor. Godfroi had been assigned to them as their religious confrere in these heathen lands. However, Haralde and Riennes suspected he had been assigned to them by the court of King William as a spy, to report back to abbot Lanfranc, William's spiritual counselor who accused the two lordships as heretics. The two young men bent their heads to him as he wanted to talk privately.

"Your men. My lords, they want me to warn you . . . . to come away from that house, and her," finished Godfroi who bristled at Magda and her son in a most incriminating way.

Haralde's face was immutable. "What means this monk?"

"Your men, they say you should stay a distance away, that you risk coming under her spell, that she has the power to gain control of you, their lord," answered Godfroi in a tone of dread.

Haralde gazed into the monk's face trying to fathom his meaning, then looked at the crowd of men, faces fearful. Riennes looked at Magda, her son, then back at the men.

Haralde roughly grabbed Godfroi by one arm, Riennes the other, and they moved him a way to one side under a great elm.

"What nonsense be this?" Haralde demanded.

"They say she is a woman who can control your soul. They say she goes through the night gathering spirits, that she is a mummer, a worshiper of trees and wild animals. People here say she is seen attending a fire up in the mountain with others, conjuring things. She is a foreigner, a granddaughter of a Pict druid priestess from the north who follows the old pagan ways."

Godfroi glared over his lord's shoulder at Magda. "They believe she is a wicked priestess of the dark. People say they have seen a black cat around her house at night."

"Who says this of my Neury?" demanded Haralde gruffly.

"The men do. They say two farmers, neighbors, have fought over her, and now are enemies to each other across their fences. She does that to the men here."

"What do the women here say of her," Riennes probed.

"I have not talked to any. The men say their women want them to stay away from her ales and mead drinks, but do nothing themselves because she is helpful to them during their women troubles, birthing times and family sicknesses."

"Fair monk, what do thee think?" asked Riennes softly.

"My lords. She is a slattern, a witche I believe," the monk spit out. "I believe she must be seized up, herself and her whelp and her house burned and purged of its dark alliance with the devil."

They stood silent under the trees for a moment. This was serious. It had to do with the peace of the community and that fell within Haralde's responsibility. Finally he stirred, an appealing look cast at Riennes. It all did not imprint on Haralde and Riennes. Neither was superstitious, nor did they hold fears of such things.

Yes, they knew of djinni, the desert devils, and ghuls that grabbed at passing strangers and dragged them to feast on them in the dark, dank places beneath ancient ruins.

Yea, but they were taught a knowledgeable heart was a strong light that withered not in the shadows cast by someone's dark talk.

"Aaah. Monk. Thee disappoint us," admonished Haralde. "Thee are a learned man. The evil eye is not of your catechism."

"My lord. I have seen such things before. It bends many a community to a distortion."

"Thee have been here but a minute, and yet thee rush to judgment," criticized Riennes.

Godfroi's eyes burned in bright devotion; a fiery faith that had found a holy cause to enjoin this pagan community to his Christianity: the purging of Magda.

He made the cross in the air before them. "You must listen to me. My faith is your armor against such evil."

Haralde and Riennes stood there, silent, appraising their good monk. They glanced at each other, then Haralde spat out: "Aaggh! I think mine will serve me just as well, monk."

And he turned, and went back to Magda and son on the verandah. Magda had been leaning an ear towards them, trying to pick up their words, yet knowing all the time she was at the centre of their disagreements.

She kneeled and quivered again, holding her son tight, as her lord mounted the steps of her verandah. His shadow was a threat to her house, her small kingdom.

"Mistress Magda. Serve us a cup of your mead," demanded Haralde. Riennes joined immediately behind him.

Again, Orim was sent scuttling and he returned with another earthen jug to pour an amber liquid into the cups they still held in their hands.

Haralde and Riennes had never tasted mead, but what they drank was superb, a malt honey relish each time it passed lips.

"Aaah!" Riennes was the first to smack his lips.

Haralde wiped his mouth and grinned. "Thee make a man laugh inside with this superb ale. I will require a keg of this also as soon as thee have made enough, do thee not agree Magda.?"

She nodded her head yes, but glowered inside, and thought of the goods she needed to purchase to do this. *I may have just lost the profit of me two pence.*

Riennes smiled gently. The pence were in his mind also.

"Work hard on your lord's needs," said Haralde turning away and leaving. "Be at peace Magda. I tax thee no more. All will know thee are now the ale maker to Lord Longshield and must not now be disturbed."

She continued to kneel, holding onto to her upright son, grateful they were leaving.

"And Orim," Haralde cast over his shoulder. "When next I pass this way, thee will be ready for your first horse ridings."

Orim suddenly grinned, and yelled out loud: "Oh, yes my lord!"

"Pray my lord, no!" Magda uttered adamantly.

"What means thee woman. Why not?" irked Haralde. He looked down on her bowed head, irritation growing over her quiet resistance to him.

"Riding horse is for warring. Here, horses are only for the plow and for their manure, for farming."

"It does no harm to teach a young lad how to ride. I would have thought thee would be pleased by my favour of the boy," grumbled Haralde.

"You would teach him to ride, then he grows up, then you demand he ride with you to warring and killing. No. If it pleases my lord, my wishes are do not with my son. He will not be one on the mountain trails to fighting," Magda answered, her head bowed, but there was resolve in her.

Haralde sensed immediately when it came to her son, Magda would rebel against her master.

Shaking his head in consternation, he walked away with Riennes and Godfroi. The crowd of men parted and followed behind.

Munch and the lads of Wym leaned on some trees or lay in the grass under, waiting for their lord, ready to go.

"They have to be wrong about her," Haralde turned to Riennes and mumbled low. "She is a beauty, no doubt. It must be that which turns men's heads."

"Yea brother. The wickedness is not of her heart but is to be found in the guilty soul of those who lecher after it." Riennes shook his head over the poison he heard in the gossip of the group. "I wonder also if they fear her intelligence. To be able to capture sunshine in an ale cup like that, that is a desirable trade. I feel no darkness here."

Haralde slyly smiled. "One must admit she is bewitching."

"Hmmn. It is a wonder she has maintained her station without a husband all these years. Such must breed contempt," mused Riennes.

Haralde felt an inner discomfort over his brother's words. His own lust pricked him. He nodded, took a deep breath, and assumed his mantle as lord. He did not want Riennes in any part of this. Women liked Riennes from the start.

"Well, my brother, we part." Haralde finally addressed the little dread that niggled between them over this. "Be not long away from me. I will be ill at ease Ren, until thee return and in a fire chat recount to me all your adventures in Wym. Thee will find it a richer, what does mama call us, a commote."

"That I will do Harry, on hoof fleet enough to meet your people there, to get our business done and to get me back," answered Riennes warmly. They touched each other on the chest, then shook arms in the warrior way and clapped each other on the shoulder.

"I will look for thee in Neury in five or six days," suggested Haralde. "If not, I will be here at sunset by a fire on the seventh day talking with my people. If I must wait even the morrow after that, I will be ahorse towards Wym seeking after thy safety."

"Good my brother," and Riennes swung up onto his mount, who snorted in anticipation. In a creak of leather, Riennes saluted him and Godfroi.

"Take care of him dear monk. We have much to do with each other yet," Riennes said goodbye.

"Goodbye my lord. God walk beside you," blessed Godfroi.

They watched him and his company make their way out of Neury, heading east to their brother fiefdom.

Haralde turned to the company of men, and singled out Geraint.

"Now master Geraint. Take me for a walk through these slaves and serfs and freemen who live in this vill. Let us root out those who hide in their hovels and barns and get them back onto their fields. And heaven thunder down upon any souls I find to be slothful on my earth," instructed Haralde.

chapter 3

*Even a blind pig
finds an acorn now and then.*

RIENNES CAME SHARPLY out of his sitting meditation the instant his horse squealed a protest and pawed hoofs upon the ground. Riennes had trained the horse to go to alarm whence bothered by anyone other than he.

He was on his feet instantly. Before him under a tree bough, a dirty, hunched figure poked a staff under the feet of his mount. The beast was tied to a line between two trees and could not move away from his tormentor. The mount was about to rear.

Riennes moved quickly towards the botherer of his beast. The door of the wooden long house under the same tree slammed open and Munch burst out as Riennes was upon the man.

Riennes stepped into the man, pressing a leg behind the legs of the woolen hunched figure, tumbling him to the ground. The Frisian, irritated, moved forwards as to stomp on him, but Riennes interrupted, soothed his beast to a quiet.

Munch was upon the man, heaved him up and swore: "Polcher! Brother, what are you doing to your lord's horse?"

Riennes settled his mount, and waited for an explanation.

"My lord. Sorry we are for this. This be my brother Polcher and the uncle to my sons. He was to bring them to home."

Munch hauled Polcher forward, and made him do a bob of obeisance to his new master. "My lord. Forgive this, my brother Polcher. This be Riennes de Montford, Lord of Wym, our new master, and Polcher, you must find him a very good man as I have," instructed Munch.

Riennes smiled, not wishing to be severe towards a man whose intelligence appeared impaired, as seemed by his hunched body, either by birth or some physical shock.

He nodded, then addressed Polcher. "Uncle! What were thee about with my horse?" Riennes charged.

Polcher was silent for a moment, either trying to understand Riennes's Welsh, or forming a reply. " My master," said Polcher. "Forgive. You see, never my life I see such large, heavy horse on such sturdy legs. I must not touch. I did. Naught have I seen ever around here."

Riennes examined the small, curled up man. Nowhere did he meet the family trait of straight robustness, such as was the tall, sturdy Munch. He suspected the sons would be the same. Yet, his healer's eyes saw something and his judgment of Polcher changed. He sensed an intelligence peculiar to the man, as one who saw life differently.

"I will ask Master Polcher again, what was it with my horse?" demanded Riennes.

"Master. I saw low down. Strong understanding of this beast such as none before," answered Polcher.

Munch grimaced, and looked to see if Polcher's way offended Riennes to anger.

"Explain thyself man," demanded Riennes as he stroked the muzzle of his traveling companion.

"Master. Your horse. Look under. What standing under it has on heavy hocks," answered Polcher.

It took a moment for Riennes to grasp the peculiar way these people described things. A smile enlightened his mind. He put his hands on his hips, reared back and barked out a short laugh. "Thee be right uncle. My mount does indeed have a sound standing under him. Well stated."

Relief freed the apprehension from Munch's face.

"But be warned uncle to stand off from my mount. If he had the inclination, he would kill thee," warned Riennes.

Munch smiled, put his arm around his brother, looked around and said: "My brother has two guardians in my sons. Where there is he, there be they."

As he said it, two strong young men strode across the field towards them, one hefting the carcass of a deer. They picked their way between the young green shoots peeking up in rows. Somehow, they had managed to get spring seed into the ground with their father away amidst all the war and strife.

They were robust and tall as measured against other young men here, Riennes noted. They had their father's blond-rose hair. They had that far-north, Nordic look about them, much like Raenulf, master of the Viking ship Heimer which had brought them across distant seas to Britannia.

"Aahh!" exclaimed Munch who released his brother from his embrace and went and greeted his two straight sons into his arms. They bruised him in their arms bruffly, almost crying with emotion.

They were dressed in the terra cotta colors of green and brown in their woolen jerkins. They carried two long wooden staves, not touching the ground as walking staffs, but held parallel with the earth. Riennes recognized hunting longbows, unstrung.

Riennes watched father instruct sons as they walked back together. At the same time, he examined the stooped Polcher.

Polcher was a bent man, down turned by life, one with an outlook low upon his world. Riennes had seen such before. Few had been as successful as Polcher. Few in this mean world reached the age he had.

"He came thusly at birth from the Otherside," explained Munch. As a healer, Riennes had examined the dead of such before. They did not last long in life. To exist and survive here in the hinterland of the Welsh March, meant one labored long and hard, crawled exhausted onto one's pallet at the end of difficult days. A serf slaved each day to meet two obligations; one to feed the belly of his family and the other to fulfill his lord's needs. Riennes watched to learn how Polcher had survived in his low, hard station.

Munch brought his two sons before Riennes and smacking them on the back, announced: "My lord! My sons, Conlan and Hefin, of who I am very proud!"

"My lord," they nodded their heads forward in the closest thing to a bow, then, as if realizing whom they were addressing, glanced in consternation at the deer hanging over a shoulder. This was the lord's deer, and therefore the king's.

The night discussion around the family pit fire answered for Riennes Polcher's position in the family. The long house was strong and comfortable, built by this family of men. No woman, no wife was here, destroyed some time ago by the hard life.

First, it was obvious the brother of Munch was much loved. Second, Polcher was in the protection of men, not because he was weak or slow or dumb, but because he contributed to their well being. None lasted longer bent over the plow for long hours in the field, explained Munch. None was better bent low tracking game through the forest to bring home supper at day's end, explained the brothers. None could go through the woods low, see the ground signs to round up their errant hogs and sheep and bring them back to the toft. Because these were strengths bolstering their daily lives, Munch and sons could concentrate their labour on other fruitful efforts through the long day's farm work. "Oh no," they claimed. "Our harvests over the years would not be so successful without our uncle." Riennes marked the boys' uncle in his mind as a bent man with a singular ability, useful in some special future endeavor. Riennes would make sure his observations would be marked down when Polcher's number was marked down on Haralde's roll.

And indeed, Polcher was responsible for putting the boys on the trail of the deer they chewed upon that night. Polcher tittered over such praise as they ate.

The boys had come in cautiously with their father, eyeing their new lord, aware they were caught carrying his deer.

Riennes had said nothing of the animal when introduced. However, he had to impress his character upon them as their master. Thus, he imposed his ownership of the animal when he ordered the boys to braise the best parts of the meat over an open fire. Then, he invited all to join him in the succulence of meat cooked this way, a gift from he to them.

It was the third night Riennes spent at the Munch farm, albeit outside and in the farmer's stable. Munch had insisted Riennes take his own night pallet, but like all these hovels and people, body odors and the close, smoky heaviness within was too much for him.

He had heard them mumble amongst themselves over his decision, and they held him in higher esteem, that this *uchelwyr* would sleep outside with the beasts. The comfort of horse smells, dung and urine suited him better. He had walked around Munch's holdings, saw his strong long house, the barn, the toft, and the rich fields green with young plantings and judged Munch a stout man of the land and a good servant of his lord's fief.

Lady Saran had listed for him the names of the principle men of Wym and what the taxes and obligations of each were to her. The wasting of her lands by warring bands over the years had seen a weakening of these taxes paid her. From Munch's farm and with Munch running ahead, Riennes had assembled with these men, and told them to work their lands, that the brigands had been killed.

Riennes informed them a time of assembly in Neury was to be declared. When that was announced, they must gather up their all, bring food for three days whereupon their duties on a new local council would be outlined. There they would meet the new Thegn Longshield and they would be instructed as to their obligations to he, Lord de Montford. When he told them the occasion would be the marriage of Lord Saran, the faces of the somber women of their households lightened. They clapped their hands or burst out in glee. Their high regard for Saran meant the gathering would be a time of celebration, that the threat they lived under was gone. This pleased the men folk. They submitted themselves humbly to his wishes.

Neury was to the west of him now. He could see it, a country of high hills and heavy forest. Beyond that, the wild Brekin country reared up in the high mountains. Here, in Wym, the land was flatter, less forested, the lowlands and waterways freer of bogs and jammed logs. Impressed he was with the better fertility of Wym, and the diversity of field crops and vegetables planted, livestock raised. The land flattened out even more to the east, toward Shropshire.

He wondered what their overlord, the earl of Chester, would think of his new fiefdom.

"I see thee with those longbows," Riennes said quietly, nodding at the two young brothers.

Conversation died around the fire, the Munch family afraid their lord was about to return to the subject of the king's deer.

Finally, Conlan not wanting his father to be singled out for any criticism, plucked up his courage and explained: "Yes my lord. Fighting and wastings of our farms have forced many here to hunt to keep families from starving."

"Yes, I see. Are there many here like thee and your father, sharp with such?"

"Some. More now than before," Munch stepped in. "It is not the bow so much as the practicing. We know now how to make them. We know how to use them. But the secret is shooting over and over. Rhys insists practice an hour every day, and all day Sunday, and families in Wym will be free from hunger in bad times."

"And the same of Neury?"

The Munch family sat quiet for a moment and gazed deep into the fire. Then, Munch nodded yes.

Riennes smiled inwardly at that.

Our Fremen. The man with a bow is freer. He is right. This company of common could now drive off bands of brigands, even Welsh raiders if organized. I must think on this, talk to Haralde.

Riennes turned the conversation to their farm, its practices, how money was made, what crops were best. Relaxed, the brothers told their father of their stay with a relative family, well hidden away from Aelfgar's recruiting. Riennes listened closely to their talk as it turned to local gossip; of young men taken away to fight against their own Lady Saran, of young maids and wives raped in families that resisted.

Finally, as the evening wore late, Riennes stood up.

"Munch. I thank thee for the help and friendliness thee have shown me. Thank thee for standing with Lady Saran and us all. Thee have been a loyal servant. I count thee a good man and I salute thee as a comrade in arms."

Munch stumbled to his feet, bobbing and embarrassed over his lord's good words.

"I will leave thee in the morning."

"I will be ready my lord."

"Nay. Thee will stay here. I mark thee as my first principle man. I need thee to attend to your farm, your sons and for your common interests for Wym. Am I correct, the next man I seek is between here and Neury?"

"Aye my lord. That be Alfold. He has a wife, children and an aged grandmother," answered Munch.

"Good. I will speak to him, then make my way back to Neury."

"But you do not know the way."

CHAPTER 4

In the delirium of the dying,
Be it truth, or be it lying.

A LIGHT MUSICAL AIR peeped from Riennes's pipe as he rode, enjoying the leisure, slow clop, clop of his iron-shod horse. He had a leg across the saddle. Before and below him, Polcher, his guide, led along the broad roadway between two fields.

Polcher had stopped in his tracks when Riennes had first pulled out his pipe and played. Polcher had grinned, swayed his head from side to side, stomped a dance on his buckled legs and told his lord he had never heard anything like that before.

Then, to Riennes's amazement, Polcher hummed the very tune he had just played. The musical notes were random, simply reflecting his master's mood. Yet, the humble man hummed it perfectly.

Riennes piped a sailor's song. Polcher hummed it perfectly. Riennes stopped. "Thee say thee have not heard this before. Yet, thee know the tunes. How?"

"Master. I just do."

Riennes grinned, played other tunes and Polcher echoed back. Riennes had seen this before among idiots. A dumb wise, is how his medical experience had concluded. It was a wonder of wonders, and he had great respect for such as one. He wondered what would happen if Polcher had a pipe of his own. He would make him one.

Riennes played tunes he knew, from the mountain tribes of the Hindu Kush to songs sung by sailors aboard ship. Polcher embraced each note of Riennes's offerings. Riennes marked Polcher as a singular intellect, thus a resource. He marked the bent man for some future use.

After awhile, Riennes's musicality collapsed, and he stopped..

When Polcher, disappointed, asked him to keep playing, Riennes shook his head and put the pipe away. He did not tell him the lightness of his soul had left him, replaced by a sad mood.

As they headed west towards Neury, the forests began to close in. Both were enjoying the late spring warmth and the messages of the wind talk in the trees.

Polcher sniffed the broad pathway like a dog as he jogged ahead, watching the ground under his feet, telling Riennes a deer had crossed here and watered, a wagon had been by just a day before, and there, the first summer bug of a type he knew had now come out.

At one point, Polcher stopped, tore a leaf from a low bush and munched on it. When Riennes asked him why he did that, Polcher answered it was good for when he was bunged up, that it helped his 'poop'.

Riennes halted at that, dropped from his beast, examined the plant and gathered a batch to add to his apothecary. He sniffed at it as he rode, even chewed a bit.

Thus he spoke under his breath over this discovery: "The desert is indeed a wonder."

Polcher, still on the move, asked over his shoulder: "Desert? Not know desert. Is it good?"

His hearing is better than most. "No my friend. It is a harsh place, but magical at times."

"What magical?"

"Something nice. A surprise that is nice and makes thee feel good in a hard place where there is little good."

Riennes turned his attention back to his surroundings and realized they were on a turf road. "Why is this pathway so wide and straight?" Riennes asked at one point.

"Old road," the uncle answered simply. The bent man prowled around for a moment, found what he was looking for, reached down and tore up some turf, and there under was a cobblestone pattern of stones.

Roman, judged Riennes. He had seen this pattern before. A powerful empire had once built these now overgrown networks of roads. Trade and goods flowed along these byways, bringing prosperity and wealth to its towns and villages.

"Where does this go?"

"Neury," Polcher pointed to the west. He turned and pointed to the northeast. "Chester."

"Is Chester a big city? A Roman city? Have you been there?"

"No me. Killed I would be in such a place," Polcher grumbled his answer.

Riennes wondered why a Roman presence in such a wild hinterland. Were Neury and the March a place of rebellion even back then? Did the Romans place men and arms here to keep the peace and trade flowing to and from Chester, a mercantile city of the sea?

Polcher led off the road and through an opening in a stone fence towards a huddle of hovels in a poor village. Smoke rose through central holes in the roofs. The fields looked to be half planted.

They stopped before the largest one. Polcher called out Alfold's name. There was no reply. A dog barked inside. The woolen cover across the door moved aside, and a small man in a shabby, dirty woolen garb stepped out.

He saw Polcher first and called to him. "Is Munch back?" he asked, and then half turned to Riennes.

His eyes widened in horror as he saw a large mounted warrior with a sword at his back.

"Be at peace Alfold," Riennes spoke calmly. "I have been sent by Lady Saran to inform thee and all here the brigands are dead and all here must come out and attend to their fields." Riennes went on to explain Alfold and his family would be summoned to the Longshield stronghold and that he, Lord de Montford was now his new lord.

Alfold stood with open mouth, trying to understand this armed man's foreign mangling of Welsh. It came around to him, and he started to nod his understanding. He was told principle men including himself would be summoned to Saran's wedding. There, he and the others would swear their allegiance to he, the new Lord Riennes de Montford of Wym, and to Lord Longshield of Neury.

When Riennes completed all, he asked: "Do thee understand?"

The man nodded, a dumbfounded yes.

Riennes told him none would be exempt from coming, that it was serious, and that his influence in Wym was respected by Lady Saran.

The man stood silent for a time, his head down, totally at a loss.

"What is it? Thee seem to be without your wits?"

The serf shook his head. "My lord. I am an empty vessel. I am incapable of following thy will?"

"What nonsense is this?"

Alfold for the first time lifted his eyes to his master, and they were empty. Riennes looked right through them and down into the man. He was an empty husk.

"I am without horse, oxen, livestock, food, even seed. I have within a sick ancient mother. My wife lives in our stable there, afraid and hiding from the ramblings coming from the filth that is the mother of my former dead wife.

"Is she sick or fevered?" asked Riennes, afraid the answer might signal a disease that could rage through this small community.

"Nay, just delirious, dying slowly, howling, frightening us all with terrible lies of an Otherness. It is like being cursed to have to bear these rantings."

Riennes told himself he had no time for this, that he had to get on to Neury. The old woman was likely to die any moment.

He sighed, dismounted, and headed for the hovel's door and the wretchedness he knew within. As he passed Polcher, he stopped and instructed: "Go to Munch. Tell him of this. Tell him to share what he can with Alfold here, a horse, food, a bag of seed, anything. Tell Munch he is to go to the other four principle men and they do also. Tell them to bring these things here so Alfold can get his farm going again. He needs to be amongst them for Neury when summoned. Do you understand? This is very important. If any refuse, their lands and livestock will be forfeit to me."

Polcher stood nodding his head even as Riennes gave him the details. He repeated in his cryptic way his master's wishes, then scuttled away quickly down the road.

When Riennes ducked inside, the smell was a wall of filth, an insult to human decency. Excrement, vomit, urine and other juices that leak from an ailing body hit him. He turned away and screwed his face in revulsion for a moment. He adjusted his sensibilities to that of a healer, and then looked around.

A small fire lit the dismal, smoky dark that was the room of the hovel. A gloom of despair crowded out of the corners and hung over the supine form of a hag on the ground. It was a miserable place for one to die.

Riennes wanted to take his kandos cleaning rag and tie it around his head and over his nose, but judged not. Such an apparition would frighten a sick person.

He walked across and leaned over her. A light came into the room briefly as Alfold came in.

The light revealed a white-haired woman with a skeletal face, skin pulled back tight over the bone of her skull. Yet, for all of that, a glow of something touched him, softened him towards her.

Why, she is beautiful for her age. Something outshines from her. I have seen this before. Mother, what wretched thing has life done to thee?

He knew first her body was without liquids.

He turned to Alfold. "Water. Is that warm water in the pot beside the fire?"

"Yes my lord." Alfold scrambled and presented Riennes with a wooden cup of full, clean warm water.

Riennes held up her head and when he touched her lips, they absorbed the water like parched earth.

Riennes shook his head in disgust. "What religion are thee?"

"We are Christians my lord."

"Then thee have committed the great sin. Stupid! Stupid!"

"No my lord. We have sinned naught. I have a good heart. I have tended her for all this time."

"Where is thy wife?"

"She will not come. This is not her mother, but the mother of my woman who came before. She will not attend."

"Stupide! Stupide!" he blurted out in Norman. Then realizing where he was, he switched to Welsh. He stood up and in a deadly, quiet, mean tone, hissed: "Get thy wife in here. Both of thee, clean her filth away. Put her on that pallet. Lift and bring her outside."

Alfold hesitated. Riennes barked at him. He fled. While Riennes gave her more water, he heard Alfold and his wife shouting at each other. He heard a slap then a struggle behind the hovel's woolen blanket door. A slap followed a blow against a body, then the light came in, a woman was shoved to the floor and Alfold followed her in.

She looked up, and her eyes went to fear as she saw the giant figure of Riennes looming out of the gloom of her house. She saw his sword in the light; then a wonder came to her over the freshness of his young face.

Riennes reared up. "Thee two. Get rags, a blanket. Soak it in your pot of warm water and clean her up. Make gruel and feed her. Bring her outside."

He stormed past them and slipped outside, into the warmth of the sun and the cleanness of the fresh air.

Why must the sick and dying always be prisoners of the dark? Such despair.

He took a deep breath. Such had he seen all his young life. He believed illness inhabited gloom and dark. Experience taught him fresh air and sunshine healed.

He walked over to a stream and washed his hands. He sat for awhile enjoying the clean breeze.

Then he rose and returned just as the hovel's blanket parted and the man and wife carried out the old woman. She wore a woolen robe too big for her. Yea, but clean it was. And her hair had been combed, swept back to lie white down her back. Now in the light of the sun, he noticed small tattoos near her finger nails.

He picked up a cut stump of wood, placed it beside her chair and sat down to observe her illness.

He glanced at Alfold and his wife, and was pleased to see amazement, no, some comprehension in their faces. It was they beheld not a hag they had sheltered all this time inside, but a vision of age and grace.

"Grandmother. Do thee hear me? I am one attending to thee. Thee can speak through me to others if thee have needs. How do thee feel?" coaxed Riennes.

Her face was turned half to one side. There was a grain of gruel on her lips. She had drunk of water and ate of sustenance. We must wait. Her face, though, was not stretched as tight across her skull as it had been.

An apparition of life flickered as a light across her face. Then her eyes fluttered open. He saw them respond to the sunlight, then recognition dawned in her eyes.

He watched as her consciousness followed the wind through the tops of the trees.

"Grandmother!" was all Riennes could think to say.

She turned her face towards him, and was blessed with a crooked smile.

"They come," she croaked, licking her dry lips.

Riennes cuddled closer. "Who?"

"The Others. My people. They approach and will take me through a thin place. They will take me to the Otherside."

"Who are they?"

"They are the Others who came long before me. I am of them."

"Who are them?"

"They are the ice people." She seemed to gain a strength, and her voice became stronger. "They are my people of the ice. We who followed and ate of the wingeds of the sky and the finneds of the sea."

He touched her hand to warm her. It was as cold as the sea.

"We followed and killed and lived off the tuskers. Rich and juicy and bloody and meaty was their flesh. We gorged on them as we crossed the sea along the ice. We carved our worship of them in the ivory of their tooth. We paid homage. Then one day, we saw the other world over there, the rich world, full of other people who fed as we did."

"What happened?"

"Some stepped off the ice and joined the other people. But the other people fell upon and killed my people. We labored back over the ice. There were storms and blizzards. It was a long, hard walk. And then we stepped off and found ourselves on a land of the sea. We came from there to here, the land of persecution."

Riennes leaned in closer. "Do thee want to join those on the Otherside?"

"Yes. Soon they will be here and will reach down and will take me where I really want to be."

Riennes considered her wild talk. Was she telling the truth? It might be, as she understood it. He had heard such ramblings in deliriums before.

She turned her head to him, and smiled. "We know of your kind. Continue to do. You follow the true way. You are favoured."

"Thee do not know me."

"Yes. We do. Do you know me?"

"No."

"I am Morog. Does that not strike fear in thee?"

"No."

"Good. I am the last of the druid furies. Once I was dressed in clothes rent and hair long. A beautiful damsel was I with flying hair, hungry to capture young men and feed upon their manliness."

"Morog. . . . Magda?"

"Aaaahh. Our daughter. So much a wica. She would have been a great priestess. She who now hurts. She who now helps. She is of you. She walks the night to find herself. Go help her hurt. "

She leaned over and whispered to him: "Why must non-believers be imprisoned behind chapel walls? Is joy not greater under the trees?

He gazed closely now upon her face full, now again turning to cold ice.

"They come," she whispered. "From the Other place."

"Where is that?"

"Turn me," she ordered.

Riennes stood and gestured for Alfold to help him.

The two slowly turned until she grunted stop. She was facing west. "The ice sea," was all she finally said.

A breeze moved her white hair, lifted up and separated it into two wings. The day brightened suddenly, a seeming flash of white light in Riennes's eyes so that for a moment, he lost sight of Alfold and his wife. He lifted a hand to ward of something, a bug or a bird that brushed his hair. Then, nothing. All was calm.

The three looked upon her face. Nothing had changed. She stared in silent faraway.

Riennes rose. Was it a slight smile or a wry grimace that was the eternal upon her face now?

"What did she mean, the ice people? Another land across the sea?"

"If thee had tended to her properly, she might have answered that for thee," opined Riennes. "Stupidity. Always it wins and we are the losers for it."

He looked at her hands. "What are those marks on her fingers?"

"Honour marks. My dead wife told me her mother was a druid, a gifted healer," answered Alfold.

Riennes nodded, turned, walked to his mount, gathered up the reins, and then for a moment leaned against the heat that was his traveling companion, as if seeking a moment's comfort.

Then he mounted and turned towards Neury. And not another word did he say to the two standing beside the chair.

Godfroi had stood under the tree now for hours. In the dying light of evening, he was barely discernible in the shadows there. He prayed all that time, his voice a low mutter. It was a prayer to God for strength and protection.

His blessings were directed at the black Frisian tied to a stone verandah post and for its master inside the house of the witch.

While attending to the sick of Neury, someone had nudged him and pointed out Haralde and his black mount splashing across the ford in the river. Haralde had dismounted, knocked on the door and when the round face of Magda appeared who tried to shut her door against him, he forced it back open, strode in and firmly closed the door behind.

Had Lord Haralde come to claim her or had the witch of Neury lured him to her threshold? Had her power reached all the way from the stone house to his wooden stronghold in the hills? Godfroi was sure it was the power of her wickedness and hurried to come under the trees and begin his prayers to weaken her incantations and spells.

Godfroi knew it was the master's second visit to the woman in as many days. The men in the village grumbled. The women were rather silent in their criticism, saying leave her alone, she hurts no one. They warned their men to stay away from her.

The monk prayed. He stoically bore the weight of this responsibility to protect the good noble alone. Then, he heard a horse rumble almost beside him. He turned.

Barely, a shadow in the shadows under another tree stood out. He squinted, then his eyes opened wide. It was Lord de Montford, also watching the house.

Godfroi ceased his prayers and was almost to go towards the Norman noble, when Riennes stepped forward into the light. The look upon the Norman's face was, what? One of envy, of jealous conflict?

Godfroi drew back further into the shadows.

Not he also. Not the gentle healer. Please lord, release him from her wickedness.

They both stood that way, a held breath for some time.

Then Riennes walked away quietly, mounted and splashed across the ford towards the stronghold.

Hours later, after rubbing down and feeding his black, Riennes reclined on his pallet in the donjon with his hands behind his head. He heard the whinny of Haralde's mount in the bailey stable.

After he heard Haralde come up the stairs and the thump of his closed door, Riennes rolled over. Jealousy harassed sleep until the early morn. He turned and tossed in green envy.

chapter 5

And has my brother taken from me,
that which I do not have?

RIENNES WAS UP early, expecting to shower with Haralde under a trough that now ran from the aqueduct into the stronghold. Ordered repaired by Haralde, much cold, clean water flowed directly into the Longshield donjon with a side trough running down into the village in the lower bailey. Haralde had designed it himself to supply water to everyone inside. Makeshift it was for now, but everyone marveled at the running water falling into a large stone cistern. There, they could fill their wooden buckets. Thence another outlet directed the overflow to let livestock drink their fill, and thence another which went on further to irrigate a small vegetable garden of the donjon's slave servants. To everyone inside the wall, it seemed a small miracle, this clean water continually coming directly to them.

Only Haralde was gone, up early and to Neury said a slave girl. Riennes had wanted them to bathe together, and then to meditate, as they always did, to resume their former, easy comradeship and foolishness. A dark mood hooded his morning expectations. Haralde at Magda again; two, three days, a week now?

He showered alone standing upon a flat rock. Above him, warm water trickled out from another Haralde construct; a black animal skin bag hauled up above by a rope and pulley. Water dribbled out of small holes through the bag. Chilled by cold water washings, Haralde thoughts turned to this idea of a black bag full of water the sun would heat up to give he and Riennes a warm shower.

He heard someone laughing and when he looked through the veil of water flushing out his eyes. Tyne, a distance away watched him, shook his head, and laughed.

He did not know it but Tyne no longer took their habit of bathing together as an aberration, not after long talks with Saran.

Now, Tyne just shook his head and laughed over their obsession for cleanliness, that and the sight of farmers' wives shooing all their children back to their huts in the lower bailey so as not to look upon the foolishness of their naked lords.

At first Riennes laughed back and waved, thinking this was a regular reply one made to a laughing Irish man like Tyne, as if he were learning a local custom.

However, after Tyne kept yelling: "Ho Lord Riennes! Dirty again?", he realized he was being mocked. Yet, he continued to laugh and wave back. Better to be affable to a comrade in arms than to take umbrage with Tyne's disconcerted revulsion for bathing.

After meditating to lift the dark mood from his mind, he went to a little stall he had erected behind the donjon to work on his pots and buckets and earthen containers of plants and herbs, powders and potions. Herbs and plants of all kinds hung down drying under a wattle roof. Open on a trestle table was a large book, his bible on apothecaries written in Egyptian Arabic. This was his true treasurer, one he had carried across half the world. Its last journey had been all the way from London under the ass of the monk Godfroi in the dray. In the middle of the stall, a fire bubbled an iron pot of plant material as he attempted to boil all away leaving just a residue. As that was steaming, he put dried plants into a mortar and ground them with a pestle into fine powder.

This was his passion; the medicinal pursuit of curatives from plants. It was needed in the stronghold village because there was no apothecary.

As in most villages, the stronghold had to fulfill its own necessities, from the slave all the way up to Lady Saran. Every village in the manors of Neury and Wym had to be self-sufficient. One man was an expert on making and repairing leather shoes and horse cart traces, a tanner to turn hides into leather, a lead carpenter, a wagon maker and wheelwright. Most important was the farrier to make iron rings and shovels and buckles and weapons and now horseshoes as demanded by Haralde for their Frisians. Even now, Riennes could hear the ring of the smith's hammer on an anvil down in the village as he made his lord small iron pots.

People baked their own bread in Lord Haralde's oven and paid him a fee to do so. Everyone butchered their own animals, but one was appointed to do the lord's livestock. Such was the way of all open field cultivations centered on villages sprinkled across the fiefs.

His Uncle Gilbert in London had told him of the feudal system now imposed on Britannia by then, the Normans. Brutal, greedy, they would take the land as was due them. The countryside would be organized tightly into units called manors, an estate with demesne directly exploited by a lord and peasant holdings from which he would extract rents, taxes and fees.

Riennes doubted Haralde could hold Neury as his own for long under this onslaught. It would either all be given to he, a de Montford, or seized by a more powerful earl. Or possibly, because they were up in this wild March country in the hinterland of Wales, they might forgive Haralde as his father was a housecarl to the Confessor king, himself a Norman king of Britannia.

The local serfs and churls would likely not notice much change. They would go on, making all their own things, looking to their own needs.

Here, the village was without a leech of any kind. Riennes had coveted the role of maker of medicines. They were aware of what he was doing. They called his medicine pack his Simple Chest. By Simple, they meant simple ground herbs like mugwort, plantain, nettle, dock, crabapple, chervil, and fennel. Also, they asked him what kind of charms and incantations he had in his chest. When he asked them what they meant, they told him charms to ward off warts, to protect them from the evil eye or a dwarf and incantations to chant a unfruitful land into one of bounty or to delay birth or against the stings of a swarm of bees. They also called him their leech, sprung from an old Saxon healing book of herbs, cants and curses called The Leech Book of Bald.

He was exceedingly qualified to heal them. What he had seen of the skills of healers in Britannia was exceedingly crude. In fact he reckoned in him Neury and Wym had the finest healer in all Britannia.

As a senior boy, he had sat at the feet of the Persian, Azat, a maker of potions and curatives, a setter of broken bones. He was the second healer of the court of the Ger Khan. Riennes fetched and carried and washed and cleaned and cared for the sick. Seeing his interest, Azat taught him how to set broken bones, wrap sprains, make ointments to soothe rashes, concoct antidotes to poison.

Later, at the Khan's instruction, he was sent as a young man to stand at the elbow of the mathematician, philosopher and the greatest physician of the East, Sena, who opened men's bodies and repaired sicknesses and traumas. One day the master told him to sew up a wounded horse soldier. When Riennes told the master he did not know how, Sena showed him. Riennes came to assist more and more when Sena had to cut into bodies. The Egyptian taught him to observe the sick, to talk to a person, to listen to what he or she had to say about how they felt, to think and come to a conclusion on what was the cause. All this he had to do before deciding if it was necessary to issue a curative or go in with the knife. After long days, Sena made him stay and read into the night the master's Book of Medicine, now used by all healers beyond Outremer. In it Sena had set down diagnosis of hundreds of ailments, some that called for the opening of the body, some that diagnosed herbal medicines.

From the bodies broken and cut on the battlefield of the Khan's conquering armies, he learned fast how to stitch up sword and axe wounds, cut out arrow heads, operate on those pierced through by spears and to cauterize wounds. In all, their real enemy was flesh that putrefied after the body was closed. In this, Sena showed Riennes something he had learned by accident. One night, as a young healer, Sena had called for a torch to be closer to a body he was about to open. The flame carrier brought it too close, and Sena had to push him away, accidentally shoving his cutting knife into the flame as he did. Later, his patient healed without any pus or flux or festering. A similar accident happened again ending with the same result. Sena examined knife after cutting knife held in a flame but could find nothing on the blade of any difference from others. He taught Riennes to do this, saying he did not know why but most times it resulted in the sick recovering without gangrene.

In the Longshield stronghold, Riennes boiled potions and ground powders and waited to be of help. His first patient, a slave whose leg had been broken under a big tree dropped for the building of Saran and Tyne's long house, was brought in. The bone had punctured the skin and was sticking out white. On seeing who was attending him, the man had protested. He wanted no part of a lord attending to his wound who cut men down with a sword. The man called out one word instead:

"Magda."

Riennes asked the man why he wished Magda. The man said she attended to women's needs, but that men would let her touch them if they were seriously injured. It was a revelation. So part of the men's fears was over her healing abilities; black magic, the men called it.

After Riennes attended to the bone, the slave's fear subsided when his pain and his leg felt better. When he grinned up at his lord and master, and bobbed and thanked him, Riennes knew this would spread throughout the two fiefdoms. What would Magda's reaction be of him?

Magda! How thee haunt me. I saw thee but only once. Now my heart has fallen within the shadow of your memory. Are thee true? How new thee are to me.

For the thousandth time, he dwelt on her memory of that one visit with Haralde. Since then, he had not seen her even one time. Yet, her face, her eyes, her bearing haunted him.

When he sat in his stall and worked, children, wives, young maids, farmers, churls, serfs, even slaves, poked their heads in from time to time to watch what he was doing. Some he knew were trying to catch him out, to find him practising his black magic.

As he was peering into his pot to observe what mess his plants had boiled down to, he heard the guard at the gate shout out the arrival of Lord Longshield.

A few moments later, a slave girl from the donjon pattered up to his stall, leaned in and said: "If it pleases my lord, Lord Longshield, Lady Saran and Lord Tyne want you at a meeting in the family hall."

"Very good," and he put out his pot fire.

A fire crackled through the morning, chasing away the cold from the night's chill in the great hall. Now only embers burned orange in one corner of the square stone pit. Smoke shrouded upwards but did not dissipate easily up in the vaulted timbers of the room. The arrow-slits up there in the crown of the room did not dispense the smoke readily.

Haralde had gazed upwards for some time, trying to design a way to draw the smoke off more efficiently. He did not like the looks of the timbers blackened by soot. He had scrutinized the great fire pit and concluded it had actually been a Roman pool, likely where military commanders had sought their ease in hot water up in the primitive Welsh highlands.

Now, meals came hot out of a swing iron pot at one end of the fire pit. Two doors had been broken through a wall and a large stone room added on to the keep to act as a kitchen and food storage area.

Thus it was when Riennes entered. All were gathered around the trestle table where the family dined, planned the defense of the stronghold and entertained, although no opportunity had arisen for the latter.

Haralde, Saran and Tyne looked up as Riennes came in. Tyne had a big smile on his face, as if enjoying the discussion's subject matter. Haralde sat stone faced.

Haralde and Riennes had devised undetectable secret signals between them when one had been away and was entering a room where the other was present and part of discussions. Such were the dangers even to one's life amidst the jealousies, intrigues and political plots in the court of the Khan that they had developed this system; the one that had been in the room silently signifying to the other entering whether the matters being discussed were dangerous or benevolent.

The trick was for the one entering to make a scene or start up a conversation to draw all eyes to him, thus screening the other to make the unseen signal with a dip of a finger or blink of the eyes.

Lady Saran accomplished the latter as she rose on Riennes's approach. She came to him, took up his hands in hers and spoke. "We have heard of your remarkable healing of one of our slaves and rejoice," she smiled, drawing all eyes to her. "Also, you bear much news of your travels through Wym. We wait with held breath your findings."

Riennes shook his head humbly and glanced over her shoulder at Haralde. There was no secret signal.

"Your servant is hardy, and heals easily himself," answered Riennes.

"No. Our people have remarked on it." She turned and addressed Haralde and Tyne. "Have you heard on it?"

"Yes. But mama, I am not surprised," informed Haralde. "Riennes brings a great gift of healing amongst us," and he told her and Tyne of the remarkable cutting into and healing of the young bandit who attacked them on their travels here.

She whirled back. "Never have I heard of such a thing. You are as a physician of the Levant, as we have heard about."

"Yes my lady. I was taught by such, yea, the best of such," grinned Riennes.

"You two. So many surprises. Come," she clapped her hands and pulled at him. "Come sit by your mother. We are talking of important things, such as the marriage of your mama to that silly man over there lechering after me."

There was a general giddiness over that around the table. Only Riennes was aware of a tightness in the air. It came from Haralde.

They talked at length about the affairs of Neury, Wym and Brekin, of what had been accomplished, what was yet to be done in short order, details of the joining ceremony soon to be held on the new estate for Saran and Tyne.

Haralde coughed to change the subject. "I have another matter to tell thee, one that thee may not agree with."

"Pray, what is that Haralde?"

"I am going to free all the slaves here in the stronghold." Haralde watched their reaction closely.

"Son. You cannot do that," Lady Saran gasped.

"Why not?"

"Without our slaves, our commotes, our holdings will be without labor, without rent, without food renders, taxes, obligations," admonished Saran. She explained all of Wales was about slavery, that all the great houses sought out and bought slaves to maintain their wealth.

On an inquiry by Riennes, she described how Wales was a land divided up into cwmwds or commotes and each commote consisted of 50 trefi, many small vills. Within the commotes, land was held for the king or the prince, or his lord. The land was exploited in large tracts by serfs, but mainly by slaves from whom farm labour, food rent and agricultural goods were delivered up to their masters.

"If you free them, they will run. Northmen will pounce upon them. If not Vikings, then raiders or princelings will shuffle them across Wales to slave markets where they will be bought by Welsh noble households hungry for their free labour." She painted an even dismal picture. "Often noble Welsh houses go to war against other noble households to secure slaves for their fields."

"Aye, I have learned thus," understood Haralde. "'S truth but I believe I can keep them from leaving."

When Tyne and Saran asked how, Haralde explained he did not intend to free them outright, but to allow them to work and buy their freedom over a period of two years.

"I will grant them land outside of the walls here, where in their spare time they can plough and plant their own gardens and fields. They will pay us a food render from these as well as from our gardens and demesne lands which they must still work. In the end, our lands will become very fruitful."

"Why, you will work them to death. It will be worse than slavery. I cannot countenance this." The iron of his mother surfaced to challenge him.

"No. I will not be harsh. They will labor within their abilities and I will not impose hard food tithes."

Lady Saran got up, stamped around, then turned on her son again. "Why do this?"

Haralde face turned grim and he looked to Riennes. "We have seen slavery everywhere we were dragged in our exile. We were slaves ourselves. We know the heartbreak of a slave, the imprisonment of his humanity. We hated being enslaved. The promise of freedom drove us to be resourceful, ambitious."

Riennes dropped his head and nodded.

"One day, a great lord freed us. We stayed with him. And we learned when slaves are guided to their freedom carefully, they tend to stay with the hand of their gentler masters. And mama, every master who did this ended up with landholders who produced three, four times what they did as slaves. He was paid ten times ten in loyalty. And in every case, he became wealthier."

Silence settled in the room after his discourse.

"I have many agricultural ideas. I want to try them here on my lands. Serfs, churls and freed men must feel they have some stake in their land.

This figures in my plans," finished Haralde. "Slaves would only be a weight around the neck of my endeavors."

Lady Saran shook her head in dismay. Tyne imitated her discomfort.

"You are strange. From my loins to foreign. What ways you follow, what beliefs you hold. They are not my ways, nor the ways of our peoples. I cannot believe what you intend. But you are my sons. You are lords here now. What you wish to do, instruct Tyne and me. We will do as you say."

Tyne stepped forward. "At first I could not accept you, both of you. I raged inside against all you forced upon me. Still I am. Yet, I have seen you do things. You know about things I have not ever thought of, and never will. You prepare us for the future, and yea, it falls upon us as you predicted. It confounds me. I do not like it, but it saves us. Like my heart here, I will do as you instruct."

Saran noted a quiet between her Haralde and her Riennes in all this. Her intuition uncovered tenseness, a rigidness between them.

As a mother and a woman, she picked up the tract that divided her most esteemed possessions, her sons.

As Haralde prepared to move on, she stepped on his protracted agenda for other things around their kingdom.

"The people of Neury, they wish a present for me and Tyne. I hear they petition you to allow a representation at our wedding?"

"Yes," Haralde grumbled.

"Thank you. I hear amongst them to come is Magda who wishes to present her best to Tyne and I."

"MAGDA!" Riennes and Haralde started, almost rising from their bench together.

That outburst told her she had hit the mark of it. Somewhere in this was the hardness, the lump growing between her sons.

"What do thee know of Magda?" Haralde demanded angrily.

"Shush you impertinent son," Saran admonished Haralde. "Far more than your little ambitions will ever understand. Magda and I have suffered a long time together. In doing so, we have held together this little clod of dirt for your father, and now you two."

Riennes was in confusion. "What do thee know of Magda that thee have withheld from us? I have certain strong opinions of her. Do thee?"

"Whatever it is of Magda, this be a family matter of which your opinion will not be regarded of any import here," Haralde flared up, his eyes shining hard.

Lady Saran twisted her hands in her lap. *So it is Magda that festers their bondship.*

Tyne blinked. Even he could sense something.

The room's air stifled everything.

Haralde dropped his head. *What did I just do?*

Riennes stared at the blank stone wall across the room.

Never in all their times together had this happened. A difference, a difficulty unmeasured in their relationship. Haralde's fang of jealousy had punctured their kinship. Riennes felt a flush of blood, the acid bite of Haralde's jealous venom.

He sat unmoving, waiting for his brother to amend, or find a way out as he had always in the past. They had fought, they had argued, they had rumbled their differences before. Yea, though, this was the first time neither could find a way out of the hurt to the heart.

It was Tyne who attempted to bind the schism.

"I think it is marvelous that Neury strikes such a delegation in this joining time. It makes your mother and me very happy. We are family and thus are together in all things," he suggested, standing up and walking around and smacking both of her sons on the back.

The warmth of Tyne's gesture moved Haralde. Such originality he didn't think was in the Irish man.

Riennes sat quiet, composed, gathered. It was his way when upheaval swirled about him. His would proceed steadily. No confusion would be allowed to dictate his direction.

Pain ached inside Saran. So, Magda again. Why do they go at her so?

Tyne smiled and announced: "Word has just come from one of our soldiers at the gate that a delegation from Neury wishes to inform us Munch is returning for our joining. He brings with him the principle men of Wym with families."

Saran clapped her hands together in delight. "That is wonderful. Munch. The boys. Alfold and his new wife. And you must all meet Polcher."

Riennes's responsibilities stirred him to speak. "Men of Wym tell me to inform your lordships the seeding throughout Wym is finished. Livestock is fattening up. Manure is flowing onto the land. And because of an early spring, some early vegetables, ale, doves, lamb and a boeuf for roasting they will give to the wedding feast."

"Oh. Wonderful. Wym and Neury again. In a feast celebration. It has been so long." Their mother's face broke out in joy.

Riennes leaned into Haralde. "I wish a moment with thee about the Wym woodsmen and their bows. I think thee should know they are significant. Rhys makes it so."

"Rhys! How that man eludes his obligations to me," grumbled Haralde somewhat in frustration.

His mother heard that. "Oh, that Rhys might come. And with his children! Oh, that we might be together again."

"I think the man owes me some coin, some tax, some service, something," boomed Haralde.

Saran shook her head no. "He is a rare man, a free man, noble in spirit and character. He carries it with him. In Welsh he is *bonheddig*, a man who serves without servility."

Haralde had heard and seen before such status in similar men. But, not here, not in the high March country."

"Hmmm. What does the laws of Cymru say of such a man," pondered Haralde.

"Yes. In strict terms, such a man owes to his lords a gwestfa, a food render," explained Saran. "And thence a commorth, a physical service to you."

"Aaah! Then I have him," snorted Haralde. "But wait! He has no land. How do I petition for his obligations to me and Riennes?"

"It can be on land, but more on the strength of his character within the community." Haralde smacked a hand into an open palm when he heard this from his mother.

"Bring him before us. By the Ger's anger, I want an ending of this. By God, I like the man and want him a servant fulfilled of his loyalties and who can thus walk amongst us," blustered the Longshield thegn.

Riennes had sat quiet, and then cleared his throat to speak: "If memory serves, he fulfilled this gwestfa when he kept us in venison and fish during the siege."

Haralde flared at Riennes, as if wishing his brother had not made it to the family discussion. Then, his face broke into a smile and beguiled, he burst out laughing. "So he has! So he has. Damn, how that Fremen squirms from beneath my grasp. Aah! I will demand heavy for his service to me."

"Well, you may see him quite soon my lord," chuckled Tyne. "He plans to be on our field, where he wishes to give Saran and I a wedding present."

"How know thee this?" demanded Haralde.

"It would seem all of Neury and Wym now know. And it would seem his proposal meets with the approval of all your principle men," Tyne pretended serious, wiping a smile his face had offered over the good tidings.

"Lord de Montford. Thee have some opinion and rights in this as thegn of Wym," Haralde said, trying to drag Riennes into his field.

"Nay. I leave. I have many things to attend to. Matters of Neury, I leave to Neury. Matters of Wym I settle myself." Riennes rose and left through the great front door.

The coldness of it shocked Saran. She looked to Haralde. He half rose, then sat down, and covered his head with his hands.

Haralde, stripped to his waist, worked with his slave men in digging a circular foundation. Slaves arrived with wagons of stone. Men of lime and gravel stone and sand and block rock arrived behind and began setting huge stone rock within the trench Haralde was cutting through the earth. At one place it touched onto the back of the family stone bastion where it had been cracked open to become a door.

The old wooden tower was gone. Now the atmosphere of the inner bailey was one of dust and noise. The sound was that of chipping stone to fit and of the clinking of stone placed one atop the other. Haralde was in the trench to make sure the foundation was sound.

Once assured all was going well, he stepped out of the ditch, wiped himself and looked around. He was sure he would find Riennes standing witness, inquisitive, questioning. He wanted his brother there, to talk to, to tell him his plans, his ambitions, which of course included his brother.

No Riennes. Haralde was bereft of his brother's companionship. Always, one visited to the other when one activated an ambition or a new direction.

Of late they had not met in the morning, bathed, joked, meditated or gone for walks to talk of the day's endeavors. And where was the stick man in the black rough woolen cowl. The monk too had ceased to be a partner.

Suddenly, like the sharp prick of a dirk, he realized his kandos was not upon his back, not upon his person. He searched around, and then remembered he had left it in his room. Not good. Not a lesson but a sharp life's practice, one that had saved his life more than once, he had let slip.

He hurried into the bastion, bound up the stairs to his room, retrieved his steel servant and headed back out across the inner bailey to find his brother. *I am getting careless over what really matters.*

Haralde found Riennes scratching with charcoal a message on a last piece of papyrus he had in his writing folder. Beside him, steam bubbled up from a big pot.

"Yea brother," interrupted Haralde as he leaned beside Riennes to see what medicinal corruption he was brewing. "A new curative?"

Riennes embroiled his head into a cloud of steam bubbling up from the pot. He picked up a stick, shoved it in and hooked up his soaking blue silk undershirt. "No. Washing. It was beginning to stink."

Haralde laughed and smacked him on the back. "Thee need not do that. The slave Ellga does all that. I would have called her to do this for thee."

"Thee have been preoccupied of late. Besides, she knows only of wool. Silk takes special care and it is the only one I have," considered Riennes.

Haralde shook his head, took Riennes by the arm and said: "Come. Thee have not looked upon my new effort. A stone tower for the keep."

"I have. Only again, thee were too busy. Your head was down. Thee were snorting at your men to greater effort. Like a hog, there was gravel on your snout. For two days now, all I have heard is the click, click of rock being laid on block."

"Riennes. It will be higher than the stone donjon. We will be able to see way across the valley to the other side." Haralde rambled enthusiastic, and Riennes began to smile inside over his brother's enthusiasm.

"It is for us. It will have a room for me and a room for thee. Thee can keep all your books, your herbs, and your animal specimens in yours. I will have my agricultural things, my arrowheads, my measurements and my metallurgy things in mine. We will discuss, nay argue in peace about all the things we have seen, the circumference of a bird's egg, the size of the world, how to make good wine, how high the sun be, thee know, philosophy, all those things we wanted to have when we got here. Beneath, our travel trophies, our war swords and bows, our battle flags on the walls, Aelfgar's weapons piled in an armory room . . . .thee are writing something? Is it about your plants?"

Riennes picked up his parchment. "No. It is a letter to Jhon of Muck. To ask if any word has come across the canalem about my Norman manor. To find out if things have changed for the better there."

Riennes's words harkened back to Jhon, a merchant, owner of the House of Muck. He was the first person they had met in landing in Britannia. Haralde remembered how they had entered into the creation of a trading company with Muck on The Thames River. He was also to be their ears on the affairs of Normandy across the canalem, especially any news of Riennes's estate there, now occupied illegally by a rebel lord and his family.

Haralde stood quiet for a moment. "Why would thee do that?"

"Brother, thee paid out good coin to inform Muck when and if things changed at my manor in Montford,"

"Well, yes."

"It is time to see if that now has rewarded us with information."

Haralde stood there, hurt, confused, and almost frightened. Again, the possibility of parting at the end of their road set him in a panic.

"Yea brother, but thee are here. Thee have a holding here. Thee now have family here. All here love thee. And a chief of the king has put thee in charge of Wym."

Riennes felt Haralde's deep hurt, and thusly, he also. Yet, he could not help pushing Haralde to feel his own hurt. "Brother. Thee are bringing Wym as well as Neury back to its pride. The fields are being worked. The land is returning to such as it must. It will yield thee much tithe, tax and coin. Thee will meet your overlord Earl Gerbod's expectations of silver coin from thee. He will be pleased and likely with my recommendation restore Wym to the family Longshield."

Haralde hung his head. He scuffed his leather boot against a cattle turd. "Why do thee this? Why now?"

"Nay brother. Not now. I write to prepare for the day that is to come. We have talked of this before, that in time this may happen once we reached our homes," answered Riennes.

"I see," and Haralde half turned. Then he stopped, turned back and spoke a bit sharply to Riennes. "I too must write Muck. If I may borrow some writing material, I will send a message with yours to Muck to ship Amont to us here, to the Estuary of the Dee off Chester. We need things here, iron, seed, wine, linen, cotton, new silk for us, new breeds of sheep, and instructions on how to prepare wool here, rather than send it to The Low Country. We also need a report on our London enterprise."

Amont, the captain of their Viking trading ship, was expected to arrive some day in Chester with goods for their holdings, and to report on the state of their trading interests.

Riennes nodded his head. The air was heavy between them.

Haralde shook himself, and stood erect. "But not now. Come. The Lady Saran prepares us a venison stew, with cheese, bread and ale. I am to tell thee, it will be so fine and so much and so heavy, we will gorge it up, drink, burp and fart until we lay ourselves down for a good afternoon's nap. She says we both need it, that we have laboured long and hard and our bones are showing. She says she knows because our bodies look like corpses when we bathe."

"Aaah! She has been peeking," and Riennes put down his charcoal writer, and stood up. "If the Lady Saran says thus, then thusly we must obey. Let us go and eat more than our fill. If she is the maker of such fare, it can only but put meat on our skinny frames. And let us ask her who of her sons has the skinniest ass. Nay, belay that. I already know the answer."

So they headed towards the donjon, walking not as friends or brothers, shoulder to shoulder, sometimes one bumping or shoving the other in rough humor, but rather as in a strangeness, one following behind the other, naught said between them.

chapter 6

Brother, we have fallen.
Jealousy has put us down.

"Aaagh!" Haralde jerked upright on his bed, disgusted, anger souring his disposition. Again, he had tossed and turned all night, slept badly. Muddled up he was with half dreams and half realities of a naked Magda and Riennes intertwined.

He got up, pushed his shutters open and looked out his narrow stone window. A weak dawn light glowed the distant highland.

He was chilly. He was naked but paid no mind, short of wrapping a leather apron around his loins. He roughed up his head, and felt longer locks. He and Riennes had not shorn hair lately.

Suddenly, he reached out into the dark of his room and his kandos leaped into his hand. He needed to do something, work out the residue of angst covering his dark apprehensions.

He slipped outside, the stone stairway cold on his bare feet. He walked by Riennes's room. His kandos sang its metal song as he pulled it slowly from its scabbard, then continued on his way when he heard the echo of fine steel being drawn on the other side of the wooden door.

He padded silently down the stairs. Above his head, he heard bare feet padding on the stones following him down. He padded by sleeping slave servants curled up by the almost dead fire.

He groaned open the great wooden entrance door of the keep and stepped down onto the hard packed ground of the clearing above the inner bailey.

Haralde strode around behind the keep to Riennes's stall to where a wooden trough overhead tinkled water onto a large stone platter.

He turned slowly, bowed slightly and Riennes looming out of the dark of early morn, also bowed reverently. Then their bodies went taut, their kandos kissed their metallic kiss, and it began. Always, Riennes allowed Haralde the first move, and Haralde knew it was to gauge his tempo, how he was feeling, and his discipline this moment with the long, curved, sharp blade.

The two steel short swords were given them by Taigen, a Manchura monk, who had forged these weapons specifically for Riennes and Haralde many years ago.

Haralde made his first pass, grunted, turned, took Riennes's retaliation on the tip and the hard steel sang in the clean morning dark. They grunted, worked up muscles. The 'aahs' and 'hai' echoed off the walls. The dance of their ritual 'air's breath' followed. Air's breath was the discipline of mercy, of the deliberate avoiding of the cutting of the skin of one's opponent. Tagien had instructed them to complete their exercise without injury to anyone. The greater skill in such an exercise visited great honour upon the holder of such a blade. The blades flashed, talked to each other, the two controlled their breathing. Sweat began to break out on their bodies.

Upstairs, Lady Saran bolted upright in her bed at the sound of ringing blades. Her hand automatically sought her sword normally beside her on the floor, but no longer there. Awake, she turned to rouse Tyne beside her, only to find him gone. She turned, and saw the naked form of her lover looking down through their window.

She was up and over to him. "What?"

He nodded and she looked down, and a fright gorged up instantly. Haralde and Riennes were at each other, the first weak light of dawn turning their swords silver. She squeaked out "Tyne. We must stop this!" and she turned to run out of the room.

He pulled her back. "Woman. Put some clothes on first. I have seen them do this before. There is nothing to fear," and added as she threw some clothes on, "I hope."

Haralde turned, thrust, and they passed through each other, turned again, took each other's expression of their mock combat on the tips of the blades, working through the intricacies, the deadliness of these delicate weapons. It was always with them, not only a dance of controlled aggression but also an act of mercy, this duet dedicated to do no harm. Thus it was Haralde began to initiate a change, not only in the ritual, but also in himself. Through his very hands, he felt his touch change. He was changing the tempo. The thrusts and moves took on a deadly seriousness. He was not losing himself to his inner spirit, to the cleansing enjoyment of their discipline. He had come out of it, and suddenly moved intently against the form of his brother.

He felt Riennes beginning to draw away. Suddenly, Haralde stepped out of the comfort of the ritual, and moved different. A thin red line with little beads of blood bubbled on the chest of his brother.

What have I done! Haralde stopped immediately as they always had in the past when one was not right.

On the porch of the keep, Saran squeaked out an alarm and brought her hands to her face. Tyne gathered her in his arms, his other hand holding a naked sword.

Riennes, breathing strongly, stepped back, pointed his blade to the earth, and slowly bowed, ending the ritual. Haralde stopped, pointed the blade down, and also bowed.

They both just stood there, immobile, little red lines of blood dribbling down Riennes's chest. Haralde felt a wound of shock flood across his face. He had broken faith with Riennes. His brother stood also, a hooded, dark, grim look of disbelief on his face.

"Why?" Riennes whispered the all demanding question.

Haralde shook his head slowly. "I do not know . . . .Thee have been visiting Magda!"

"I have not seen the face of Magda since the day we first met her, Lord Longshield," answered his brother.

"Ren. I have been told thee have been seen with her at her house."

"Standing only under the trees Harry, watching thee visit, going in."

"But? . . . ." Haralde stopped. His brother never lied. His own jealousy had betrayed him, turned him. "Ren. What have I . . . . Ren! She will not see me. She turns herself away from me. She hides Odim. Closes doors against me."

Riennes felt a lightness of spirit rise up in him. The dread of his night tossings, of this morning's breach of their brotherhood, left him. He turned and went into his stall.

Haralde stood there, black of heart, bitter of soul. "What is wrong? What have I done? Why will she not see me?" Haralde, confused, angry with himself, let his head fall in disgust. "I just wanted to talk to thee about this."

Riennes looked down at the thin line of blood dribble on his chest. "Yea brother.   I believe thee just did," he observed, his lips grim. Inside, relief flooded through him. The lump, the growing stone between them, now was not hard anymore. Haralde's news of Magda's rejection rolled that rock away.

Haralde gripped his kandos hard. He looked skyward in anguish. His hand eased its grip and his kandos fell to the ground. The compact of brotherhood he had foresworn to Tagien, he had now broken.

On a decree by the Ger Khan, they had stood before the Manchura monk on a sandy ground courtyard to submit themselves to him. He warned the weapons he would unfold, unseen by anyone before, would test not the strength of their sword arms, but rather the faith of their very souls. "If there be no honour in thee, thee will but bear swords that will conspire against thee." He warned of the secret of the small swords made of the hardest steel in the known world. "It lies not with the Khan nor me, but with thee." They had sworn to dedicate this secret way of the kandos to the protection and service of others. "Thee choose. Let not the Khan choose," their master had admonished before unveiling blue silk and green silk coverings, Thus were the strange, shinning steel curved swords first revealed to them.

Now, Haralde had disgraced not only his oath, but himself.

On the porch, Tyne drew his lady back into the shadows of the door. "Come. Let us go upstairs." They hurried up the stairs, over to their window again and huddled together looking down. "What are they doing?" asked Saran of her man. "What is all this going to mean?" Then they heard Riennes the healer speak first.

Riennes returned from his stall with a rag in his hand. "Harry, here," directed Riennes picking up his brother's kandos, flipping it in the air and presenting the handle to him. As Haralde moved to accept it, Riennes moved so fast that it was unseen by the two peering out the upper reaches of the keep. Haralde felt it before he saw it, and a thin red line across his chest began to bead blood that ran in thin dribbles down his chest. "I am sorry my dear. I have done so in anger." And Riennes let slip his kandos, and it fell into the dirt.

Haralde stood there, diminished, deflated, looking at the curve of silver on the ground. Then, maybe for only the third time he had ever touched Riennes's blade, he picked it up, flipped it and presented it to his brother.

"There be no harm here. The bond between us is unbroken. Thee and me have simply made a mistake. The honour remains, in that we admit it. Only a good man does that." Riennes produced the oily rag and cleaned the blood from his blade. He handed it to Haralde who took it reluctantly, wiped his blade and watched as the blood of both seeped together into the cloth.

Riennes sheathed his blade. Harry slowly did the same. "Come Harry. Let our water bond wash it away."

Riennes turned and Haralde followed slowly. When they approached the water leaking from the trough above, they set down their scabbards and stepped forward. Riennes, playfully, forgiving, bumped Haralde under the water first. The blood washed away, and puddled at Haralde's feet.

Haralde felt the cleansing action of the mountain stream upon his body, and more intimately, upon his soul. Playfully, he grabbed at Riennes and pulled him in. He watched the blood also puddle around his brother's feet.

Never will this treachery heal in me, he thought, even as they laughed a bit, pushed and shoved as of old.

They let the water clean them, then Riennes stepped out, went to his stall and came back with a small apothecary pot.

Haralde stood out and shook the water from him. "Ren. I was wrong. Forgive me . . . . I want to talk to thee about Magda."

Riennes shook his head no, delved into his pot with a small flat wooden spoon and smeared yellow paste across the thin wound. He handed it to Haralde, who did the same for him. "Do not touch it. Leave it until it dries to a yellow powder and falls off. Thus will there be no festering."

When they walked back to his stall, Haralde tried to return to Magda but was interrupted.

"We must talk about our Fremen."

"Rhys! What about him, that scoundrel? He walks our land. Eats our deer. Owns nothing. Returns nothing to us."

"Do you remember what Saran said of him?"

"Yea. That he at least owed us a commorth, his labour, some physical service."

"Yes. And he has done so."

"I have seen naught."

"Aaah brother but thee have! A great physical service. Have thee forgotten the brown-stained goose feathers of the arrows that ended Aelfgar's ambitions for your death?" Riennes pointed out.

Haralde opened his mouth as if to object, then shook his head at his ignorance.

Aelfgar the Wild would have split his skull open with a big broadsword if two arrows had not stopped the brigand. Riennes and Haralde had chased Aelfgar up into a wooden mount where the brigand leader had ambushed Haralde. Aelfgar had surprised Haralde and would have heaved his broadsword down upon the Longshield thegn if two arrows from out of nowhere had not buried themselves into the bandit's body. All that was left to Haralde was to behead the still living body of his adversary. In all this action, Rhys was never seen.

"No greater service can a subject render his lord," Haralde mumbled, agreeing with his brother.

"Aye. Good for thee," smiled Riennes as he pulled off the cloth around his loins and squeezed the water out. "Rhys also has done thee a great service in another way. I saw serious bowmanship amongst the farm men of Wym. I suspect the same of Neury. Rhys is behind much of it. Harry. I need to talk with thee about this. I saw how many here are skilled in serious shooting within the longbow. They do not realize how well together we now can defend our interests against marauders."

Haralde rubbed his face, and then peered over his hand covering his mouth at Riennes. My friend. My brother. I know thee intimately. Yet, thee surprise me again. What a wonder thee are.

"My lords. Come eat! Lady Saran says to fetch you," a slave woman holding the hand of a little girl, yelled from the porch of the keep.

Haralde whirled to Riennes. "Brother. We must cover up."

"Why? I be not ashamed," Riennes signaled by spreading his arms wide of a naked body covered by only a rag across his loins.

"Please!" urged Haralde, touching the line of yellow paste on their chests.

"Aaah, yes." Riennes went into his stall and pulled on his silk undershirt. Haralde quickly pulled on a tunic his brother threw him.

As they walked around from behind the keep to its front door, Haralde added: "Let us be jovial. It is the day of her joining. Carts with night pallet and linen tents have already left for the longhouse being built on the land I gave her and Tyne. I am afraid it is nights under the stars again for you and I brother."

Riennes nodded, "Aye. For her, all excitement. And where is our monk, our Godfroi in all of this?"

They walked, this time shoulder at shoulder.

Consternation also walked Haralde. He was all ahoo inside, unable to pull the pieces of his problem and forge a solution. He was disconsolate over his shame. The bits and pieces would not come together.

Magda's fire burns too hot for me. She is just too close to her flame for my wings. Best I not hover near her anymore, lest she singe me and I fall.

Riennes walked with a lighter step. Always he knew Haralde worked harder at dedicating himself with fire greater than his to the inner spiritual discipline of the kandos. Yea, he also knew a day would come if this became too restrictive, too binding when this led to no solutions, his brother would break out of it and cut at the heart of his problem.

He just never thought he would be the one cut.

chapter 7

Death's door slams shut.
The window of life opens.

A SLIGHT SORENESS IN his arse region again reminded Godfroi he swore never to drive a cart again. Yet, here he was thumping across a meadow in the midst of an excited host of farm families on the first day of Lady Saran's joining with Tyne.

Some of these families were supposed to be here. Only principle men of Wym and Neury and their families were invited. Instead, a whole host of families had trudged in from near and far.

The Neury villagers pushed Elder Geraint ahead of them. If their absence from their fields without permission angered their lord, best push an old man at their thegn to suffer the first beatings, giving the rest time to scatter. The old man led them up from the river across the meadow towards where slaves toiled lifting the last huge cut log into place and setting the last stone in the walls of what was soon to be Lady Saran's and Tyne's longhouse manor. They had deserted their fields to celebrate their lady. They risked their lord's anger for her of course after she had protected them all these years.

After years of wasting of the land, this was a chance at fun. They wanted to present their lady with a joining gift, they had said to Godfroi, who was more amongst them now converting pagans and doing church work. Would he lead them to where Tyne and Lady Saran were expected?

Of course he would, Godfroi had replied, as he more and more had looked upon them as his charge, his flock. Besides, he must get on site to prepare himself, to learn what arrangements were being made, and to launch an idea that had been growing inside of him. When better to petition the lord of the land for the building of a chapel than on such a happy occasion, a Longshield joining.

The mood was festive. A farmer broke out in song, and he was joined by his farmer neighbours who sang the supporting chorus to the ditty. It was a short lilting piece about livestock copulating in the spring, copying their masters, and the song ended with men laughing and their wives and daughters tittering.

Godfroi turned around to smile at this jovial company. Then he saw Magda and her son Odim and his spirits turned down. In the back of her cart were wooden barrels, her gift to Lady Saran and Tyne, so the wives of Neury had told him.

A roar burst out from the crowd around him. He swiveled the other way and looked to see what was happening. Look! They shouted. Rhys joins us! Godfroi looked up to where they were pointing and along a high ridge with two children in front walked the excellent bowman. The Fremen, he remembered the two lords called him. Some of the farm children broke away and ran towards him, as did some of the young village maids and a few mothers following after. All rushed up to him, embraced him, some of the maids each pulling the other off to have their turn, while some of the farm wives picked up his two children.

Some of the older men broke away and went forward to greet him. "Oh! This is going to be a grand old time with Rhys here," one man walking beside Godfroi uttered. A few young men walking with him whooped, turned and ran back down the meadow to return to Neury.

Godfroi, puzzled, turned to the man beside him.

The man smiled, "They did not bring their staves with them. They have gone back for their bows. With Rhys here, there is going to be some grand shooting."

When the Longshield entourage of carts and horsemen topped a knoll overlooking the Saran and Tyne land, and they looked down at the crowd and the noise and the trestle tables set up in the meadow and some archers shooting at wooden targets, Haralde groaned.

"I feared some such thing might happen," growled Haralde. Riennes stood up in his stirrups, looked around, sat back down and grinned. "What good is a wedding if no one showed up to stand witness and wish the couple good cheer."

Lady Saran's cart slid up beside them. She stood up, clapped her hands in joy and cried out": "They should not do this. Yet, I love them for it."

"Look at that. They have food on those tables. They have been holding out on us. They expect to stay the night." Haralde turned, and nodded to the two soldiers they had brought with them. "I will have them out of here and back to their fields in a heartbeat."

"My Lord Longshield, let them stay," Saran pleaded. "We all have fought and suffered much together over the years. Now let us enjoin our loyalties."

Haralde sat, muttering to himself. Tyne, gauging Haralde's changing heart, moved his horse beside him. He struck Haralde on the shoulder. "Aye, my lord. Might it be a time for dancing? Tonight let us get drunk together."

It hit the mark right. Haralde threw up his hands. "So be it. But by the Ger's beard, I will boot all in the ass if I find any man here in two days time."

Saran sat down. "Thank you. I am much pleased with my son this day, as I have been since all the days he has been returned to me."

Haralde wagged his finger at her. "Thee knew I could say naught. I think thee also knew about this all along. Mama, thee got your way again." Then he barked out loud, "And I swear an oath now before all here I will endeavor to make sure thee do always."

Everyone laughed. Haralde had struck a good note. It would be a grand wedding.

They started down.

The crowd below, spotting them, started to shift. A delegation of women holding branches of flowers and with some woven in their hair, broke away and came forward. Amongst them was their thin, dark-robed Godfroi, acting proper and somber. In his hand he carried a bowl of blessed holy water.

The small figures of the serf women surrounded Saran, giggling and wishing her a happy day. Plain they appeared, shabby in their course, and in some places, repaired brown woolen clothing. Yet, their hair was braided in colorful flower garlands. A few ribald jibes were made about how a wife can rule her husband. Lady Saran took it all in stride, smiling, collecting some of the flowers, holding the hands briefly of some of the women she knew. Haralde and Riennes moved past them to Godfroi.

"Good morning my lords," wished Godfroi.

"Good morning monk Godfroi. And what in the Ger's name is this all about? What are these men doing here?" demanded Haralde with feigned gruffness, but secretly warmed by their loyalty to his mother.

Riennes sat astride his black, bemused by this solemn air Haralde affected as lord and master here. This was not the brother he knew.

Yet, maybe this formal, dignified mantle he wore was a role he knew he would adopt when he arrived back to Neury. Or, maybe it was the weight of his obligation to his overlord, an earl of the king, sitting on his shoulder. That earl waited for an accounting of Haralde's tax payment in silver to him and thus to the king. I wonder if thus it will be to me when I get home to Montford?

A few men had followed behind Godfroi with some trepidation; a delegation.

"Go ahead then Master Geraint," Haralde spoke seriously as the men shoved the Neury elder out front to speak for them.

"My Lord Longshield, we ask to stay, to give Lady Saran our respect. You did say maybe a wedding was a good time for a hallmote and the swearing of loyalty," he said, then dropped down almost to a whisper. "Also, we have a wedding present to give her and her betrothed."

"Hmm. Is it a good gift, then? It must not be anything shabby, nor what is mine. It must be truly thoughtful," warned Haralde. "What is it?"

Geraint glanced at his lady and her man slightly behind Haralde and Riennes, then asked if he could approach Haralde in quiet.

Haralde motioned him forward, disregarded the stink of the man as he leaned down from his saddle, and listened as the old man whispered.

When Haralde sat up, he was beaming. "Now that, Master Geraint, is a fine wedding gift. Aye, thee all can stay. Light fires tonight. Be merry. But mind thee behave. I will have no drunkenness at my mother's joining."

The bunch of men behind broke up with a whoop, and they raced away with their news towards where the trestle tables were being set up and wood cut for fires.

Riennes was curious. Haralde leaned over and whispered: "They have captured a *clerwr* and dragged him to Neury for these festivities."

A what?"

"Aye. A Welsh poet, a storyteller, more for thee, a jongleur. Master Geraint told me he is one of laughter, who tells jokes and does tricks. He will sing and recount sagas tonight and tomorrow after the ceremonies," answered Haralde.

"Oh, ho! ho!" chuckled Riennes. "How did they do that?"

"I suspect they have pooled some coin for him. I also suspect they hope for some generosity from thee."

"Me? I have no money. Thee are the keeper of our purse."

"Oh, Riennes. Let not thy pinch-penny soul rule thee. I am sure thee have coin stuffed away in that stall of yours. Remember. This is for your mama's betrothal."

"Godfroi. What is that you bear in your hands?" asked Tyne as he on his horse sidled into the group.

"Blessed holy water Tyne. It is for you," answered Godfroi, bowing his head.

"You mean, thusly we are to do this now, here?" demanded Tyne, his bush of red hair bristling.

"Aye my lord. Right up there, under that tree, a pagan place you asked of me, in the privacy of the outside and with your betrothed."

"Aaagh!" Tyne growled. "Damn this whole business."

"My lord. Do not curse at this very holy moment of your life," admonished Godfroi. "Your very soul is to be saved."

"Saran! Saran!," barked Tyne as he turned his horse around clumsily and trotted back to his lady to complain about Godfroi's choice of this moment.

Thus, for the next little while, Haralde and Riennes kneeled before their horses a little way off, and respectfully watched Tyne kneel under a tree before Godfroi with Saran kneeling beside him as witness.

He and Saran had discussed it and the mad Irish warrior had agreed to give up his pagan beliefs to become a Christian on the day before their wedding.

Tyne never discussed any inner conflicts with Haralde or Riennes, but they did hear him grumble under his breath from time to time about pleasing Saran. However, they did ascertain he would let not Godfroi turn him into a Latin Christian.

After, as Tyne and Saran thumped away on their cart towards their longhouse, her arms around her man, Godfroi strolled down past his two young lords.

"He is difficult over this," whispered Godfroi. "He resisted me, said he would become only a Celtic Christian, not a child of Rome."

"Aaah. So for thee, he is only half way to heaven?" chided Riennes.

"You Welsh and your Celtic gibberish at religious ceremonies. The church feels it is an abomination still. Yea. Half way to heaven. I will work on him, and get him and the rest of you half Christians the rest of the way."

Haralde bellowed in good humour. "Holy man. That be the closest thing to a joke I ever heard thee bespeak."

"Look. There be Magda and her son. I must speak with them," and Haralde's heels thumped his horse in the ribs. He thundered down towards the building site of the longhouse.

Riennes watched him go, and switched his gaze ahead of him where the woman and her son unloaded barrels aside of the trestle tables and the high pile of wood that would be a great blaze tonight.

He progressed not. He knew to stay away. Yet, he sat and watched the woman work, and admired her lines, her movements, and her deftness. He could not take his eyes from her, from the workings of her body, from the joy of her son and her purpose with the barrels. He closed his eyes momentarily and felt a glowing. Such a warming he had never felt before. It chased away all his apprehensions. The only memory left was of her face, of her character, and then he opened his eyes again.

He watched as Haralde joined them, as he dismounted, as he talked to her, as she cowed her head, as he raised his arms in a kind of emphasis, and his heart gladdened as she shook her head in rejection.

He also smiled as he watched Godfroi pass by the two, then with a stem of many leaves and casually flicked the remainder of his holy water over Magda's barrels.

Shortly, Haralde mounted and he and his black trudged up to him. "She rejects me," he confessed. "Again. And then again."

"Have thee listened to her. Or, has she spoken ill of your character?"

"Nay. She just shakes her head no. There be something wrong with her," Haralde said adamantly.

"Listen brother. Talk to our mama. She knows all of them," suggested Riennes. "And I have heard her intimate something of Magda."

"HO!" Haralde bellowed suddenly. "Who pokes at me?"

Riennes turned with Haralde to look down and discover Rhys standing behind them with a long staff of wood investigating Haralde's leg.

"I beg my lord's pardon," Rhys bowed respectfully and spread wide his arms. "You were engrossed in a matter trivial, and yet here was I and you took no notice" said the aggrieved greenwood man.

"Did we now!" barked Haralde. "Shame Riennes that thee noticed not our Fremen."

Riennes sat back in his saddle, feeling so good over Rhys being here. Taken in all, Riennes enjoyed the fun of the man. This wedding, Rhys' support of it by his very appearance, Godfroi's enjoining of Tyne to his new Christianity, and Magda's rejection of his brother's advances, all suddenly endorsed his life's journey and his continuing support of his brother. He threw a leg across his saddle and embroiled himself in stirring the wit of their Fremen.

"My Lord Longshield was engrossed in serious matters." Riennes kept a straight face. "May I hazard it was gross of thee to . . . . grossly poke at his person like that."

Rhys laughed, sat down on a stump of a tree, and poked and pried out a thorn from a bare foot. "If I had not, like this thorn, my Lord Longshield would not have gained any relief from at least one matter pricking at his mind."

Haralde smothered a grin, knew he should not cross wits with this man, but did out of sheer enjoyment.

"Pray man, what relief?"

"Relief from your worry about what entertainment and amusement you must provide at your mama's wedding. Something that mad Irish man will also enjoy, as well your guests and even you, my lords."

"Must! No problems have I over entertaining anyone," groused Haralde. " . . . . what kind of entertainment?"

"Why, a two-day archery contest my lord."

Riennes's eyes widened at the suggestion. He swung down and stepped out in front of his mount to better witness this whole thing unfold. "Watch out Lord Haralde."

"Two days to watch the finest bowmen in all of your lands," went on Rhys,

"What be thee about, Fremen?" Haralde finally asked.

"My wedding present to Lady Saran, my Lord Longshield. Two days of the finest, skilled, most deadly shooting in all of this land. Over two days, men and women will watch in fascination, and praise your love for your mother for providing such fare. And I will organize the whole contest, so thee can be about other business."

"Fremen. I have held thee in short regard," Haralde went on, waiting for the end of this. "Go ahead. Indeed, a fine thing thee do."

"You approve?"

"Excellent idea. Yes."

"Good. Then there is just the small matter of the prize money."

"Prize? How did we get from archery to money?" asked Haralde, already suspecting the trip wire this poacher was leading him into. He dismounted and stood with Riennes.

"To bring in archers from all around, two gold coins should be put up as the prize."

Haralde's body stiffened at the mention of gold and his eyes widened aghast at the woodsman's audacity.

"Wait, wait, wait," demanded Riennes, knowing he could not hold laughter in much longer. "Thee poke Lord Longshield in the leg and now thee expect coin?"

"You are a Norman, so I do not expect you to connect the points of this very important proposal very quickly," Rhys said with a straight face.

"Gold! Gold, here in Neury, from me. Are thee sure thee are not referring to the king's treasury for such a prize? And . . . and . . . ," Haralde spluttered. He rubbed his hand across his face, and then stared over his hand at his mouth. "And do I understand rightly thee intend to enter. Is not the best bowman in the land thee?"

"Aaah my lords! Some say yes. Some say no. And a breeze or a slip of a bow ring could turn the skill of an unknown into a great archer."

The three men stared at each other over a brief blow of a breeze. Then all broke into hearty male laughter.

"Fremen. Lower your aim. Two Saracen silver coins will we hazard," admonished Haralde. "Gold just does not figure in the Longshield household."

"Then we must accept such a prize, one of such generosity that your name will be praised throughout Neury and Wym," agreed Rhys.

"How do you propose to do this?" asked Haralde, wiping a tear from his eye.

"Short targets the first day. That is where we will get most entries. Then long bow shooting the other day. And I mean long. Here, the tough nuts will endure," suggested Rhys.

"Done. And I and Lord de Montford will be able to enter."

"That be interesting. I know not how you shoot, but by your suggestion, I sense the prize could be snatched from me," Rhys poked them.

"Or from us," laughed Riennes. "Thus, I know not how my lord feels, but I will put up the silver for Tyne, who will judge the short draw."

"And I silver for my mama who will judge the long draw," followed Haralde.

"Naught could be fairer, for no woman in this land is as fair of heart as she," finished Rhys in seriousness. "It is done then. I will go arrange the targets."

"Hold there bowman." Haralde stopped Rhys in his turn."

"My lord?"

"I propose a third contest."

Rhys paused, trying to catch what Haralde was about. His eyes flicked to Riennes, then back to Haralde.

"I propose horse shooting at targets."

"I do not understand."

"A silver coin for the best shooting from the back of a running horse." Haralde's eyes glinted. "That would give us a chance at winning."

"Yea, but no one here has any skill at such a thing."

"Let us find out. It will be very entertaining, and as thee said, an errant breeze could make a hero out of a farmer."

"Very well my lord. But who will put up the third coin?"

"Thee will."

"What! I cannot. I am but a poor woodsman. I have no coin."

"I suspect thee will after the first two events."

"But that just means if either of you win I will have to give you back your . . . . Oh ho! You crafty knave. Pardon me my lords, but you two are buggers. To put a fine point on it, I am now shooting under pressure.

Haralde put out both his arms, turned the palms of his hand upwards, shrugged and grinned.

Riennes, the bystander in all this, put his hand over his mouth to smother a chuckle.

Rhys stood fuming for a moment. Then: "So be it. But I wish to enter this event."

"It is open to anyone."

"Good. Then I ask a boon of you."

"Yes?"

"No one can shoot a longbow from a horse. As I have no short bow, I need to borrow yours, to practice a bit."

Riennes roared at that. "Harry, I think he has thee there. It is only fair."

Haralde grimaced, then agreed and shook a finger. "Yes, but not without me telling thee first that thee are the greater bugger here, Rhys of Gwent. A sneaky varlet!"

All three laughed. They remained there, bemused. Haralde walked to Rhys, put a hand on his shoulder, and said: "I thank thee for my life. Such shooting. He was a breath away in cleaving me half in half. If there be a commorth due, it is one I owe thee."

The face of Rhys went a deep red. For the first time, a lord had caught him out. He thought of his children. He was truly embarrassed to be spoken to in such a manner by a lord. He stepped back so that Haralde's hand fell away. Always, such uchelwyrs, such high born men, demanded even after his service, some kind of payment of him. Always he ran. But not here. For the first time, not here.

Haralde eased his hand away slowly on seeing the Fremen's embarrassment and changed the subject. He could have been insulted by the Fremen shrugging him off, but let it go. Haralde could see Rhys was genuinely confused by his gratitude.

"I see two children," observed Haralde, nodding over Rhys's shoulder. Up the meadow Lady Saran approached them holding hands with two small ones.

"Are these your two? If so, would they visit upon Lord de Montford and me?

Rhys stood immobile. That overlords such as these two would inquire of his children! "My lords. I do not know what to say. Surely yes. You honour my wife."

Lady Saran approached and the two children eased in behind her when she stopped. Two shy faces, a wee boy with a thumb in his mouth and a girl of about six or seven, peeked out. The two were dressed in the skins of wild animals and wool. Haralde could see by the stitching the tailoring was done by their father.

"My Lord Haralde and Riennes, I want you to meet Rhys's children, Gwenna and Hugh. Gwenna, Hugh, bow now and say 'My Lords' just as we practiced," suggested Lady Saran smiling.

The two looked up at the giants in front of them, and then at their father, who nodded encouragingly. The girl hesitated, then bowed behind Lady Saran and said, "My Lords," and the boy then, over his thumb, "Lords," then both dashed for Rhys who gathered them in his arms. Everyone laughed.

The two turned in his arms, proud of their achievement, and smiled at everyone.

"Rhys, they are beautiful," remarked Riennes, stepping forward. He took Gwenna's small fingers and bowing low, greeted: "Lady Gwenna, I greet thee." Gwenna giggled and buried her face in her father's shoulder. Hugh took his thumb out his mouth and offered his fingers. "Master Hugh. I greet thee too," and Hugh then buried his face.

Haralde then stepped forward and put his hands on both their legs. "Thee must bring your father one day and come visit me. And I will take thee for a ride in a cart pulled by a horse. Would thee like that?" They both looked at their father who nodded and they jiggled their heads up and down to Haralde, and then burrowed into Rhys's shoulder again.

All laughed again, creating a jovial mood amongst them. Rhys put his children down, offered his hand and Saran took it. That was more than a gesture of familiarity or politeness, it seemed to Riennes. The touching of hands was of gratitude. There is a story here.

"I thank you my lords, Saran," nodded Rhys. "They will chatter away at me all night about this. They will be very grateful, and so will I. Now I must be away to that group of families down there. We have a certain thing to do," he nodded to fellow conspirators Haralde and Riennes.

"Do you wish me to mind Gwenna and Hugh," asked Saran.

"No. You have much to do this day. Besides, there are friends down there with children to play with. My Lords. My Lady." The children took off running before him down the hill yelling all the way.

"Sit down, both of you, beside your mama," said Saran, patting both sides of a big log. "I have two stories to tell you. These are things you should know. When I finish, you will understand more."

They both dropped their reins and complied.

And she related two tales:

It was winter. A cold rain had fallen from the heavens for two weeks. It was the worst kind of bitter, cold, wet weather roaring in off the Hibernian Sea. We knew nothing of Rhys. We did not know at that time he had been living up in Brekin for almost a year. This night the wind howled against the Longhield stone. We huddled around our fire pit, piling in the logs to keep us warm. There came a thump on our door and it was pushed opened by one of our people who motioned me to come to him. I did and he nodded outside to a figure of a man, water streaming down off his hood. In his hand stood a wee girl child soaked to the skin, and crying. The guard said the man told him he was in dire need. I had him brought in immediately to the fire. The little girl shivered from the cold. My people stripped off her excuse of a clout and dried her down. When we stripped off the man's capuchin, under a covering in his arms was a babe, wet through, coughing, crying, red of face, fevered. I immediately cleared every one away from one side of our big fire pit and assigned a place to set the babe down to get warm and dry. My girls would not let me attend, but chose one of them to do so. None were then allowed to go near that place for fear others could catch the same cough. The man we stripped down was deeply worn out, trembling for help. We dried, and brought him to the fire and fed him and his wee girl.

He told us his story. He was Rhys of Gwent, a wounded survivor of a battle way to the south years ago who ran and fled into the woods. In time, he passed out, was found by nearby villagers, attended to and was healed. It was there he met and married his love. They had a baby girl. And then again, tragedy. A band of roughs raided the village, killing, ransacking, and raping. He and his family fled into the woods. The son of a woodcutter, Rhys knew forest craft. Tired of the brutality of other men, he swore never to come into the open again, rather to stay within the safety of a forest. They moved slowly north through the trees until they reached Brekin. His wife gave him a beautiful son. However, even the forest ceased to be a refuge. The winter came, the rains, a flood and washout carried away their fur sleeping coverings, rugs, food and other belongings. His wife caught a chill, a fever, and then died in his arms. He did not know how he was going to care for his baby boy, let alone his daughter. He tried to make his way down through the mountain forests, slipped and sprained his ankle. He struggled on, saw a light, and came to a cave. In its mouth he saw three old women cooking, stirring a great pot. He went in and they took care of him. A fourth, a very young woman, the pride and joy of these three old dammes, directed them.

This young woman had magic in her eyes and in her hands. She was some sort of Druid, but of her own strange sort. They bound up his ankle, fed them all and then said he must hurry on for the babe's sake, that his daughter and especially his son needed special care. They directed him to me. The babe's fever broke two days later. The child rebounded in great health, his daughter began to run around here, and he within his grief, to laugh. I told him he was to stay with us. 'My name is Rhys. I have naught to pay you for your good heart. I will stay until spring. My name will I give over to the protection of your house. I am a forester. I will give you of the bounty of the forest from time to time'. He left in sunshine. I gave him names of our good families he could stay with when he needed to for the sake of his children, that I would tell them to watch out for him and his babies.

"And the young priestess?" asked Riennes.

"She was Magda."

Magda showed up here years ago when she was fostered out by her mother to an old woman, an Old Religionist priestess. It turned out it was her grandmother. Her mother was carried off by a man from Wym. This old priestess was renowned through the area for her herbs, chants and healing abilities. They say she was a Pict, from the far north, way up where the ice forms sometimes. I let her stay because she became a comfort to the women here. I count one of her potions as my salvation, when I came down seriously sick. Stoerm returned home one day with Odard, a comrade in arms who had stuck by him during a pursuit of a rebel Welsh prince and his raiding band. He was a Breton, originally from across the canalem. One night she came to me, and told me she was pregnant by Odard and asked me what should she do. I asked her what her chief concern was in this and she answered, her child. Then, you must marry for the child's sake. She did, and from then on turned away from the Old Religion. Her grandmother disappeared shortly after that. I heard she is down country, living with her daughter in Wym.

"The old priestess, was she Morog?"

Lady Saran turned a surprised eye upon Riennes, struck again by his foresight. "Yes. That old one left because Odard was a Christian and there was turmoil between them."

There came a day when one of my people who was on the coast of the Dee Estuary north of us came riding home quickly. He warned a Hibernia-Danish army had landed there and was moving inland. I warned my people and closed Longshield Fortress. The main raiding party did not come our way, but a remnant of it foraging ahead did. Magda was tending to her baby, a lovely little girl, when she heard the clash of steel, a thump of bodies, and her husband fell dead into the doorway of her new house. Thus was to begin her nightmare. Two armed beasts jumped over his body and hurled themselves upon her. While one ransacked the house, the other beat her almost senseless, then ripped her clothes off and commenced to rape her. That is when her baby began to cry. She cried so much, the beast upon her became irritated. She cried out no, but the animal reach into the child's crib, flung the baby up into the air and pierced it with his spear. With the baby screaming, he drove the spear into the wall, then knocked Magda down again as she tried to stick him with a knife. He raped her just under the spear, which stuck out horizontal to the floor. The spear began to sag, and she under him, watched in horror as her disemboweled baby began to slide down towards them on the grease of her own bloody guts, screeching all the way. The butchered babe came to rest just behind the beast's head, looking down at them.

Three things happened at the same time: the man seeded in her, the baby died at that instant and then the man slumped over her, two arrows in his back. The other man ransacking her house ran outside and fell, killed by two other arrows. Her rescuer came in, hauled her out from under her rapist and carried her outside. Men and women in the area came running and took her.

"Was her rescuer Rhys?" asked Haralde.

"Yes".

For almost a year, Magda lived in a state of silent, living death. Nothing we did could bring her out of it. In that time, a baby grew inside her. Midwives literally had to do everything themselves to birth the baby. It was the boy Odim. Then, a strange reversal happened. She came around, began to brighten and attend to the child. I brought her here so we could care for the two. One night, when she told me all of what had happened, she said her son was not the offspring of the beast, but of her husband Odard. She explained that at the moment of conception, her baby girl died looking down at her, and her soul jumped into her womb. She is inside Odim. Odim carries the soul of her little girl, the daughter of her husband and her. She said she can prove it. She said watch as Odim grows up. He will be magical. He will be exceptionally smart. He will accomplish much because he has two destinies. What she has predicted, I think has come true. Watch Odim in the days ahead. There is something about him.

Haralde who had been holding his breath through the tale let it all whisper out. He shook his head. Now he understood what was in Magda, the madness and the magic and most especially, the rejection.

Riennes had dropped his head. He stared at the ground, brooding.

"Now you must understand one thing. Magda hates violence and hard men. She rejects them all, those horse warriors who ride weaponed. She longs for a peaceful life, for healing, for goodness, for the simplicity of her people. Once she rejected her grandmother's Old Religion. Now she practices her own kind, to nature, to the secrets to be found in it. She works hard to know all things.

Riennes raised his head. "Is that why she rejects us? Is that why she kneeled, trembling before us like a frightened mouse when we met her? She will not even make eye contact?"

"Yes. You two terrify her."

She watched her two sons out the corner of her eye. They both just sat there, hand clasped together.

Then, as if a signal passed between them, they rose, took up the reins of their mounts, and simply just walked away from each other in different directions, much shaken.

CHAPTER 8

A wedding binds two joys,
The families argue over the differences.

HARALDE STRIPPED RIDING pad, stirrups, and reins from his black and turned her loose with others in the pasture. The beast nickered at Riennes's horse grazing across the way, and moved off to join him.

"My Lord?"

Haralde turned and two farm boys were there with arms out to relieve him of his tack. "We will stow it for you in the longhouse outbuildings. They have just been completed." "Very good," he thanked them as he made off.

People shouted with glee all around him. Children dashed by him laughing, chasing one another. Some of his Neury vassals walked by and in deference, bowed slightly, waved and called out his name.

It pulled Haralde out of his somber mood over Magda. He smiled. More and more they were anticipating his needs, appearing suddenly when he needed something, or anticipating something he needed done. They were freeing him from the little nuisances, the little many niggardly details that crowded his mind, setting him free to address more important problems. What he liked was they did it not out of servility, but out of respect. They honoured Haralde out of their duty to serve him, yes. Yet, they had judged him and his personal code of service towards them, and were imitating him. He was home, amongst his own people. It was happening now as he had dreamed it.

"Haralde. Thee wished ….? Is this a good time for our gathering?"

Haralde turned and nodded to Riennes and his entourage of the principle men of Wym and Neury approaching him from the river.

"Oh yes. A good time. I meant the wedding to be an occasion when we all could sit down together quiet. However, it seems many more of my people and Lord de Montford's have come here than were invited."

They assembled down by the river. The men had cleared a circle, erected hasty low benches and wooden stumps before higher ground from where their masters would address them. As they stood for a moment in the murmur of conversation, Haralde and Riennes moved amongst them, greeted them, made recognition here, an introduction there.

"Munch! It is good to look upon thee again," grinned Haralde honestly, his hand on the farmer's shoulder. "Where are your young men? I would meet them?"

"Where they should be my Lord Haralde, working my fields. If I had brought them, and they saw all this, I would never get them back behind a hoe," grinned Munch.

"Haralde, I want thee to meet Munch's brother," and Haralde looked down upon the back of a gnome of a man.

"Lord," answered Polcher, not having to bow, but turned his head sideways to greet Haralde. "God bless to you. You son of Lady Saran. I wish I be."

The crowd chuckled, and then looked to see how Haralde would take in the bent man.

Haralde was somewhat taken aback. A hunchback almost. Gibberish. An idiot maybe? What was he here doing amongst this company?

Riennes stepped up beside him, smiling. "Polcher runs the Munch holdings, can out plough Munch and the boys, run a deer to ground." A low chuckle rumbled from Munch. "And besides that, he has an ear for music. Master Polcher. Sing the sailor song I played thee," requested Riennes.

In a strong baritone voice, Polcher sang a tune. He added his own words to the song, words that really did not come with the tune but which Polcher embellished. His voice was beautiful, strong, filling the clearing. The others around them cleared their throats and tried to catch up with him, to pick up on the tune. He finished.

"Wonderful," Haralde clapped his hand when it ended. He had caught on. There was more to this bent man than it seemed. "Then I welcome Master Polcher. Thee must go give your best wishes to Lady Saran before this is all over."

Polcher winked at Haralde. "He tells me he has a surprise," said Riennes as he took Haralde down the line to meet Alfold, and the other men of Wym. Then it was the turn of Neury.

Haralde greeted men like Bleddyn and Dafydd who had helped in the removal of the body Aelfgar, and Aled and Geraint the Elder of the Neury ford.

Then, for the next hour, they sat to hear the demands of loyalty and vassalage to their two lords: when they would be registered in a great book, dictums about agriculture, defence of the manors and their fields, religion with the presence of a Latin monk they had brought with them, of the health of the communities, and of their future according to events unfolding to the east: the coming power of a Norman, now king of the Anglos and Saxons.

"Now, listen to what we say," Riennes ordered as he slowly paraded his authority before them as he passed by and looked each man in the eye. "We are your master here. We will demand of thee tithe, tax, food render, service, rent, and just as important, obedience. All will be done fairly."

"Know thee we owe loyalty in turn to an overlord," explained Haralde in his turn. "We are vassals to another who owns all here. We are subtenants, enfeoffed to a higher baron of the king. We must pay rent and tithe to him, and thus his to the king. In short, we owe all to our new king. Know thee then Lord de Montford and Lord Longshield are king's men. This higher servant to the king, if he receives not his due from us, all here can be burned to the ground and the land turned over to other families. This cannot happen. So we will serve thee, your masters, well so that the king's representative is satisfied and need not come here."

Both walked up and down, explaining, giving them insight. They were thunder struck. No one, not even Lord Stoerm Longshield, had ever talked to them this way before. Some sat, mouth open. Others leaned forward, eyes bright, realizing what was unfolding here was new. They kept up with Haralde and Riennes as best they could and found gratification in being told things. They were being exposed to something never as before, and most knew it. These two lords were as a light leading them through what was a long night.

To accomplish a peaceful community, their two lords chose them to be members of a council: that their neighbors would come to this council with issues of land, trespass, lot disputes, of planting decisions, of expectations of harvest, of communal efforts to meet harvests, of animal husbandry, of civil disputes such as taxes, marriage, divorce and infidelity.

They were to hold meetings separately in their own manors, and thusly together as one joint council in the fall after harvest. On the morrow, they were to circulate amongst the people, tell them of their meeting today, and ready them for their vassalage in a hallmote.

"So that our interests are attended to, we will oversee the fall meeting of council," informed Riennes.

"And if we cannot attend, our representative . . . . here he comes now…..," and Tyne came into the circle. . . . "the man who is about to submit himself to his own overlord, Tyne of Cumraugh, to be the husband of my mother." With a sweep of his hand, Haralde presented his rough leader of the soldiers of Fortress Longshield.

The principle men stood up and whistled. Of their rough country humour, they wanted to jibe at him about his virility, about his courage in the nuptial bower, but they knew him not, nor did they totally understand what was unfolding.

"If either I or Lord Haralde cannot be at your council, Tyne will be there as our reeve, to instruct our interests to thee," outlined Riennes.

"It be we may have to travel to Chester, if the Earl of Cheshire calls a session of the shire's council. Tyne will represent us here," instructed Haralde.

Tyne made a little bow. "And if any of you buggers gets in my way and makes me mad in this council thing, I will heave a fletch blade up your asses," warned Tyne.

Haralde coughed at that, glanced at Riennes who shook his head and put his hand over his eyes. They had not had time to talk in detail to Tyne before the wedding about his new duties as reeve. No doubt, a rough start.

The gathering broke up, unsure of what had been done on this patch of ground beside the River Clee.

Munch sidled up to Riennes. "My lord. My fellows are confused. My neighbors, my friends, we do not understand all this. It is all foreign to us. We have naught done things like this before," Munch pondered.

"Thee know your people. I have seen them come to thee with problems. Have thee not sat with your men and talked of problems, what to do?"

"Aye, but this, this coming in a way to air their problems to be witnessed by everyone, this is not our way. We do it quietly, slowly. And if they do not like how we want the problem solved, some do not do it."

"And did some ill feeling remain afterward"

"Yes, sometimes."

"Well, Haralde and I do not wish to see this here. Under our seal, the problem will be discussed, then your lord's wishes will be carried out. The thing is quickly done. And whatever decision thee arrive at, we will enforce it. Lord Haralde and I have an idea how to do this."

Munch was still perplexed. Riennes went on. "We wish to go back to the days where Cymru was a place of peace and order, where laws were created and people followed them."

Munch said he had heard that was so long a time ago, that an Irish monk had told him how Wales was a centre of religion, music, law, learning.

"There! Thee see!"

"Yesss! I see."

"Talk amongst yourselves tonight. Pull Master Geraint to you. Thee two meet with Haralde or I on the morrow with questions your council may have. Mayhaps we can help thee along."

Munch went away, nodding his head.

Tyne came up to them. "Did I say well? I hope I was tough, as you asked?"

"Thee did well," answered Haralde, putting his arm around him. "Rather roughly put, but yes. Riennes nor I may not have been so strict, but it works none the less. Obey thee they will."

Haralde turned to Riennes. "I am tired. I am athirst. Let us go tap one of Magda's barrels. I suspect ale. I need to drink deep."

"You cannae," jumped in Tyne. "Saran has sent me to tell you, quick, come to her. It seems a trestle table has been set up and she and I are to sit there. A line is forming. She says many are anxious to present gifts for our joining."

"Oh no," groaned Haralde.

"What Haralde?"

"Who is doing this? Who is master here, thee and I or them? We are losing control here. Let us hurry. They will have them wedded, bedded and with a family even before I can get to my own mother's joining."

It was too late.

Neury and Wym were lined up under the late morning sun, some bearing chickens or a pig or a cage of doves or cloth or wool. One man held a shovel, another an axe and some farm tool for the household. Women carried pots of cooked food, stew, bread, vegetables to put on the table before Lady Saran for the grand wedding feast.

As Haralde and Riennes walked up the line, he heard one man say his neighbors' gift would be a huge pile of cut wood to warm them at night.

Haralde wanted to chastise them for hiding all of this from him, that some of this should be brought to the Longshield keep, that it was render they owed him.

However, as he proceeded up the line, this irritation eased, to be replaced by a satisfaction. They loved her. They were loyal to her. Out of such deep feelings, peace and order had settled onto the land. Such would make it easier for him and Riennes in the days ahead.

As Riennes and Haralde and Tyne came around behind the table to stand with Saran, Master Geraint went down on one knee and with a flourish of spreading arms, presented what he said was the overall wedding gift from Neury and Wym.

"What is it he said?" asked Tyne slipping into the chair beside his lady.

"I do not know Tyne. He made a flowery speech, something about a special gift from all here, one that will follow us all day, even to our wedding bed. Look at them all. I cannot believe this is happening."

Geraint, squeezing his woolen cap, bowed deeply, and then found himself in trouble with bones and muscles that would not answer directly. A neighbor straightened him up to his feet. With a flourish of his arm, he turned to present something.

Everyone turned their heads. The action was like a ripple down the line. Each head swiveled in turn to look back. There was silence. Nothing. What gift? The crowd murmured.

Then, a pipe. Riennes was the first to hear it. He whirled around and all at the table turned.

Out of a bush behind them stepped a young man, one half dressed in cloth the color of wine and the other half, green. He had a funny peaked hat with a red ball on top hanging from a string and as he played, it swayed.

"Oh! A clerwr!" Saran's hands came up to her mouth. She had not seen such since Stoerm took her as a young girl to London. It was not possible for one to be here in these rough uplands.

The man played a lilting piece, did a little jig, spun around, swayed his head, tipped off balance and kicked up some dust.

"Why, he is drunk," whispered Tyne, as the player swayed, staggered a little bit, tripped over things that really were not there.

Riennes saw different. The musician had the crowd laughing at those antics. And he was a piper. He was hitting every note right. And he was young man, athletic, flexible. The villagers had found a good one. The piper came round their table, got entangled in a small bush, fought the plant, fell forward, his pipe flipping way up into the air, went into a forward roll in front of them, bounced up on his feet, spread his arms out in greeting, and the pipe came down and settled perfectly in his hand.

A roar went up from the crowd; giggles, laughter.

The clerwr threw his arms back, did a perfect back flip, and landed on the grass with his legs split. Men groaned, as if in pain and women eyed his strong thighs, tight out. He brought his pipe to his lips and with a lilting flourish, brought his song to an end.

Everyone at the table laughed, and then clapped their hands, especially Riennes who knew how difficult it was to do two or three physical things at the same time while attempting to keep perfect pitch.

The jester attempted a funny verse:

"Lady Saran and Master Tyne,
I will play thee all in rhyme. Oops!"

Laughter, as he acted surprised he had accomplished a rhyme.

"For Lady Saran I will lewd in song,
To erect tonight your warrior strong. Ooooh!"

He clapped his hand over his mouth, to prevent further naughty from slipping past his lips.

The crowd roared at that. And then for the next little while, he cleverly composed a poem to Saran, the lady lord who as a warrior woman held these lands against the beasts, until the hills echoed with the legend of her, until her man Tyne came to stand with her to fight together, until the sun came out again.

He then cart wheeled down the table, bounded up and with another pipe flourish, composed another poem, a stirring saga to the courage of her two sons who appeared out of the mist of her past to slay the brigand devil, the Longshield family's true paladins.

"That is us," Haralde grinned gleefully, jabbing Riennes several times through the whole act, until Riennes moved out of range from the continued bruising of his ribs.

His lines were quick, intelligent, adroit, full of wit and meaning. And he was composing as he went along. Then he stuffed his pipe into a pocket, pulled some colored balls from a pouch. As he walked, more balls joined in. Soon there were red and blue and green balls flying way up above the crowd.

He disappeared down the line, only the colored balls in the air marking his receding presence. He slowly left, instructed to save himself for the wedding dinner and to get out of the way because others needed to make their presentations.

The wedding table laughed, clapped, and gave over generously their appreciation to the people for their gift.

And then it began, the line shuffled forward, gifts were presented to them on the grass in front and food and provender on the table: thick, fur sleeping rugs, special food treats, hanks of pork and beef and venison, gifts of chickens, ducks and wild birds in cages, and household things and tools for Tyne, a wood bed, intricately carved with animals and birds, stuffed not with straw but with wool to keep them warm.

Haralde stood watching not only the quantity but also the quality. His eye told him Neury may be rough ground, may never be rich in crops and livestock as was Wym, but it had a wealth of its own. These goods were good. It bode well for him if he could turn some of this into coin somehow. An idea began to grow.

Something else was welling up; a growing awareness about custom hereabouts. Was now the moment he should present his mama with wedding gifts? He preferred to do it later, in the private moment just before her joining. Then again, wealth was power. Presentation to her before all could have a powerful influence, elevate his stature and give him more sway over his people.

Indecision began to worm around inside him. Then, events squeezed any further hesitation out of him.

The line was coming to an end. The gnome Polcher was bending his way forward. Behind him, Magda with three grandmothers from the village, was struggling forward with a small barrel of what he was sure was her famous ale, or mead.

Riennes anticipated her. He stood up, caught the eye of two farmers standing nearby. "Thee two there! Help those grandmothers." The men hesitated seeing it was Magda he signaled to. Then, they jumped to when they saw Riennes angrily gesture again.

Haralde motioned for two girls and a boy, kitchen slaves from his stronghold, to attend him. The one girl hurried over. "Hellga," he whispered instructions. As he had planned with them earlier, the three hastened away to fetch their Lord's special bundles stowed away in a nearby cart guarded by one of Tyne's armed soldier.

"Polcher. Thee did come," greeted Saran. She stood up and scrambled around their table. Haralde and Riennes were somewhat taken aback over what she did next. Such public affection was not normal. Riennes's nose reminded him Polcher's body bouquet did not exactly attract women. She went out front, bent down, hands on her knees, and looked into the face of the bent. "My eyes are so happy to behold you again. You have not been coming to see me much." And she put her arms around him and helped him shuffle forward with his box.

Suddenly, she shot up and stood back. "You smell smoky. My God Polcher! You have bees about you. What have you been up to?"

A sound of wonder went up from the gathering.

Polcher signaled with one finger that she was to go back behind the table. "Lady must sit," he instructed. "My gift."

"Oh. Yes I see," and she hastened back to sit in her chair.

Sure enough, as Polcher put his box down and opened it, a few bees flew out and stung him. Inconsequential to him were the bites. He beamed over his wedding gift.

Honey! A whole big massive comb of it!

"Oh Polcher! You are hurt?" she asked, then: "No you are not, are you?"

Polcher smiled and shook head no. "Sweet on porridge on wedding morning. For house. For husband."

"What a wonderful natural gift," Saran clapped her hands. "I accept it most joyfully. Where did you get it?"

Polcher's head turned slightly to Riennes, a certain glint to his eyes as he said: "From desert. Let desert provide."

Riennes stood straight up from his chair and barked out laughter. Polcher had struck him wonderful.

"Polcher! Thee onto yourself are a gift to us all. But it is the forest. Let the forest provide."

"Desert magical."

Whereupon Riennes laughed again, wiped a tear from his eye and sat down. They all looked at him. "I will explain later. It is a wonderful joke. Polcher feels this day is magical."

"And it is a wonderful gift," said Tyne rising. Tyne struck it perfect. Husband and host of this gathering, he thanked Polcher and said he was sure he and his betrothed would sup on it delicious in the days ahead.

The slave girls and boys hustled over to Haralde and lay his bundles before him. He instructed them to carefully pick up Polcher's gift and take it up to the longhouse to the food table there.

One of his gifts would mate with Magda's, that is if that small keg she was stepping up to present, was what he thought it was. The idea of the two gifts mated together brought forth a strong sexual blush in him.

Then another event broke over them.

One of Tyne's soldiers, now a horseman riding with one of their new fighting lances with a pennon on it pointed straight up, forded noisily across the river through a wall of splashed water to the whole of them. Men and women stepped back as he pulled up a distance from the table.

Haralde was about to get up and attend, but Tyne was up and running. Haralde sat back down and waited.. It is as it should be. He now is your general. It is his matter to attend to. Haralde set a look of dissatisfaction on his face, irked over this disruption of his mama's happiness.

Tyne hurried back and leaned over Haralde and Riennes.

"We have unexpected visitors. It seems a party of rough, armed men on horse has entered Neury and is on their way here escorted by my men." Tyne had placed his remaining four horse soldiers in strategic spots in the valley to protect everyone against this very thing, a surprise intrusion on this special day.

"Do we to arms?" asked Haralde standing.

"Nay. It seems . . . ." and he turned to Saran . . . . "it is a relation of yours, come to your wedding."

"I see. Then, go greet them Tyne. We will remain seated." Haralde turned to Magda and gently addressed her. "Mistress Magda, stay where thee are. We will take but a moment for this."

Riennes had hurried away at this news. He returned from their cart with the soldier guarding it and with their two kandos.

He handed Haralde his, and the two strapped the scabbards onto their backs.

"They say your marriage day is the busiest day of your life," joked Riennes.

"Nay, hectic. I believe it," answered Haralde cinching tight.

There was the thunder of hooves now, and horses breathing, and neighing, and huffing and leathers squeaking. Then, there they were, down into the water and throwing up spray everywhere.

Tyne stood on the bank and pointed a finger to his left, indicating they should come up to him on that side away from the host of villagers with women and children.

His four soldiers turned that way, but the stranger behind kept riding straight on. There were four heavy men in black with leather vests, and wrapped leggings each carrying spears pointed down. Their leader was dressed dark also, but covered in a white tunic with a red castellan dragon on it. He was fair-haired with it streaming long behind and he wore a head band with things sparkling in it.

They roared up the bank and barely slowed coming into the villagers. Men and women grabbed children and scurried to get out of their way.

"Where have we seen his kind before?" Riennes whispered as they came around in front of the table and stood between the visitors and Saran.

"A dandy. Wants a show," answered Haralde, looking all over carefully.

"A dolt. Haralde! They are well armed."

"Not a gracious way to enter a wedding party. Our horses are in the field and our bows tucked away for the day. Riennes. Get Tyne back to us and let us three greet them here. Let them come to us. Good. There is Rhys come up. His bow is strung."

"Good." And Riennes strode away to catch Tyne's eye.

Tyne and Riennes came back with their horse soldiers and Tyne lined them up on one side facing the clearing in front of Saran.

Riennes came over, bowed gently to Magda and her grandmothers and escorted them around to join Saran behind the table. Before he left, he gazed impolitely into her face. Her eyes went dead to him. She dropped her head.

Haralde motioned to Tyne to come to him. "Riennes and I are going to stand over there with our soldiers. I want thee to act as if thee are in charge here, that this is the wedding day of Lady Saran and thee. Be angry that your people were endangered by their charge through them, and demand who are thee. Do thee understand?"

"Aye my lord. In charge, angry at their behaviour, who are you to disturb us thus."

"Good. Good. I want to take the measure of this party before Riennes and I make ourselves known.

Everyone moved away and took their places.

The interlopers rode in. The four horse soldiers dressed in black were experienced spearmen. They actually were dressed in dark linen shirts and linen drawers. These were covered in black woolen cloaks to their knees trimmed in black fur. Over that each wore a leather cuirasse studded with iron. Tied to their saddles were shields. They were bare headed, some with moustaches. Bare feet hung down. No stirrups had they.

Haralde made them out as foot soldiers. In a fight, they would drop from their small horses at a signal and throw their spears.

These burly soldiers turned their horses inward and lined up facing Tyne's own horse soldiers. They sat there gazing coldly at them. Some started to chuckle, to unnerve, belittle.

The fancy Welsh leader came in on a prancing horse, bigger, likely taken from a Norman or a Saxon, thought Haralde.

He stopped, smiled and bowed low in his saddle. "Greetings. I am Arwel, a prince of the Teulu Bleddyn. I bring greetings from my chieftain Bleddyn ap Gwynfor to Lady Saran Longshield."

Teulu. Fighting family and Welsh battle unit. Riennes sharply appraised the black fighters sitting ahorse. *Might we one day meet in battle?*

The young man loved the attention, all eyes upon him. He slid slowly from his horse, bowed and made his way towards the table. "We have heard so much of the lady lordship who has battled so many incursions onto her lands. She has become a legend in these mountains."

Magda, on a little plot schemed by Lady Saran and her even as the dandy arrived, asked: "And what business have you with Lady Saran whose wedding day this is?"

Arwel, his eyes catching on Magda, smiled as he beheld something bewitching, which Magda seemed to accentuate.

Arwel quickened his pace, leaned over the table and buried Lady Saran in his shadow, as he tried a silver tongue on Magda. "That legend said she was beautiful, but no bard has come even close. I am your cousin, Arwel. Remember me?"

"Yes," said a voice below him. Saran stood up, brushed her head against his chin and bumped him backwards. "And you are still as impolite and rude as I can remember."

Arwel looked at her as she rose, then at Magda, and then back, and then at the noble bearing of the older woman, and realized his mistake.

"Aaah. But you always enjoyed the tricks I played on you. Do not you remember this one." Lady Saran had to smile. Yes. He had indeed been a rascal and caught her out in their youth. Arwel was the son of her father's brother, her uncle. Though her father and mother had died a long time ago, she had sent notes down into southern Wales and her uncle and aunt had sent back similar snippets of news, until he died a few years ago.

Arwel, she remembered, had been fostered out to a warring chieftain when very young. The business of war interested Arwel even then.

Tyne stood up, openly angry. "I am Tyne, betrothed of Lady Saran. How do I address you?"

Arwel took one look at the short, stocky Irish bulk, and knew to be respectful.

"Call me lord . . . .my Lord Tyne."

"Then Lord Arwel. We are taken aback by your rude arrival. You could have injured a child or a mother in your charge into us. I signaled you to enter to the left of our people."

"My Lord Tyne. I apologize. I thought you were instructing your soldiers to come left, opening the way for us to ride directly in. I remember thinking in the saddle, how hospitable my cousin was."

Arwel bowed with a wry grin and asked to be forgiven. "We have come a long way to join Lady Saran and you on your joining day."

"I did not know you wished to be invited," smiled Saran. "However, you are most welcome if that is what you wish. I would advise you though to ask your host."

Arwel turned on Tyne, and was about to begin, when he was interrupted. "No. Them," nodded Saran.

Arwel turned, then whirled around. His eyes went up the two young giants with the swords at their back. Their commanding stare measuring him up and down unnerved him. His façade, always his courage, wilted.

"I am Haralde Longshield. This is Lord Riennes de Montford."

Arwel stared at both, especially Riennes. Then he let slip under his breath: "A Norman, up here?"

"Get on your horse," Haralde ordered.

"You can not order me to do so. I am her cousin."

"We can. We are her sons and lords of these lands. Get on your horse lad, before I heave thee up there myself."

Arwel turned and looked at Saran who said: "It would be wise to do so cousin, for you see he is our thegn."

Arwel turned again. He looked at the line of his horsemen, then at the line of Tyne's men, then stomped towards his horse and mounted.

"Now. Thee came to this marriage with good feelings in your heart, to wish your cousin great joy and happiness, did you not?" Haralde demanded.

Arwel did not answer, he just nodded.

"So thee have brought a wedding gift for Lady Saran?"

Arwel smiled and answered: "The finest Chieftain Bleddyn could find to so compliment my cousin."

"And thee must be with coin?"

"I am."

"Forgive me then. Let no rudeness mar this day. Thee may dismount. Thee are invited to your cousin's betrothal."

Arwel's brow knitted in confusion over the strange accent and behaviour of the son of Saran. However, as he made to step down, it was his behaviour that was thrown into his face.

"Uuhh. Before thee do I think thee should wipe away the rudeness thee inflicted on my people of Neury. Give me a coin or two."

Arwel froze. "I what?"

"Yes. Your men and your horses kicked a pig and stove in its ribs. It will have to be slaughtered," went on Haralde. It was going to be anyway. "And thee smashed a chicken cage with a bird in it, as well. Thee frightened a wee girl. To make all amends, I think thee should pay for the damages done to my property by your hasty entrance." Haralde put out a hand.

Arwel looked down in disbelief onto the face of this impertinence. Something in the face of this man, something of the bearing of Stoerm Longshield he once saw, told him not to resist the suggestion.

Arwel stepped down, pulled out a pouch of clinking coins, reached in and gave Haralde a couple of pence.

I am making a profit here. A grin passed over Haralde's face. He acted the hearty fellow. "Well done. Come cousin. All has been repaired by your generosity. Come sit with the Lady Saran and us."

Arwel did so, bowing over his cousin, glancing as he did at Magda's beauty. His eyes went to her breasts.

"Let your men be at ease cousin," suggested Haralde. "Cold mountain water for them, and some bread and cheese," he ordered.

At Arwel's signal, the men dismounted. Tyne signaled for his men to do the same.

"Let the gift giving continue," ordered Haralde who sat down, a hand on his bundles.

Magda left their company, gathered up her grandmothers and they lifted the small keg to the table. Larger kegs had been assembled up in the longhouse earlier.

Then Magda turned to face her mistress and alone before them, she came alive. Her eyes came up and silence settled upon all there. A loveliness glowed from her. It was a genuinely beautiful woman who stood there, paying homage to another woman who had played such an important part in her life.

All there looked upon her in different ways; heat in the loins of some males, black regard in the eyes of others, warmth in the eyes of the women who had been healed or some member of her family saved from death by her ministrations.

Godfroi, standing nearby in the crowd, turned and walked away. He would not endorse her place in this community with his presence.

She stood erect. Haralde and Riennes took her into their hearts, each in his own way.

"My Lady Saran." Strong was her voice. All attended, glancing to see how Saran reacted to her. "You who have been our goodheart. You who have been our fortress, our hearth, our walls, our leader, our healer, our protector, lord, and our gentle mother. We know of your loss. We know of your pain. And now we know of your happiness. He has found you, and you have found him. We will obey him and come to love him as you have. May you find happiness together. We of Neury and Wym wish to toast that happiness of you two. May it accompany you through the years. And may it bring peace and gentleness upon our land."

Magda went over and drove a spigot into a bung hole. A single, blood red drop fell on the back of her hand. She moved a hand to a pile of wooden drinking bowls.

"Magda. Pour it into these," whispered Haralde who had positioned himself near the keg. She hesitated, but would not look directly at him. "It would please me greatly. It is a gift to my mama." He handed her a wooden box.

She looked at the box, opened it and a little gasp escaped her. She looked up, and smiled. Riennes sitting beside felt a warmth flush him from that happy face. He held his breath as a powerful feeling of joy warmed him.

Magda set the open box down. In it were six silver chalices. She took one, filled it. A wonder murmured through the crowed. She filled the second, turned and walked to Saran and Tyne.

Presenting them to the couple, she whispered to Saran. "From a little boy and a little girl." Then she shouted: "To our Tyne and our Lady Saran. We here give you joy, May God bless you."

Tyne and Saran stood up, touched their cups of silver together, and drank deep. Saran went: "Oh! Wine!" Tyne exchanged cups and they drank again.

A roar went up, then everyone started clapping, some hooraying, some crying.

Magda turned, went back to the keg, and started pouring wine into the other chalices. She presented one to Haralde, bowed, one to Riennes, bowed, and then went down the line to Arwel. He grinned at her, drank, then licked his lips sensually, looking up and down her body as she turned away.

Haralde and Riennes came up for air. "My God. Wine. And it is very good. Like nectar. How can she raise wine here?" puzzled Haralde.

"She has a way with drink does she not? Ales, meads and now wines." Riennes sipped again. "Thee do not suppose she is a witch," Haralde whispered, and then shook his head no, indicating a bad joke. "Superb!" exclaimed Riennes. "She is a jewel in your crown my lord. What men would give to have her in their holdings." His eyes were direct over his cup at Haralde, looking to see if the arrows of his words hit any mark.

Haralde sipped, shook his head, and said: "A jewel yes, but not in my holdings. She is of herself, not of me. I wonder if one will come to her one day, one to gladden her heart." And he looked directly back at Riennes over his cup to see how well he had struck back.

Saran grabbed Magda as she came by. They laughed and tittered together and talked quickly as women. "How did you do this?" "I have been making barrels of this from wild berries. These are years old, sitting hidden. I never told you but I knew this day would come for you." She clapped her hand, happy that she had pleased her Saran. She started crying. Saran joined her, a tear running down her cheek. They leaned over the table and hugged, two women happy in each other's company of memories.

Excitement began to move the villagers. People started running elsewhere. A number of farm lads came up and asked the wedding party to stand. "Come," said Master Geraint waving down to an open range with targets set up. "It is time for the archery contest. Bring your drinks, your wine will follow. We have a table for you there."

Saran and Tyne, surprised, turned and looked at Haralde and Riennes. The two shook their heads no, then pointed to Rhys who was walking by, readying himself. Saran walked over to him, took his hand, and asked: "You?" "For you Saran and Tyne. It is all that I can offer you on this special day." And before she could embarrass him with her gratitude, he continued: "Besides. I could be a rich man at the end of this day."Haralde and Riennes approached. Saran stepped between and put her arms around their waists, and just stood there, warm in the company and talk of men, especially her's.

"Well Rhys. Is your hand steady today, or would thee like to pay us our coin now?" chided Riennes lightly; doing what Rhys was doing, sniffing the air and checking the tops of the trees.

"It is a fine day to shoot a bow," said Rhys, wetting a finger and holding it up. "The breeze is light, and steady, but it will gust soon. Watch yourselves. It may catch you unaware."

Haralde wet a finger, put it up. "There is not going to be any gusts. How do thee know . . . .?" He stopped. Rhys had jerked him. They both grinned at each other.

"I understand another young bowman has entered the list, one who has ridden a long way." Haralde and Rhys raised eyebrows at Riennes. "Arwel. When he saw this kind of crowd, he rushed off to his men and got his bow. All this adulation."

"I suspect more to impress Magda," Rhys slyly suggested.

That brought Riennes up. He looked around, and saw Magda leaving the field with Odim holding her hand. "She is leaving."

Saran uncoupled and strode past them. "I will get her. It might be she shuns such a display of weaponry and male arrogance."

Rhys leaned on his unstrung stave and watched Haralde and Riennes look over their horned bows, also unstrung. "Will they put an arrow a good distance?" he asked. "The targets will be set at 60 yards, then set further back after each shoot."

"Such was what we were taught on as children." Haralde then smiled at Rhys. "Only unlike here, the targets moved."

"Hah!" and Rhys did a little bow. He had been jerked. Then he dropped his voice and spoke serious. "I suspect my Lords the desert air is drier, that your arrows just fly there. Here in these valleys, and with the Irish waters nearby, the airs tend to hold more moisture, and thus be denser. Under the rules, you be allowed one ranging shot. Aim a tad higher. Allow for more drop."

It was a noble gesture. To compete fairly.

"Thank you Rhys."

"Thank you bowman."

Saran hustled by arm in arm with Magda. Odim came jumping up in excitement. "Are you going to beat them Rhys?" "I dinnae know little one. Our lords here are mighty fine bowman." "Then I will cheer for only you three."

Haralde laughed and bent over. "That is very smart of thee Odim."

"Odim! Come!" and he skipped away to join his mother at the table with Saran and Tyne and Arwel, who standing with his bow, admired her approach.

Saran was to later tell them she convinced Magda bows were important to her and everyone because they were a hunting tool, not a weapon, and kept all in venison. Besides, she had said, she and Odim were here today because of Rhys's arrows.

Tyne, as judge and prize master, yelled out: "Practice!" across the range. "Five step forward." The first five were farm boys, except Arwel who with his bow pushed his way in between two. One boy grumbled and stepped back.

They released independently, and the arrows like little black lines flitted down to the targets. The targets were made of wood, long thin slabs sliced through the round surface of a small log. They were set up vertically tight to each other, and nailed to cross pieces behind.

A black line was drawn through their middle horizontally. The closest to the line and the middle slab would qualify for the second movement of the targets.

It was exciting, it was colorful, it was interesting to see all the different styles. Haralde moved closer and kneeled to take it all in.

Rhys held back waiting for everyone else to shoot first. Riennes stood with him, curious.

Finally, Rhys: "Aaah. My lord. See the end target, the one closest to those small trees?"

"Yes?"

"It is calmer there. The trees are holding the breeze back from that spot. An arrow will fly truer into the target."

"Aaah. It is in the lee of the trees."

"Yes. Come on. Let us go pick that one as ours. We will shoot independent of each other."

They tapped Haralde on the shoulder as they passed. Riennes explained what Rhys had discovered as they came up to that target.

Some of the crowd moved to their side. Rhys's ability was known. Yea, but what of their lords with those strange horned bows?

Riennes came to the line first. He breathed deep and went quiet inside. His eyes focused on the target. He closed his eyes and focused on the mind's image of it. Then, he opened his eyes, drew smoothly, let his breath out slowly and loosed. The bamboo arrow rushed to the target and hit a tad high, but into the centre slab.

Haralde stepped up, saw where Riennes's arrow hit, tested his bowstring a couple of times, notched his bamboo, repeated Riennes's routine and released. His arrow hit closer to the black line and missed the centre slab but one.

The two young lords got a respectful round of applause. Two young farm boys ran to the targets, ran back and handed them their arrows.

Rhys stepped in. He was quiet, smooth, still in himself. Then in a liquid motion his hunting longbow came up, the arrow flew and struck fair into the target. The favorite of the crowd got a round of applause as he joined Haralde and Riennes at the wedding table.

More young men came forward. Shouts of: "He is my son" or: "Do well my husband," floated along the front lines of the spectators. Arrows thudded into wood down range. A festive air settled about the whole thing. Older churls and serf men sat in a bunch close to the front. They analyzed each release, each style, made insulting noises with their mouths when young men, still green in bowmanship and wilting under even the pressure of a practice shot, missed their targets altogether.

"I see those funny arrows had enough legs to make it to the wood," prodded Rhys as they came up to the wedding table.

"Pluck that mote out of your eye, sirrah. Your aim was a tad off centre," Haralde baited back.

Lady Saran clapped her hands over the banter. Magda smiled openly for the first time and it was if the sun shone brightly. Riennes's heart swelled. Saran was sipping wine. "Would you like some of Magda's ale? She has brought some?"

The three begged off until after the shoot, but Arwel swept up a wooden drinking bowl. "Aye. I would sip of anything Mistress Magda offered," he smiled directly at her.

"Finished," said Tyne of the practice round as he slid down the table and accepted a silver chalice of wine from his lady. "My lords. It is time."

"My sons, approach me," requested. Saran. "Will my sons accept their mama's favour?"

Haralde and Riennes looked puzzled, knew not this tradition, but leaned over the table on her motion. She tied a green ribbon on Haralde and a blue one on Riennes. "Do well," was all she said.

Magda stood and Arwel saw she had a red ribbon in her hand. He walked in front of the table to her, but she regarded him not. She motioned to Rhys, who stood surprised. She motioned again, her eyes directly on him. He jumped to and leaned over the table. She tied the red on the leather strap holding his arrow quiver.

"Do well," she said boldly and directly to him. Rhys, not wanting all eyes to come to them and embarrass her, nodded briefly, turned and walked away. All, though, saw the red flush on his face.

The day was beautiful. The people for the first time in years were joined in a happiness. Their men, young and old, strutted their male power up to the lines. The event plucked at the very heart of their competitive nature. Releasing, letting go, loosing, directing an arrow down range, thrummed at something primal deep within them.

Haralde could see it, he could smell it, he reveled in it. He looked to his brother to see him once again as he knew him and saw a bright joy in his face. It was with him too.

Time and time again, as they came to the line and let loose, one would point to the other as he came off, or joke about his style, the one trying to throw the other off. Rhys came in for the same attention, and he gave back as good as he got.

Lesser bowman dropped away after the first round, the target was moved back, better bowman fell away, and when Tyne called out for young men to move the targets to their final position, 10 remained.

It had been fine shooting by all. Haralde now knew what Riennes had been hinting at, that Neury, Brekin and Wym had a corp of deadly archers, and it was due to the tall greenwood man who now approached them.

"Well done my lords," grinned Rhys. "Impressed am I with those little horned staves of yours. They bite the wood well, and with some force. Methinks you have taught me a thing or two today."

"And well done to thee bowman. We have learned something ourselves about our people here," nodded Haralde as he touched Rhys's longbow in open admiration. "Vassals they may be, but there is something of free spirit here. Archery seems to bring this out."

"From where we have been to where we have come, we have naught of this in our travels," said Riennes. "It confounds me. . . . it seems another way."

Haralde looked around at the 10 waiting for the targets to be set back. "They are all stalwart in their hearts right now. . . . Rhys? Riennes and I have been talking. Be honest. Our chances of winning, they are now less?"

"Aye my lords."

"I saw my arrow flutter just before hitting that last time," said Haralde. "My attempt held on just enough, but I noticed a faintness myself," enjoined Riennes.

"The distance now may be a shade too much for your kind of shooting," explained Rhys. "I have an extra hunting bow with me. I would be proud to share it and this with you on the next go. Our longer arrows and these goose feathers will carry the day."

"And let thee walk off with my silver, I think not bowman," grinned Haralde. "I will stay the course."

"He is crafty, is he not my lord," grinned Riennes. "Secretly, he fears our bamboo as the better wood than his ash."

Rhys grinned, nodded in admiration. "I do my lords. You are two fine shooters. As good as any hereabouts. I mean that truly. May I make a request of my lords?"

"Surely Rhys."

"May we walk up to the line together. If I lose, I would rather go down in your company."

"Stoutly said Rhys of Gwent," nodded Haralde. "What say thee brother? Should we favour him?" "Agreed," said Riennes and as they turned to go to the line together, continued . . . . , "although I think he means to sweet talk us, leave us over-confident and snatch the silver from us."

They chuckled together as they moved to the line, then each went quiet as they prepared themselves. Haralde and Riennes stopped just back of Rhys, quickly released the tension on their bows, took away the strings, quickly re-strung with heavier ones, and did something at the end nocks. Rhys saw none of this.

"You will face two targets and you will loose five at each," Tyne instructed. "When finished, no one will touch the targets, but all will walk down range and I will declare my judgment there. The archer with most to the centre wins."

Thus, the first five walked to the line. Tall, strong, impressive in the eye of all, four young men and a gritty old man, a shepherd from the upper hills, thrilled the crowd. Some hit their mark in the centre.

No one uttered a word as the final five stepped up. A large black raven cackled nearby. Rhys shot a warning glance at the bird. A dog barked across the river and a baby bawled momentarily, to be silenced into contentment by a breast.

The final five stood and waited until a quiet settled. Each in their own way prepared themselves. The tension grew, until one bowman lifted, hesitated, loosed. A hit. Then each in their own way, and the arrows turned to black darts down range. All hit. Even from that distance, one was heard to hammer into wood. Rhys.

A roar went up from the crowd, and some started to run for the targets.

Tyne walked out in front and roared at them. The crowd came up short. He had his soldiers hold them back. He signaled for the 10 to follow him. Down they walked. The crowd held their breath.

Saran and Magda stood behind the table eyes wide with interest. Arwel who had dropped out early, stood behind the table trying to shift closer to Magda.

The shooters gathered round their targets. Tyne went from one to the other and back again with a piece of string. Their five leaned in close and checked their arrows. Rhys straightened up, and looked at Haralde and Riennes, somewhat in amazement. The bamboo shafts were there, not tight to the centre to win, but were thereabouts.

Tyne came back, arranged the shooters in a line to face back towards the wedding table. The men released their bow strings and stood loosely, some leaning on their staves.

Tyne walked behind the line, took out a red signal rag, stopped behind Rhys and waved it over his head.

The expected roar went up from the crowd, then applause. Tyne led the other competitors past his guards, so that they could come down and look at the results. All of Rhys's shafts were in the centre slab, closest to the black horizontal line. All shook their heads in amazement, pulled out their arrows, shook hands with each other, especially Rhys, bobbed their heads to Haralde and Riennes, and headed back.

Haralde and Riennes congratulated Rhys in their own way. Rhys bobbed his acceptance of their good words, grabbed his arrows and the three headed back.

Half way there, he stopped them. "How did you do that? What I beheld was impossible."

"Aah! Now that he has his prize, he seeks to smooth our ruffled feathers Haralde," joked Riennes.

"No brother. Our Freemen would not stoop to such baseness," Haralde retorted. "One day when we are old and are gumming at each other over a winter fire, we will tell thee how we did it." As they approached the table, Rhys continued to pick at them. "You buggers. You resorted to some kind of trickery here. I will find it out. No short bow should have carried that far." And Riennes and Haralde laughed out loud and smacked him on the back.

Gwenna and Hugh came rushing across shouting: "Dada! Dada!" and their father gathered them up in his arms. Much kissing.

Tyne brought Rhys out in front with his children and a roar went up from the people as they witnessed the presentation of the coin.

"Come. Let me pour you all an ale of Magda's finest," quipped Saran, clapping her hands in grand enjoyment over the spectacle they had just put on.

"No, no. Wine for me," demand Haralde, smacking his lips lightly. "Come congratulate your lords on their excellent shooting today."

"Indeed let me smooth my son's feathers." Saran took one of her wedding chalices, poured a good splash of red wine and gave it to him. He sucked deep, then a sip to enjoy the fine berry flavor.

"Nay. Ale for me. I am thirsty, not pompous," grinned Riennes. Saran, holding a pitcher of wine, turned to Magda for help. Magda took a proffered chalice and poured ale. She offered to Riennes, her head down, but a smile on her lips. He looked down her long black hair as she did. He quaffed deeply and appreciated the slaking of his thirst from her gift, her offering. She moved back to Odim.

Arwel watched Haralde drink again of his mother's wine. He watched the young thegn turn and look down range at the far target being set up for the long shoot. He joined Haralde with his drink. Arwel avoided the Norman. It was obvious to everyone. There was an obvious ennui there by the young Welsh princeling.

"Methinks my lord is measuring his next effort with the bow," mused Arwel. "You are very good at it my lord."

Haralde stared for a moment, then drank again. "I think not. I think to sit down and enjoy myself. I will leave the field to my betters."

"I think as thee brother," said Riennes joining them. "I am no threat to these hawk-eyed archers of Cymru. Not at that distance."

People now had fires going. Quick noon meals were prepared. Men snatched up food, then started walking down the range, taking up a spot to best watch the shoot. Soon most were lined up on one side.

Saran and Magda took Rhys's children in their arms and sat them on their knees behind the table. They played little games with them or bounced them. It was to let Rhys stand alone, to gather himself as he checked his bow, his unnotched strings, himself.

Then, Haralde and Riennes went over to him, talked lowly, shook their heads no when he expressed surprise at their decision not to compete, wished him well, then went back to the table to leave him in quiet.

Rhys stood for a moment, his head bowed, his hands resting on his stave before him. Then, he went over to his children, kissed each, and walked away.

Arwel made a point of avoiding the Norman, and went again to Haralde, to fill in the hush with his chatter. Haralde begged his pardon, put a finger to his lips for quiet, and said: "Let us be still for just this moment. I feel we are to see something."

Riennes walked down to the range not far from the shooting line. People parted to let him through. He sat on the ground to watch. His eyes went to Rhys and did not leave him, not even when the bowman was finished. He was not interested in the shot. He was interested in the man.

The bowman walked up to a stick driven in the ground. It was his shooting line. With his foot, he drew a line in the dirt; his own shooting spot. He drove three of his own arrows into the ground before, and watched them. He did not look down range.

He is gathering himself in his own way, thought Riennes as he watched the forest man. Riennes felt the man settle himself, still himself. He sensed the Fremen's breathing grow shallower. A word struck him of this, the bowman's moment. Samadhi. In reading Hindu and Buddhist tracts, Riennes had come across a Sanskrit word, which referred to a state of consciousness and total unity; an individualism and a onenesss.

Watching the bowman's face, Tagien's quiet voice entered Riennes's mind. In archery, one must cultivate an inner balance of mind and outer mastery of the body so total that no physical movement will occur without the intervention of thought. To attempt to take conscious aim is to deny this principle and he will fail the target. The suppression of ego is necessary. A state of no-thought achieves for the archer the perfect moment of release.

"It is mushin, the absence of self," mumbled Riennes under this breath. *Our bowman has not had the advantage of these kinds of instruction. I wonder how he will master the long attempt.*

Rhys put one foot forward, then looked around, at the trees downrange, at the sky, at some birds.

The crowd was absolutely silent, a drawn breath.

Then, up came his heavy war bow. He lifted it to the sky, as if an offering. With a loud intake of air, he began to lower the wood, slowly pushing it away from himself. The arrow notched within slowly lowered, slowly came down, close to horizontal with the ground.

Riennes heard a creak in the bowstring as it was drawn tight. The bow line came past Rhys's ear. The tension suffused outwards, from the bow, from the bowman, to the air around him, to the observers fearful for him. For one glorious instant, Rhys stood within the compass of that tension. Riennes sensed the bowman's joy, his happiness, his sense of completeness. The man of the forest achieved for one split moment, mastery over himself. Then he shot within the bow, he loosed, he released, he let all go.

The crowd 'oooohed'. It matched the 'thrum" of the released bowstring.

Rhys turned and walked away even as the arrow went upon the wind. He passed through the knot of his competitors, then stopped for a moment when he heard a heavy thud down range. Someone yelled: "A hit!"

A roar went up. He had hit the target indeed, not centre, in fact just barely catching it in one corner, but a hit nonetheless. An impossible long shot.

He resumed walking back towards his children. His fellow archers did not cheer him. They let him pass quietly. One fellow reached out and brushed him lightly, as if wanting a touch of that magic.

Riennes watched Rhys come towards him, pass by. The bowman did not acknowledge him. *How could he? He was somewhere else, somewhere inside himself, Riennes sensed. He is somewhere up there, in a Brekin meadow, shooting at a faraway deer, because he has to, because he must for his children. Nay. Because he wants to.*

The crowd quieted. They had seen something incredible.

Rhys had his second silver coin.

chapter 9

Family quarrels complete a wedding.

"**A**ND LOOK AT this," Saran directed Haralde.

She was showing her son all her joining gifts. This one was a beautiful cape made of finely spun wool dyed red with a full black fur lining. The collar was trimmed in white ermine. "To ward off winter's cold and chill. The wool is from the Low Country and the fur lining, from the forests north of the Vikingland, or so Arwel claims."

There was little doubt Arwel's gift from his chieftain to his cousin Saran was a rich one indeed. "Is it not heavy?" Haralde pondered.

"Haralde. I never wanted for all these gifts. I just wanted to join with my Tyne as God as our witness, and to disappear into the woods. I just wanted to go anywhere for awhile, to escape. My obligations to your father after his death have been onerous."

"This is a rich gift. I did not know your cousin held thee in such high esteem," mused Haralde, fingering it. He was standing in the main room of the Saran longhouse with his own wedding gifts, a bundle and a beautiful brocaded pouch.

Haralde did not want his mother to live in a wooden longhouse, no matter how big and how well it was furnished. He wanted her and Tyne to live with him, but his mother said no. She praised him for the gift of the land and the orders he had given for the building. "It will be warmer than your stone in winter," she argued. She was right.

A fire burned in the big open pit. Slaves, servants and friends scurried to lay food upon the big table on a dais in front. Other food was cooking in pots swung on iron hooks over the fire. His chalices on the table twinkled red and silver from the light. Other gifts were scattered around the room.

In a few minutes, she was to go to her and Tyne's room and put on her wedding dress, Riennes's blue silk. The silk Haralde knew of. He had helped carry it half way across the world.

"Mother," he said, taking her by her elbow and going into an alcove. There was no time left to do it any other way. He handed her his bundle, she smiled, opened it, pulled out an off-white material, held it up and looked at him puzzled.

"It is cotton. There be none like it in all of Britannia and Cymru. It comes from the Valley of the Indus. I know thee love that blue silk, but in time thee will come to value this more than your gown. It is soft, light, warm, flexible and comfortable. Where we come from, it is valued greater than silk. When thee wake on the morrow, look at it. Think of whatever clothing thee would like to wear daily. This is it and I have given thee enough there for a number of clothes . . . . I know naught of those things."

Saran held it up again, felt it, began to understand, then made as if to hug him, but he put up a halting hand.

He handed her the pouch. "And this. Vikings would gather a fleet together for to come a-raiding against your longhouse if ever they heard about it. Wear it sparingly, then hide it from greedy eyes."

Saran took the pouch, hefted the weight, smiled at him, then opened it and reached in. Out came a necklace weighed down by blue stones that once put on, would cascade down each side of her bodice, to arrive in adoration around a large, blood ruby.

Lady Saran's eyes widened in wonder and awe. Stunned she was. Naught had she ever seen thus. The distant pit flame ignited an inner fire within the stone. She put her hand over her mouth and dropped it, her fingers singed by its priceless beauty. Haralde caught it before it hit the floor.

He came around behind her. "To go with your blue gown." He undid the clasp, put it round her neck, turned her and looked into her eyes. "Where did you get this?" she asked. "One night, when winter has us huddling around our fires, ask me to tell thee the story of the where and the how. It deals with the Ger Khan, his siege upon a city, of me running with sword after the city's royal guards through underground caverns and discovering a rich temple there."

Riennes came thumping into the family room, spotted them in the aside. "It is time," he reminded. "Godfroi and Tyne are pacing up and down in the clearing. A bower of flowers awaits thee. A great wood fire lights up everything."

"Do you know about this?" asked Saran touching the necklace.

"Yes my lady mama. If thee knew how Harry . . . ," he glanced at Haralde and caught the faint negative signal . . . . "kept it for thee for years and how he carried it across mountains and deserts and seas for thee, thee would declare him your favorite son right now, in front of me. How shabby now is my prize to thee of the silk."

Something was not right about his answer to her, she sensed. She looked up puzzled into Haralde's face, then into that of Riennes. "Hurry mama. Get dressed. I am getting hungry," exhorted Haralde.

She threw herself into his arms, kissed him, ran to Riennes, kissed him, and then fled to the other side of the house, a necklace drippings precious stones around her neck.

And thus was the last vestige of his mama's union with his father now ended. Up until now, the childhood memory he had that of his mother and father was of a union. Now that was no more. Even now the face of his father was fading. He would never see that union again. Up until this moment, at least she was still his wife. Now another man replaced him.

He looked at Riennes down the table and wondered how he felt. At least his mother and father had gone down together, man and wife to eternity.

The joining had gone swiftly. That was Lady Saran and Tyne's instructions to Monk Godfroi. They had stood under a bower laced with flowers and blessed their union. The monk had scowled at some of the good-luck charms and wooden figures tied into the flowers, but no objection did he lodge over this paganism. He judged them to be a positive aspect of this joyful of Christian ceremonies.

Now they were feasting. He enjoyed the moment when their guests started eating the fare provided by the Longshield family. Everyone tasted, looked up with wide eyes and smiles and told each other how extraordinary the food tasted. Unbeknownst, he and Haralde had sprinkled tinctures of pepper, salt and spices they still had left over in their cart from their London. Both showed the cooks in the back kitchen how it was to be done.

Riennes watched Magda as she supped, her head jerking up. She kenned immediately what she was tasting. Her head turned suspiciously to Riennes. He smiled at her.

Aah. Magda's wine and ale. Yea, but the food also tasted better because of her. How his stomach had shrunk over so long at sea and little food on the road home and the days of strife and warring. Now, that he could gorge himself, it was plugging up, and he could find no more room for all the different foods he had not even tasted yet.

Many guests glanced at each other when they heard Riennes and Haralde say: "Thank you for our food," put prayer hands to their foreheads, and bowed slightly before eating. Such an unnerving and foreign thing.

However, they ignored it and began to eat. With all eyes on the two lords, no one saw Magda in quiet wonder slowly emulate their ritual.

Haralde was thinking about Godfroi's request.

Shortly after the ceremony, the monk had pulled him aside. "My lord. It was unfortunate your mother had to be joined outside. Would you not have preferred it was done inside."

"Inside monk Godfroi?"

"Yes. Inside . . . . your own chapel, here, in Neury. Your people need one. Wym needs one. It would join your people more together, bind them to you and the church, bring stability, and . . . ."

And it went on, reasons why Haralde and Lord de Montford should be magnanimous. A Latin Christian church here? It was not one of his priorities. Haralde made excuses for not considering such a thing right now. He told Godfroi he would have to discuss this with his overlord, ask permission of Lord Gerbod. He quickly pardoned himself, saying he had to greet Gwengarth, Lady Saran's uncle, who had arrived late.

Gwengarth had promised he would see to the plantings of the Longshield demesne. Everyone had serious tasks elsewhere and Gwengarth took the weight of this important task off Haralde and upon himself. He had just completed it today and had rushed to catch the joining.

Now, with his mama on his right and Riennes on his left at the feasting table, and with Godfroi down near the other end, he felt safely away from any more suggestions of a chapel. Yet . . . ?

Tyne on the other side held his wife's hand, beaming out at the noise and the feasting and the drinking and the good wishes coming from around the fire. On his right were Gwengarth, then Arwel, then Godfroi.

Around the big fire were trestle tables and there were people they liked having around them; Munch and Polcher, some of the principle men of Wym down one side, and Master Geraint and others of Neury down the other.

It was not Haralde's doing, but his mother's. He was uncomfortable with such familiarity. A lord must stand off from his vassals.

On the end sat Rhys, Magda and Oswald, Tyne's soldier who acted as his second in all things.

Gwenna, Hugh, Odim and some other children sat with their parents, or ran around chasing one another with adults leaning over, grabbing them back away from the fire, warning them to be careful.

Riennes watched the fire play on Magda's face. For the first time, she seemed relaxed, alert, not a fearful doe ready to bolt.

Seeing where Riennes's eyes were, Saran spoke across Haralde to him. "I am become a convincing old woman. I would not have believed Magda would accept my invitation, but she did. What do you think of her ale."

"As good as any I have tasted," answered Riennes. "My lord Haralde here is assured of a good supply during the long winters."

"Yes, many in these uplands will run out by Easter. In other parts of Cymru, that is when many start getting sick." commented Saran. "That does not happen here. Many say it is because she puts a spell in her ale."

That interested Riennes, who leaned over with a questioning look at Saran.

She knew this would grab his interest. "It is true. Since Magda has been here and everyone has been drinking her very good ale, I have noticed a general better health in the people of Neury. Wym, no."

Riennes mulled that over. It could be true. Not the spell part of course. Maybe it was not the ale. Maybe it was the water. Riennes remember something he had read in Sena's book, something about diseases and bad water seem to keep company. After a full day of treating people, Sena and he had sat up one night discussing philosophy and most especially, history and medicine. Sena had wagged a finger at him and told him many of the disciplines such as medicine and history were related. Keep your mind open to all things. Pull all information into your centre. For example, he told him his Egyptians were an agrarian people. It seemed when they found the secret to making ale long ago, they rose as a power. It was because drinking diseases stabilized and they could turn their race energies to other things. Because of ale, master? Maybe, said Sena. Or maybe because they drank less bad water.

His lady mama had stirred his mind.

Saran looked at her son, and then at Riennes, and was pleased at what she saw. Only Riennes now was interested in the affairs of Magda.

"Maybe someone should give some of Magda's to Wym," Saran suggested slyly.

Haralde sat up at that. "Give? No. Coin must pass hands for ale and it will be my palm that feels that first."

A child's squeal pulled the attention to the open area in front of the table. One child rushed to her father and buried her head.

The clerwr cart wheeled into the centre area, put a leg out, spread wide his arms and presented himself. All the children started squealing in excitement, so to quiet them he started prancing around juggling balls or cups which he snatched away from people and even legs of fowl, which he ate as he juggled. The children forgot to squeal and grew quiet. Fascinated, their eyes followed each as they floated up into air and down again.

When all was quieter, the bard pulled out his pipe and began to play, then stopped to sing a sweet song of love and fighting men, and Welsh sagas of great heroes and kings, of wizards and dragons. He sang portions of the Four Branches of the Mabinogi, poems composed of the sagas of great Welsh kings and Breton warriors from centuries ago. He made jibes and jokes of people in the villages. Then he got everyone to clap their hands, a rhythm started, and he sang a clever lewd song in step to those hands.

For the next half hour, he pulled things from the ears of children, danced and played his pipe. One long piece interested Riennes, who pulled out his pipe and began to catch up with him.

The jester's eyes widen in amusement and he danced closer. Riennes got up, and walked around the table still playing. The two sat down at the base of the table and the two played a duet. When it ended in a beautiful flourish, everyone stood up and clapped.

The bard waved to Riennes to follow him as he headed down the hall and out the front door to entertain others sitting around outside.

Tyne stood up. "Outside everyone. Follow him. Let us get some air."

Riennes agreed, walked out playing behind the jester, and everyone behind the table followed outside with them.

Outside, fires glowed across the meadows. Everyone stood around and watched the juggler walk into the night. Riennes stopped suddenly, and did not follow. Something had changed. The lightness left him.

He looked around. Arwel came up to his brother and said something. Haralde nodded, then the two walked away down through the dark to a fire where a knot of Arwel's men stood, drinking around a table.

"Where is everyone?" Suddenly Riennes noticed Saran and Tyne were gone. Magda could be seen walking with Odim back to her fire where her carts were. The guests and principle men of Neury and Wym, sensing all was coming to an end, also drifted off into the night.

Rhys stepped up beside him. "Bowman. I think our new two have given all the slip. They have gone off to be by themselves. Like a young couple, I suspect they have a secret bower set up somewhere."

The stars were out and it was fairly warm; all in a beautiful night. Yet, Riennes was unsettled. He was uneasy. His sensed something.

Rhys was about to say goodnight. "Rhys! Stay! Something is amiss."

They stood there listening. Somebody was coming towards them in the dark. Riennes put his hand up, and then remembered no kandos. All weapons had been set aside for the wedding feast.

A bent man stepped out of the dark.

"Polcher? What?" demanded Riennes.

"Lord. Bad men. Around other lord. Talk bad." Polcher pointed to Arwel's fire.

"Thank thee uncle. Listen. Go to my wagon. Fetch me our little swords. Then go and find any of our soldiers and your brother. Understand?"

"Yes." And he disappeared.

"Rhys. Do thee have even a knife?

"I have not."

"Go find your bowmen. I am going down to Arwel's fire. Meet me there but hang back in the shadows. Quickly man!"

Rhys slipped away without a hesitation.

What could be wrong? He approached the fire slowly, looking for Haralde. He was there, sitting at a trestle table. Arwel faced him on the other side. The position and posture of Arwel's men made Riennes hasten; a ring of them hunched behind Haralde. All had spears.

Riennes realized he still had his pipe with him. When he got close where he could hear Arwel talking excitedly, he took a deep breath, began to play and stepped into the light of the fire.

Arwel's men whirled. Surprised, he stepped past them and up to the table. He stopped and spread his arms.

"As good as the juggler, am I not. Does anyone have any wine left," he said in a jovial manner. "Nay, well I should play another something then?" Riennes babbled, as if too much wine. All eyes were upon him. That was the idea. He glanced at Haralde. There. The signal for danger, beware.

Arwel stood there, leaning on a sword, one foot up on the bench across from Haralde.

Coldly, his voice dripping venom, he bullied Riennes. "Shut up. Norman! You should not be here."

"Cousin. Thee are impolite. Let us have a drink. It is Saran's wedding night." Riennes collapsed on the bench beside Haralde, his back to Arwel. He faced the knot of men ringed behind Haralde. His eyes went over them. One closest had a dirk in a sheath hanging on a leather thong. He estimated his chances. They were serious men, all of them dangerous.

"NORMAN!" Arwel almost shouted it. "I said you should not be here. Not in Longshield, not in these mountains, not in Cymru at all."

"Say again what thee want from us," demanded Haralde.

"Not want. What Bleddyn and I are going to do, come through Neury to go araiding to the east. You will say nothing. Your people will be quiet."

"East. What is there?"

"Shrewsbury. Hereford. We will strike at the Normans there. Drive them back from the March." He was tapping his sword into the ground. Riennes could hear the metal point tinking against gravel. His sensibilities were very acute now.

"And carry off some loot and women while we are at it."

"Are there many Normans at these places?" Haralde asked quietly.

"Yes. Many have arrived. In both places. They have many horses and are armed. They are here to take land away from us, to settle here. We must push them back."

"These are king's men, then."

"They fly many banners. I want one for my hearth."

It was quiet for a moment, and then Haralde put him down.

"NO! Thee insignificant man, no! Any move against them is a move against me. I am a king's man. Do thee understand?"

Riennes put his hand on Haralde's arm to make him sit fast for what was about to come. He sensed it immediately. He held Haralde firmly down.

Arwel cursed, grabbed his sword two handed, swung it over his head and brought it down.

Haralde attempted to half rise as if to defend himself but Riennes held him.

The blade came down slowly and stopped at the top of Haralde's head.

"I can open you like rotten fruit. Do you not understand? I can do it any time. You have none here to stop us." Arwel's face was a mask of anger.

One of Arwel's men hefted his spear upward and cocked his arm, as if to throw. There was a rustle of the air, something slammed into him from behind, and he pitched forward into the dirt. An arrow stuck out of his shoulder.

Out of the dark loomed figures, many men holding cocked bows.

Arwel's eyes went wide as he made them out.

"Catch Lord," shouted a voice from the dark.

A scabbard came to Riennes He flipped it to Haralde. Then another. He caught his, was up on his feet and his kandos out pointing at the knot of Arwel's men. Rhys stepped into the light with his bow. He put a foot on the back of the groaning man on the ground and shoved him down.

The whole scene before the crackling fire then was still, as a frozen pantomime, even to Arwel still standing with his sword almost touching Haralde's head. He glanced around, a simpleton look upon his face.

Haralde, holding his scabbard, slowly lifted his hand and pushed Arwel's blade to one side. He rose, bunched with one hand the clothing under Arwel's throat and with the power that was in his big, young frame, hauled the stupefied man across the table and hurled him to the ground beside his moaning fellow.

"Thee young bastard," hissed Haralde lowly. "Thee come. Thee buy your way into my mother's wedding day with a gift. Then thee insult her with these petty demands. And thee expected all to fall at your feet and obey."

Haralde looked around at the scene, and then at his people; at Rhys standing on the man on the ground, at his farmers in the shadows, at the face of a grinning Polcher seen just at the light's edge, and at his brother guarding his back. And he smiled.

"None to stop thee, eh? One word from me and an arrow in each of your eyes."

Rhys bent down and with one heave, jerked his arrow out. The man cried out. He was lucky it had no broadhead tip, but rather was a sharp pointed target arrow.

"Get up," Haralde hissed at Arwel.

Arwel rose, done for. Haralde took away his sword and threw it on the table. "A contribution to our armory in my new tower." He grinned as he walked to his brother's side. "My, but how it keeps growing day by day." He walked to each of Arwel's men, took away their spears, daggers, another sword and an axe and threw them rattling on the table. "Our desert sure does provide, does it not Polcher," he said, grinning down as he came to stand beside the bent man in the half light.

Polcher grinned, bobbed his head up and down. He uttered one word. "Magical."

There was a noise of more men arriving and Oswald, Tyne's second at the wedding feast, stood with a spear. "My Lord?"

Haralde went and stood in Arwel's face. "Go now. The next time we see thee, we will have it out, thee and me." He turned and instructed Oswald. "Ride them to the end of Neury, to where the bones of Aelfgar rattle in the wind. Then see them on their way."

Riennes bent over the bleeding man. "Give me a moment to bind this one. The arrow struck nothing serious." He went looking for his medicine bag.

Oswald and his soldiers led horses to Arwel and his men. Haralde motioned each of his vassal archers to step into the light. Then he walked through the bunch and grinned at each lightly.

Riennes appeared, sat the wounded man on the bench and bound him up after applying a poultice. The man sat stiff and stared ahead stoically through his pain.

Then when Riennes finished, all the archers and everyone saw the wounded make a strange little gesture. Everyone would talk about this the next day.

The man suddenly grabbed Riennes's wrist, bowed and touched his forehead to the back of the healer's bloody hand, then stood up, walked to his horse, mounted and sat astride, his head down. The rest of his company mounted.

"Go Oswald. Get rid of them," instructed Haralde.

As they stood there and listened to them ford the River Clee, Haralde turned and said: "Well done thee men of Neury and Wym. Now go to your fires, get some sleep."

The company broke up. They talked lowly in the dark and one laughed as they faded into the night.

Rhys turned and leaned on his stave. "They are taken with themselves at routing so easily these armed louts."

"I know," Haralde nodded. "And we will talk about this very thing on the morrow. After I get my silver coin back from thee."

Rhys objected. "Nay my lord. I have been practicing."

"As I said, a sneaky knave. Good night to thee bowman. Sleep well."

Haralde and Riennes made their way back to the longhouse and entered the family room. Food and implements had been removed. Six polished chalices stood shinning in a row on the table. A low fire had been set.

"Come here Ren," ordered Haralde as he took Riennes's hands. With no water about, he poured some of Magda's ale over them, and wiped the blood away with a corner of the table spread.

"A bloody waste, do thee not think?"

"Aaah but there is her wine still." Haralde poured wine into two chalices and walked to stand with Riennes by the fire.

They stared down into it. Then Riennes: "What did thee say, a wedding day is one of the busiest days in a life?"

"Hectic. I said hectic."

"Aye. It was all of that and more," Riennes lifted his cup. "It is her wedding night. May our mama not be too rough with him tonight."

Haralde laughed and they tinked silver cups. "May Master Tyne be up for it."

chapter 10

The brotherhood of the arrow.

ARALDE, RIENNES AND Rhys were in a greenwood away from everyone.

In the meadow before the longhouse, people were awakening. Women were stirring fires to life for cooking while men were bringing in more wood. Children were down by the river looking for fish.

Haralde stomped back and forth across a clearing. Riennes sat on a stump watching him, yawning, chin in hand. The two had been at Rhys for some time now, trying to convince him of something.

"We need thee Rhys. We all need thee. Neury and Wym still are weak to bandits and raiders," argued Haralde. "Thee saw that last night."

Rhys leaned against a tall ash tree, his arms straight before holding his longbow stave. His head was down. In his cloth Phrygian cap, a twig of leaves stuck out. He was deep in thought.

An idea had been growing in Haralde, one first posed by Riennes. Then yesterday at the archery contest, it fulfilled him. The defenders of his fiefdom were right there in front of them; serfs, churls, yes even slaves, organized into bands of archers, one to support the others, the others to support one, all to answer the call of his lord in times of dire need. He and Riennes represented the sharp head of the arrow; the rest would be the brotherhood of the shaft and the feather. The brotherhoods would enforce the decisions of their respective councils. No farmer family need feel alone and defenseless any more. He had no idea how many were in the fiefs.

"All we ask of thee is to teach them all the bow, how to shoot well, how to make their own longbows, organize them into brotherhoods." said Riennes. "Thee have already made a start at that."

"We will teach the children to make arrows. Give them some pence at harvest celebration. I will put the smithy here to work and we will hammer out hundreds of arrow heads, hunting broadheads, target arrow heads, war heads, whatever we need," Haralde outlined.

"It is not my nature to be common among men," whispered Rhys. "They will make demands of me." Rhys spoke his thoughts out loud. Pulled into their schemes, they will demand tax and tithe of him in time.

Riennes sensed this as reason for his reluctance.

"We will build thee a house, on the edge right here, with Brekin just at your back or wherever thee would like, and no tax, no food render would we ask," volunteered Riennes.

That brought the Fremen's head up.

Haralde stood before Rhys and crossed his arms. "Thee have babes bowman. They are growing up. Thee need a place of their own, where thee can care for them, where we all can care for them. They cannae run like wild cubs much longer, unprotected while thee are out for food."

That struck the mark. Rhys nodded at that.

He looked up at them. "No tax. No tithes."

"I demand only one, a commorth of your service, of your physical support of we two lords. And thee have already been doing that for Saran since before Aelfgar. All we ask is it continues, that when we call, thee will answer immediately and bring our fighting host to us."

Rhys stood up and walked around the clearing, then came back.

"You struck me deep when you brought my children into this. Then I must do this," he finally agreed. The three came together and shook hands. "I do so because I know you to be men of deeds, not just words. So say you, so do you. But you must convince the others of this."

Riennes shook his head and smiled. "No. Thee did that yesterday. The moment thee took the long arrow to the far target. Farmers, carpenters, stone workers, wheelwrights, fishers, woodworkers, millers, fletchers, all wanted to do that. They fell in behind you."

"Good. Good." Haralde rubbed his hands together. He chattered all the way out of the woods. He was effusive in his joy as they crossed the open meadow.

They walked down a line of men and women and children lined up before Godfroi under the tree. They all were holding or flipping stones. The children would fire them at a passing bird. Haralde or Riennes would nod yes, when stopped by some to be asked if his or hers was the right size. The monk was busy scrawling in his big vellum book and painting numbers on the stones. Helping the cleric was Owain, the gentle youth.

As he was a comrade in arms, Haralde spoke to the youth, asking if he was enjoying the wedding. "Yes my lord. Everyone seems to be having fun here. It is something I have naught seen here ever. Many here are trading things amongst each other. Families will be the better for it after this."

The fact they were trading caused Haralde to hesitate. "Not for much longer, I should warn thee lad. As soon as I get the final archery shooting over, everyone better be away and home to their fields."

"We understand my lord," the youth smiled. "It will be alright. This will be something we all will remember. We your people will now adhere to my lords for this."

"Lord Haralde. Owain here has come to help with your wishes," beamed Godfroi. "We need to keep records of Neury and Wym in a safe place. Like a chapel. He is another who thinks we should have a chapel built in Neury."

"Ah good monk. Keep that thought," remarked Haralde as he walked away. "Like an oak tree, a nut of a good idea grows in time."

They passed on, pulling men like Munch and the others with them, calling out to others to come to a meeting at the spot by the river. Haralde wanted to tell them immediately about Rhys.

Riennes begged off. He felt tired, listless. The morning was beautiful and he wanted to be alone. A bath maybe in the River Clee and to meditate, he thought.

He walked down to the tumbling water and sat quiet. He watched a heron stand reed thin, eyes cocked into the water looking to spear a fish.

He thought about events of the last few days. His brother and he had been busy indeed, even of their personal selves. He touched the light line of scab on his chest where jealousy had touched there. Beautiful black eyes smiled at him from everywhere, in the trees, in the water. Long black hair framed these eyes. She comes alive when she smiles.

She had spoken to him in his Norman French. In his mind he placed her amongst his apple trees in his Norman manor at Montford.

His mood changed instantly. His thoughts dispersed, his mind became cloudy. He stood up and looked around, his stomach feeling bad, as a morning after too much wine.

He heard yelling around a bend, and then a woman screamed hysterically.

He started running along the shore towards the yelling. The yelling was coming towards him. His eyes caught something in the river's current. It was a body floating face down, a small body, going to pass him.

His momentum carried him splashing into the fast water. The spring flood flowed swiftly. He went under, came back up, grabbed at the body. The body came into his arms; a little girl, water streaming out of her mouth. He turned and pulled for the shore. His feet struck a gravel bar and he was up running for the bank with the babe in his arms.

Women, children and some men came running around the bend yelling and shouting. He dropped on his knees and laid her on the grass.

Do something! Do something! What?

Odim suddenly dropped onto the grass beside him. The boy grabbed his playmate and screamed "Leela! Leela!" The boy pounded her chest. Then, the boy did a strange thing; he started blowing into her mouth, as if to give the girl his own breath, something of himself into her, to make her wake up, to come back to him.

Puff, puff, puff he did right into her mouth.

The crowd rushed up to them. A screaming mother bumped Riennes to one side as she gathered her daughter in her arms. "No! No! Not Leela, my Leela! Help us. Someone, please!"

A line of writing surfaced in his mind, resurrected by Odim's actions. A Greek reference. Sena had commented on it. Breath of life. Someone had written a reference to Sena about a Greek fisherman who, holding his drowned brother in his arms, kissed him goodbye full on the mouth, which prompted the dead brother to cough and come back alive.

Riennes grabbed the girl and pushed her mother away. He turned up her face to him and began puffing into her mouth like Odim. The mother came back at him, pounding, screaming at him. Magda suddenly was beside him, pushing at him. "What are you doing!" she screamed.

"He is smothering my baby. He is killing her. Killer! Murderer!"

Suddenly, out of sheer inspiration, Riennes leaned into the babe's face, put his mouth on hers and puffed. Imperceptibly, he saw the girl's chest rise.

Magda suddenly pulled the pounding mother off his back and held her. Men stood around, helpless. One lunged, her father, and tried to pull Riennes off. He persisted. Nothing. Yet the lips were still warm. He blew, more gently now, more regularly. Blow. Blow. No. Breathe, breathe regularly. Softer, softer. Easy. Easy! Nothing! He went back at it. Then, a cough, then lungs heaved for air, for life. She vomited up into his face. He grabbed her by her ankles and hauled her up, up into the air upside down. Water streamed out of her mouth. She heaved and vomited again, then cried, then twisted as young lungs sucked for more air, then she started crying regularly, crying for her mother.

Her mother rushed in and grabbed her, hugged her. Her father grabbed them both. The girl wailed, coughed, tears streaming from her. People stood around, confused. Then, someone clapped their hands and yelled joyfully.

Riennes stood up and wiped his face, his breathing heavy. The crowd began to look at him, then at the girl. They dropped back. One man started yelling. "Lazarus! Lazarus man. He brought her back from the death." Another whispered "Black magic. Black magic." Another shouted: "Sorcerer, sorcery!" They had seen drownings before. Living by the River Clee, others had lost children to the water. Never had one come back from The Others.

Odim stood beside him crying. He had his hand on Riennes's breeches, jerking at some of the material. It was just a reflex action. Glad his playmate was crying, alive. Subconsciously, he was acknowledging Riennes.

Magda fell on her knees beside them and Odim rushed into her arms. The girl's father turned away from his family, and came to Riennes, snatched off his cap, dropped to his knees, and rocking back and forth, cried repeatedly. "Thank you! Thank you! Thank you! My lord, thank you!"

Riennes lifted the man up, patted him on shoulder and said: "Up man! Up man! All is well. Go hug her again," he directed.

Riennes started shaking. Reaction was setting in. A life not lost, saved. It happened this way with him sometime, whenever he won. He lost more than he won.

Magda stood up with Odim in her arms. She regarded him with a strange look. In that look she came alive to him briefly. There was confusion there, but something else; as if she was on the other side of mist or cloud and she could see through it for the first time, and the one she saw first was him. Something inside touched him, just as if a flash, standing a distance from him with her child, she touched him, inside, somehow.

"It was Odim," Riennes whispered. "It was Odim. He did it. Somehow he knew."

She drew her son closer to her. She staggered back as if someone had gently pushed her. "I know," she whispered. She gathered up her son, quickly struggled up the riverbank and disappeared over the top following the people and the parents who hurried to get their baby dry and warm.

He desired her. From this moment on, he desired her deeply. He wanted to run and catch up to her, and take her in his arms. A sudden joy flooded through him. He felt a kindness, a freedom. *I have just discovered something wonderful. A healer, I can save the drowned. That little girl was dead, or on the verge. I snatched her back.*

Or had he? Her lips were still warm, yet the life had left that little body. He sat down where he was in his own puddle. He was soaking wet. He jumped back and began to run. He wanted to catch Magda and shout out his joy to her, to share his discovery.

He topped the bank and looked after her, but she was already joining with the other farm families. He saw them gather round her. Those at the river told the others what had happened. They were pointing to the river.

He dropped back down, walked along the river, cut up through some trees and crossed over the meadow further away, heading for their fire and their dray. He needed to get some dry clothes.

Polcher found him shortly. "Reeve here. Lady here," said Polcher who had just come down from the longhouse.

"Are they getting ready for the contest." he asked.

"Yes. Sit table again," Polcher smiled. "Lord set targets. Rope."

"My friend. How are thee today. Did I tell thee this day is wonderful," Riennes scrambled around in their dray, pulling out their horned bows, quivers of bamboo arrows, some getting worse for wear, and Mongolian riding boots.

"Here my friend. Hold these for me. I have to get our mounts." He ran for the pasture, went to their mounts and whistled at them and removed their hobbles. He ran with the two blacks back to the cart.

"Thank you," he said. He looked up and saw Haralde running across the meadow towards him.

Haralde arrived out of puff. "What did thee just do? I heard. The little girl. She is well?" Riennes nodded vigorously yes, grinning wildly. Haralde grabbed him by both shoulders. "Let me look at thee" He looked his brother directly in the face and saw joy there. He laughed. "Thee are happy. A near drowning and thee are happy."

"Near, yes. But not a drowning. Haralde. I have learned something new." And he shouted what had happened and how he felt. He, a healer had discovered how to save a drowned person. "I think I have anyway. Until it happens again and I can repeat it."

Haralde slapped him sideways on his shoulders. "I give thee great joy. Thee have saved a little girl and now her mother comforts her and she is in great joy. Odim told me. He stands there now stroking his little friend's hair."

"Yes. Come. Let us ready. I must tell thee all later about Odim. Here are your things."

Haralde scrambled into his things, flung his riding pad, saddle up and adjusted his stirrups. "We are the only ones. The silver is ours."

"What of Rhys?"

"Oh he counts for nothing. He cannot match our kind of skills in this."

"Polcher. Tell Lady Saran and her reeve we will be there but momentarily."

Polcher put a knuckle to his forehead, and scuttled away.

Haralde watched him go. "For a bent little fellow, he moves quickly."

They swung up. Riennes handed Haralde his unstrung bow and Haralde slid it into his saddle scabbard.

They pulled out and trotted across the field. Riennes wanted to go faster. To heat up the beast under him, to do some fancy riding, to show off, but checked himself. It was time to concentrate and quiet his inner self. Time later for this other thing.

As they approached the crowd, Riennes and Haralde looked to the tops of the trees to see the wind. Beyond, was the shooting range. There were the wooden targets, set one after another. A rope had been set long before them. They were to stay on one side of the rope, ride fast, and launch their arrows over it into the targets as they came abreast of each. They had done this many times before in competitions before the Khan. They had also shot like this in battle.

As they trotted up to the table and a standing Tyne and Lady Saran, some in the crowd began to point to Riennes and shout: "There he is!" Then some began to chant his name.

Lady Saran stood up with her husband and joined in the clapping. She motioned Riennes to come to the table and to lean over. He did so, she stood up on a bench and she clasped him to her. She cried into his ear. "I heard. I have heard," she shouted above the applause. "Wonderful! You are wonderful . . . .my son! My gentle son."

"Thank thee lady mama." Saran whirled around, grabbed up a blue ribbon and tied it to the leather of his horse. Then she went back, got another, and tied a green ribbon to Haralde's tack.

"Do well. Oh, my sons do well," she shouted, and clapped again.

Haralde stomped his black closer to the table. "Where is Rhys? Will he concede the contest?"

"No, no," shouted Tyne. "He said for you two to start. He is just getting his mount ready. He told me the animal is acting a little skittish."

"Where is Magda?" asked Saran, looking around.

"She is back there," said a little voice and Riennes turned his black around. Odim was standing behind him just off to one side. Riennes looked to where he was pointing and saw Magda in the crowd looking at him.

"Mama wants me to ask if you would wear this?" Odim stepped forward and held up her red ribbon. Riennes swung down, picked him up and swung him onto his horse. "Go ahead Odim. Tie it in the mane."

Odim grinned and did so. Then, Riennes undid the blue ribbon tied onto a leather strap, reached up and tied it in the boy's hair. "Will thee wear my favour, my colors?" "Yes!" Odim reached up and touched it as Riennes swung him down. "Thee did a great thing for your friend at the river. Wear it proudly lad."

Tyne stood on the bench of the trestle table, put his arms up. The crowd silenced.

"Lord Haralde, Lord Riennes . . . ." the crowd began to shout and Tyne had to shout them down . . . . "and Rhys will ride down the line and shoot three arrows each at three targets from the back of a running horse. The hits will be totaled. It will not be a single arrow closest to the target but the best of nine arrows that will win the silver coin."

He pointed down range. "My lords. Will you start?"

Haralde and Riennes moved the Frisians away. They had agreed who would go first.

"Haah!" Haralde started his black away first, getting the war horse up to speed, then began to direct it towards the line of the rope with his knees. Proud of his skills, he showed off by arming his horned compound bow in his saddle with his animal in full flight.

The beast huffed and huffed and wind whistled, and the leather saddle creaked and he let the joy of hard riding take him up. As he thundered to the first target, he stood in his stirrups and loosed three quick arrows. The thud, thud, thud of three strikes could be heard by all back around the table. Again another target, again the thuds. At the third target, Haralde declined in his mind to show off his riding skills while shooting. Rather, he bore in, determined to be the one that relieved Rhys of the coin, leaned out and his bow string thrummed three times. Every arrow was in the targets.

He slowly brought his beast around, thundered up the meadow to the crowd and dismounted in a flurry that had children squealing. His mother's mouth was a big O.

"Haah!" And Riennes was away. The black hurtled down the slant of the meadow to the range, gathering speed as he did. Riennes had already armed his bow. He had three arrows in ready bunched in the same hand that held his bow. He steadied his beast, slowed it, not wanting to run full out as Haralde did. He felt he might win by moving past the targets at a smooth, slower pace. He loosed and they thudded into the first target three times. The second came up and he leaned towards the target, and released and was rewarded with three hits. The third was coming up.

Riennes decided he did not want to beat anyone. He broke his normal calm, calculating reserve in physical action, spun himself around and released his three arrows while riding backwards standing upright in his stirrups. Two thudded into the target. The third clipped the top and flipped off and away.

He brought his beast around and thundered back up the hill to the crowd and the table.

Riennes pulled up and swung down. All was quiet.

Haralde walked over to him. "What is happening?" Riennes asked as he looked around at the silent crowd with their blank face. "Yea, I know not," Haralde whispered back. "What was all that about?" he inquired of Riennes's performance. "I have never seen thee play the dandy before."

They turned to look at Tyne and Saran. Tyne was standing, speechless. Their mama had her hands over her mouth. She shook her head. Her hands dropped away. Upon her face was wonder, admiration. She looked incredulously at them. Never had she seen such a display of horsemanship or fighting prowess as this.

No one here had ever seen such a thing either. At first there was just a clap, then a second, and then it grew into a tumult, shouting and clapping. The people of Neury and Wym had seen something totally beyond their experience. However, it signaled one thing to them, and it was most reassuring: their lords were very capable fighting men. Such would insure future security, and thus, prosperity.

The roar began to lessen, the clapping to ease. People began to look around, in expectation of something.

Expectation pricked at them. Was the wedding now coming to a close? Was it time to go home?

Haralde walked over to the table. "As Rhys has declined to compete, it appears the coin is mine. Riennes missed with one arrow."

Tyne came around and stood beside Haralde and Riennes. "No my lord. It appears Rhys is about to make his run." He nodded to the range below.

Haralde whirled.

There was Rhys, cinching up his quiver onto a saddle of what looked like a horse. Man and animal stood just below close to the run along the rope and the targets.

Tyne began walking down the hill, getting ready to judge the shooting once Rhys had finished.

Haralde vaulted onto his beast, sped past the walking Tyne and pulled up in a spray of mud and grass. He dismounted almost on the run and ran to Rhys and his broken horse. Rhys had just launched his belly onto the back of the old animal. His flop left him horizontal for a moment. He kicked his legs, regained his balance, and swiveled so that he now was mounted.

It was an old equus. A horse long past its prime. No. In fact it was once a young foal born old, constant of old skin and old bone. Never did the horse achieve its full expectancy. It was born that way, and it continued through life that way. Its owner never thought to slaughter it come winter for its meat because it never achieved that kind of maturity. It just stayed bony. Kids rode it. It had become a village mascot. Farmers just tolerated it, because of its gentle nature.

"What are thee doing? What is this?"

"Aaah. There you are. My lord. Stand back. I am about to make my run. By the way, I saw your shooting. Never have I seen archery such as that."

Rhys went "ccchhhh, cchhhhh." The horse began to move. It jigged along. Rhys jabbed it in the ribs a couple of times, and the horse managed momentum. When urged on, as the children did on a summer's day, it could get up to the speed of what everyone agreed was a 'clip, clop, clip, clop'. As it managed to pull its rider along the rope range, Rhys let go with three arrows from a small hunting bow. The crowd, the table and Haralde witnessed nine hits by Rhys, each one hammering even.

Tyne then walked the targets with his string, made his measurements, then walked up the hill towards the table.

Haralde jumped on his big black, urged him to go quickly up the hill, and then dismounted quietly.

Tyne walked up to the table with Rhys. His horse fatigued he left below.

Tyne and his lady talked and talked and talked. A titter began to ripple around the crowd, although it was subdued as no one wanted to show any disrespect to either Haralde, Riennes or Rhys.

Riennes, sensing a great moment in local folklore was unfolding, bowed his head and kept a growing bemusement to himself.

In exasperation, Haralde went to his mother and his father-in-law. "The competition was for shooting from a running horse at targets. The total best shots win. This horse was not running. It simply walked, nay staggered to the end. It must not be allowed."

The final contest was Lady Saran's. As agreed in the beginning, it was her's to award.

"My son," said Saran, raising her head from deep discussion with her new husband. "Did you say shooting from a running horse?"

"Yea I did. That was the contest."

Saran ducked her head again, mumbled with her husband.

Then she came to the table. "I have ridden that horse myself. It runs, sometimes."

Lady Saran risked much when she did a dangerous thing this day. She challenged the pride of Lord Neury manor.

Rhys kept his final silver coin.

chapter 11

Everywhere be magic,
Especially in a child.

AGDA BOLTED UPRIGHT in her bed.
She was late. She had slept in. It was still dark but she was late and she knew it immediately.

Working from dawn to dusk was the fate of all in her village and out beyond into the meadows and even up into the uplands. Their lord's needs so decreed it. Since Lord Longshield demanded her tithe, her render to his house and his family to be her ale and mead and nothing else, she had to work harder to meet his needs as well as her own.

That meant she and Odim had to rise even earlier than before. That is what it took to produce that extra barrel or two of ale. Since the Longshield wedding, and her surprise gift of wine to Lady Saran, it was likely her lord would demand a barrel of that also. As wine-making took more effort and the wine had to be put away to sit for a longer time, it would be a more arduous obligation.

She swung her naked body out of her pallet, and looked down at her belly. Flat was it after some years of bearing a girl and boy. Lithe, round and young and voluptuous it was, as men's eyes constantly reminded her.

That thought halted her in mid-stride as she rose to get dressed. She smiled. She was not adverse to men's admiring eyes, and thoughts.

Then, she realized she was smiling. By the gods, what is happening?

She never smiled. Not in years. Not since her unnamed baby girl was taken from her. Something, however, was happening to her. The shroud over her soul was lifting like a mist. The constant sadness that was her life did not awaken with her this morning. Her innate feelings about things, her perception of the real world, were coming back.

Something is happening to me. And I like it, long for it. The wedding. It started then. Or was it Leela, the saving of Leela from the ill gods of the river? Or . . . . him?

She jumped at that thought. Do not visit that. She bolted to her day's work. She hurried to Odim's room, then sensed immediately he was not there. When she found his pallet empty, she tumbled down the stairs throwing her clothes on as she scurried across their main room.

She scrambled outside and ran to the smaller stone outbuilding. There was smoked curling out a hole in the top of the roof. She pulled the wooden door open, and there he was, fires going under all her kettles and pots, things burbling.

She ran to him, and kneeled and he turned to look at her.

"Mama! What is wrong?" he asked. Then, he smiled, something he rarely did. "Mama! You are smiling. Are you happy?"

"Yes! Yes my little sweet boy. Yes! Yes! Today I am happy and it is because you are here with me. And do you know what?"

"What?"

"Tomorrow I am going to be happy again. And the day after. And the day after."

Odim clapped his hands. "Me too! Me too!" And he hugged her.

Magda cried, kept it inside so that he would not see her do so. And it was because he was a six-year-old boy doing the work that would be hard even for an eight-year-old working beside her from dusk to dawn. This work be too hard for his small body. She just knew he had risen early, let her sleep in, had come out and started all the fires under the pots and stirred them.

The pots contained their daily survival. Most of it was barley being converted to malt and allowed to ferment into ale. There was much demand for her ale. She could make it in large batches because it was consumed quickly. Farmers came from Wym to buy it, and carted barley and oats to her, which she either traded for or bought outright when she had coin.

They boiled various herbs. Some were rendered right down and the precipitate residue scraped off the bottom and as a powder, mixed with other precipitates.

They bubbled stews and rendered chicken parts down to its thick essence, and then combined with herbs. These she sold as her magic medicines to the sick of her community. She sang magical cants over them, called it her charms, and then fed it to the sick old and young. When they recovered, the cure they attributed to her black magic. She knew good nutrition was the likely source.

Magda had a strong knowledge of the natural world. She encouraged the belief amongst the local Christians she was a wica, or a Celtic Druid priestess of the Old Religion. It kept them away from her places. Those places were back in the woods or up in the Brekin mountains. They claimed she worked at night with old hags stirring magical potions in big pots over fires. In truth, they were three old grandmothers who had no supporting family and would die without her.

She supported the three by sharing the food and the warm clothing and other things she traded for. The grandmothers lived in their own huts thanks to the good stews they all cooked. They helped gather in her places where certain roots, plants, mushrooms and fruits were found at certain times of the year, or months, or nights. They helped in the brewing of her ale.

She knew about the cycles of life; about plants, animals, humans. She knew about boiling things, evaporation, changing the state of things, the properties of plants, hop flowers, fermentation, and baking fruit in maslin dough. One day, by accident, she discovered properties of certain clays she found in the mountains, that once smeared into seams of stone fire pits, cured and became as fire brick, able to withstand great heat.

All these things she had learned from her mother and her grandmother. Other things she had learned herself. It was not magic. It was knowledge. As she had no man to protect her, she cloaked herself in the mantle of black magic. That was her armor. No man would go near her, lest she fix him with an evil eye.

She sold or traded her potions and her herbal mixtures and her charmed liquids for eggs, barley, wheat, a hank of beef or mutton, a tool, a man's labour, anything that she in turn could trade for something else, something she needed to help her, her son and the grandmothers survive each day.

Magda and Odim worked through the morning, sometimes laughing when they bumped into each other. Never was it thus in the times before. Then, when his young body gave out and he started yawning and fell asleep stirring a pot, she put him down on a pallet and watched over him, her eyes straying occasionally to make sure everything was bubbling and cooking properly.

And still she continued to feel better. Something nice was happening.

Comforted by the warmth of the fires and the fact they were nearing the end of their morning's work, her head started to nod, to seek a moment's sleep.

Her head jerked at the music of a distant pipe.

Odim sat up, instantly bright and awake. He got up and bolted out the door.

"Odim!" she shouted and followed.

She burst out the door to see her son running up the road towards a man leading his horse peeping on a pipe.

She brought her knuckle to her mouth. Lord de Montford strode towards them. She heard her son call out his name.

Magda called to him to come back but his little legs pumped him swiftly towards the man. She saw him unbuckle that dreadful thing behind his back and sling it over his saddle.

As Odim rushed up, the man bent over to accept her son's leap up onto his back. The two swung around and she heard them both laugh.

What should she do? Her fear of such violent ones as he made her hesitate. Her concern for her son made her walk towards both of them. Or, was it also because she wanted to know how this man had saved little Leela from drowning? How was it he had blown his own life into the near dead life of the girl? She wanted to comprehend the mystery of that, to possess that knowledge.

She bowed her head as she came up to them, and kept her eyes down as she greeted him. "My Lord de Montford. Please forgive my son's outburst."

Riennes came to a halt with Odim on his shoulders. His mount following obediently almost bumped into both of them.

"The laughter of a child is a joy of the world Mistress Magda," smiled Riennes as he swung Odim up onto his mount's saddle. "A single man like me does not get much."

She turned and the three walked together towards her house. She walked with her head down, but stole a glance or two out the corner of her eye.

"I have not seen thee since the joining. Thee two are well Magda?" inquired Riennes, trying to gain her attention, to raise her head and eyes to him.

"We have been well my Lord," she answered. Was she being demur with him, as a woman interested in man's talk.?

"We are making ale mon sirrah," exclaimed Odim.

Magda knew Riennes was going to say it even before he did, that Odim had said it to give him the opportunity.

"I have ridden far this day from Wym to here, and . . . uh . . . a drink of something for myself and some water for my horse would serve well," said Riennes.

The three just naturally drifted under the trees and up to the stone verandah of her house. They stopped there.

"Odim. Go fetch Lord de Montford a tall horn of our ale then. From the large pitcher cooling in the well," she decided.

Odim gave out a little squeal as Riennes lowered him. He bounced up the stone stairs and burst through the house.

Magda stood beside Riennes. The two were silent with each other. She glanced sideways at him, he at her. Then, she did something she had not done for years. She continued to look into the eyes of an armed man without flinching.

He looked at her demeanor. She was dressed in ragged working clothes. Her shabby wool cloak hung loose, done deliberately to detract her full womanly form from the gaze of others. She had pinned a sprig of mint with a little sharp piece of thorn on her left breast. It stood out, as would a valuable broach on a woman of wealth. In fact, she smelled of mint, and nothing else. He looked at her long black hair, then into her eyes.

"I have been with the council men of Wym," he said to prolong the moment, to frighten her not so she would again not look down and avoid him. "What news thus of your meeting and of Wym?"

"The council has made its first decision. They have set a time and place to meet with me, to hold a hallmote, and to swear their loyalty to me. It is the first time they have done this, to come to an accord I mean. They were confused at first. When I approved their decision, they left, proud of themselves."

"This is a good thing?"

"Aye. For men to come together, to discuss and to come to an agreement, this is a thing Lord Longshield and I greatly seek."

"Why not just tell them."

"When men arrive at a thing together, they support it as their's, and it is done swiftly. When men are told to do a thing, they may grumble and drag it along as a heavy stone." She stared at him, and a warm realization flushed through her, turning her face red. A gentle warrior was this man, a healer. She had heard the stories from others in Neury of his going amongst them and making many feel better. Here was a brute, a man who had killed with that thing on his back. Then there was the image of him, Leela, lifeless on her back on the ground, his mouth smothering hers, Odim's crying, smiling face after as he stroked the hair of his friend, coughing, and crying also, but alive. At this moment, I fear him not.

Her face blanched over what she was feeling. She did not want to be vulnerable. Confusion. She struggled to raise her defences against the feelings of this moment. Her fear trapped her between him and her wonder of him, of his violent role in life and her recognition of his gentleness.

Riennes looked at her, sensed what was happening, and quickly changed to something else.

"Magda. I need your help."

"Me? What can I do for you my Lord?"

"I need to find a yew tree"

She stared up at him. She did not comprehend the meaning of his words. Why ask me about trees? Her apprehensions turned into curiosity.

Finally: "My Lord. I do not understand?"

"Lord Longshield, I and Rhys met a few days ago. On our request, we are to have our own longbows. Rhys agreed, but he said to possess a longbow into our reality, we best make it ourselves. I had to go to Wym, so I could not join them in their search for the best kind of yew wood. Yet, Rhys told me what size of yew tree is best. I said I would bring my yew wood on my return. He told me not to cut one, but simply to choose one."

Odim came bounding out with a horn cup of ale. Riennes quaffed it and for the boys efforts, he slurped and made much noise of his enjoyment of it. Odim grinned and clapped his hands.

"Odim. Go bring Lord Riennes a pail of water for his horse. That might let you back up into the saddle again," his mother suggested.

"Yes! Yes! Yes!" And he was away again.

"My Lord. Why a longbow? It is not a thing agreeable to this house," she asked quietly.

"My short horned bow, thee saw me shoot it at the contest, is giving up its life. Rhys says it is because mine was born in the dry air of the desert, while here the air is moist where a longbow lives. A man here must need have a bow to bring in venison to his house, to bring game, to bring the goodness of wild food to those he holds true. Rhys says this."

Magda reluctantly nodded her head in agreement. A bow brought in much needed meat here in times of drought or starvation. Many a family had survived a winter on wild game.

"My Lord. Rhys told you to tell me that, did he not?"

"No Magda. I ask because thee know of things that grow here, of trees. I must have one. If so, I will take a true one, and do it properly."

Odim came puffing, splashing water out of a full pail. Riennes leaned over and helped him place it under his black's head. The horse leaned down and quietly drew it up. When finished, the beast lifted and slobbered some out.

"He likes it!" exclaimed Odim who then reached to pet it.

Riennes gently intercepted his hand. "He does not know thee yet lad. Give him time. Here!" and Riennes lifted him carefully up into the saddle. *As your mother does not know me yet.*

Magda watched all this, the actions of this tall, young Norman, and was not afraid for her son. She could not remember when an armed man anywhere near her son did not alarm her.

"Come with me then," she instructed.

The three with horse walked around behind her house, through her toft where pigs oinked and hens chuckled, past her garden and out across a grassy field left unplowed in fallow. There were village huts scattered around. Women looked up at them from their work, then stared as they realized who they were looking at.

She left the village and field cultivated area and climbed up a rise onto a shoulder of a higher upland mountain. Above them, the heavy forest line presented a solid wall. Below, the farms and villages showed a checkered pattern of plowed and unplowed fields. Magda's house poked large through the trees of Neury near the silver rapids of The River Clee. Some men worked the stone water weirs for the last of the salmon and eels.

She took them into a clutch of trees that were not too high. They were yew, twisted tree of needles with many trunks and small thick limbs. It resembled low junipers.

Magda bowed her head a moment and stood silent, worshipful.

"I have watched these grow for many years," observed Magda. "Do you understand yew is regarded as sacred in Cymru. The Old Religionists still hold them in special regard."

Riennes stepped forward and examined them closely. They were rather low-lying, unstriking in appearance. The branch of one turned down and had grown back into the soil; seemingly another tree was formed where this branch sprung back up through the soil.

"Rhys told us he has sometimes come across Old Religionists worshiping them in the night." He glanced sideways at Magda as he said this.

"I understand this to be true," she replied meekly. "Do you wish me to choose for you?"

Riennes shook his head. "No. I will do thus."

He stepped forward, looked each up and down. His eye tried to follow a limb upwards and to see a bow stave somewhere inside it. He thought of the Greeks who eyed a piece of marble carefully. They claimed a figure was already fully formed inside. It was the responsibility of the artist to chip away the excess and find it.

He examined the ground around it and found the soil to be weak. Magda watched him, taken with his smooth physical movements and his intellect. He examined things as she did.

"Which ever one you choose, you know you cannot cut it down, not now," she informed him.

"No? Why not?"

"You must wait until winter. Rhys will instruct you. You must wait until the sap leaves the tree. Only then can you take it. And then you must dry it out, and work it, and your stave will come slowly to you as a longbow in a year or two."

What he did next jolted Magda.

Riennes stepped into the grouping of trees, put his hand on one, then another, then another again. Each time he bowed his head and went silent.

She stepped back and her eyes widened. His was an ancient address, reflecting an ancient ritual steeped in ancient knowledge. This foreigner could not possibly know this.

Then it hit her: He is of us. He is of me. He believes as I do.

Riennes stepped back. Then: "This one is a sister, young, flowing life. This one is a brother. That one there may be a mother." He stepped forward and touched another, and immediately jumped back. "There is someone here. A spirit. I have felt this before."

Magda stood transfixed. She lowered her head and would say nothing. He was of her kind. From far away, he had come here, for this moment in this time. This was no brute. This was an intelligent man, a thinking man. He was a man of his own power.

"How do you know this?" she whispered her question.

Riennes came and stood uncomfortably near her.

He is doing this deliberately. He uses the body language to speak. A foreigner knows this? "It has happened to me before, here in Cymru, in these highlands." And he told her the story of the night camping place of great oaks, of a shadow that passed between him and Haralde and the monk, and which returned to the trees.

"I awoke later and saw something inside the trees. It suggested a thing, an idea of something unimaginally small, yet that was also the size of heaven. What was that Magda? Thee know of this?"

Magda stared almost affright straight into his eyes.

"Please, we have to go now. Odim come down now to me. We have work to do."

Odim shook his head lightly. "Mama. Please listen to him. He asks a question." Odim's senses told him this was important. "Can you give him an answer, please?"

"What was that Magda? What was there I cannot understand."

She held her breath, and then let it out. "You were in a sacred place. You were in a thin place."

"A thin place?"

"We believe there are places around us where the world of The Others, the spirits, and our world of realities touch, come close together. It is a place of mystery, of beauty, sometimes foreboding because we humans cannot understand it."

"I saw it again, where someone made a thin place where there was not one. Magda! Who is Morog?"

Magda's face went white. She shook her head no. She went to Odim and put up her arms to receive him down from the horse.

"Shhh! Shhh! Magda! I will say no more to thee. Come away. Leave the boy ahorse. I will walk thee back to your house and your work. Do not be frightened so." Riennes's voice soothed like a soft, warm summer breeze.

"Please yes," was all she could answer.

They turned and slowly trudged down, not saying a word to each other.

When they got to the outbuilding behind her house, Riennes lowered Odim to the ground.

Magda took his hand and they went into the building without speaking another word. She shut the door behind her. Shut him out, and her in.

chapter 12

The sky of his life, Was full of light,
Yet, he hungered for more bright.

SUMMER PUSHED SPRING from its throne, and usurped the
pretender.

Too warm now, spring's cool mornings and rush of showers
ceased to be in the days. Bare arms, chests, and feet enjoyed the soft airs,
as they did now in the evenings around their pit fire in the family hall.

Haralde waggled his bare toes, the soles warming from the far end
where pots hung cooking over a low coal-glowing fire. He looked out
through the open great doors of his stone hall and the sun shone with its
sky still full of blue bright light. Yet, it was their supper hour.

The smell of cooking meat worried their bellies. A second cup of
wine beggared their appetites. Haralde understood there would be a
dessert tonight; fruit berries baked in a kind of a light bread with a little
honey poured over it. He was impatient for that. He always did have
a sweet tooth. One of the slave girls now busy with the other kitchen
girls had tried her hand at it. The girls whispered the lords and their
friends would enjoy it because they had sampled some, and it was good.

Rhys's two children, after a fun bounce around the meadow in a cart pulled by a horse, now in the kitchen stuffed the treat partially into their mouths and partially across their faces. The purple of berries stained their faces.

Haralde had loosened his leather vest and hunting belt, and freed his belly to the jovial airs around him. Rhys sat beside him, his bare feet also on the fire pit lip. Riennes was beside the bowman, in a similar state of undress.

They had been hunting. They had flushed a deer. It had fled them and almost reached the sanctuary of the Brekin highland deep woods. Haralde had put a long shaft into the animal, his first kill with a longbow. Rhys also put his wood into the animal, but moments later.

Haralde offered to share it, but Rhys had begged off, said no my Lord, you struck first. So, Haralde shouldered it and carried it down the mountain. Riennes joined them half way down. When they reached their horses, Haralde hefted the carcass onto the back of a spare horse.

While he stood there puffing, sweating, and rubbing his sore shoulders under a hot sun, Rhys cleared his throat. "You know my lord. Your generous offer. I think I will take half after all."

Now the beast hung upside down in a cool cellar place to bleed through its slit throat and to let the wild gaminess settle out.

. Haralde suddenly guffawed in a short burst of laughter.

"What moves thee Haralde?" asked Riennes.

"Rhys's offer to share my meat. After I carried it all the way down." He leaned forward and shook his cup at the bowman. A little wine spilled onto his hand. "Thee are a low fellow, a trickster. I knew it the moment we first saw you. Know I have thee in my eye." He licked his hand.

They were feeling replete. To complete the hunt, Rhys had surprised Riennes and Haralde with a small barrel of wine. Obviously, he had got it from Magda. Riennes wondered if he had paid for it. He hoped so. He also wondered what the relationship was between them.

Rhys just grinned and he relished the moment.

"This reminds me of something," Haralde burped.

"Uh, oh. Look to thyself Freemen. When he starts this . . . ."

"Thee and me, it reminds me of two rams I saw once. Each to the other on a short chain. Tugging each other, constantly trying to get loose, trying to get back enough to take advantage of the other."

"Are you calling me a goat my Lord" Rhys also burped.

"Constant tension they were, like thee and me. I pull to get my taxes from thee and thee pull back to avoid it. I pull, thee pull. Round we go. Thee owe me, thee say thee do not owe me. Now this."

"What?"

"The wine. Thee do this and catch me by surprise and I fall back on my tail. Unfair. Thee unbalanced me sirrah, without warning."

"If you are on your duff my lord, it is because you fight the chain. This is a gift. I give it freely. Pray lord the tumble did not bruise you." Rhys smiled then, said seriously: "I give a gift because of what you have done for me, for my children, for all here. I choose to. I say to you. Each year from now a keg of wine will I give to the Longshield manor, to he who employs me, not orders me, to do a thing I am good at. It puts me on an even."

Haralde beamed at that, and nodded in agreement. "And we thank thee of the gift of the two longbows thee made. We will return them when we fashion ours."

It was good fellowship. It was a good time together. He enjoyed his brother and his forester; the first real time of enjoyment of his dream, his home, his brother, friends. He signaled one of their secret signs of good cheer to Riennes. Riennes beamed back at him, knowing exactly what his brother was feeling. Riennes pulled away some more clothing and he too stretched out more and relaxed.

Haralde had worked hard with his men to finish his tower. Haralde had given Riennes a tour. On the first floor was their armory. Their horned bows, all the spears, shields, and the swords taken from Aelfgar and from the upstart Arwel and his men. On the wall hung their two silk battle banners stained with blood. With a finger to his lips signaling silence, Haralde had tapped on one stone cemented into the wall. "Our chest of gold coins and our treasures," he had whispered. They climbed stone stairs to Riennes's room. There, his clothing, pots, apothecaries, and sealed jars lined the curved walls on shelves. His three volumes of the big Book of Medicine lay on a slanted trestle table, where he could write in the back of it notes from his own experience. The table was beside a large opening with shutters so he could look out across the meadows. Then upstairs to Haralde's room with his things, his notes jotted in a vellum portfolio on agriculture, metallurgy, about his travels, comments about things Haralde was witness to around him. On a similar desk was a rectangular box of sand. With no paper and only a small supply of sheep vellum, he drew his diagrams in the sand on improvements he wanted to make to his stronghold.

He had been busy constructing. Mysterious ledges ran around the upper rooms of the keep where he and Riennes slept. The ledges pitched downward ending in the kitchen. For weeks Haralde had walked along them, sat and examined them, trying to figure out what they were used for. Then one day one of the senior slave women came into the kitchen, poured a pail of water into the ledge and the water flowed down to the end and into a large pot she had placed there under a fire. He shouted at that, ran upstairs and poured water into the ledge. It ran through the rooms and down into the kitchen. The Romans, he shouted out loud to everyone. The Romans were here once. Indoor water but from where? He raced outside. The aqueduct, he pointed out. It was at the same level as a ledge along the outside of the upper floors. Now he was drawing diagrams in his sand box to solve how to run the water throughout the family donjon. Also, he drew ideas on how to heat the water inside for bathing.

His ever industrious mind infected those around him. The men slaves, their bodies incited by their lord's promise of freedom in the years to come, worked hard almost into the night. Those men had begun a very large vegetable garden outside. However, before they started, Haralde had sat down with them, come up with a plan to terrace the land on the sloping sides of the meadow near the aqueduct and to run a water line to the terraces. Everyone worked hard in their spare time hauling good soil onto terraces. Manure went there, human waste, leftover food stuffs, the leaves of dropped trees, ashes, human slops went there, even such thing as fish guts, blood from game.

Down lower in the meadow, Haralde had a shepherd separate the better demesne sheep into a flock separate, away from all others. At night, he discussed animal husbandry with Riennes and ideas on how to improve the quality of their mutton and wool. From an old Turk shepherd, he had learned herds improved if good sheep and rams were brought in from other areas. Good wool brought in good money, Jhon of Muck had so instructed them.

"Enough!" Riennes had finally shouted one day. "Thee fatigue the mind," he accused Haralde. "It is time for enjoyment. Let us go hunting."

Thus they were around the fire after two full days riding and yelling and driving deer and tromping over the hills.

"Yet bowman . . . ," Haralde continued to worry the point. He touched the Fremen's worn clothing and at some of the rents in them. Like scabs on skin, the sewn patches were splotches on and around his garment . . . . "surely now with the silver thee tricked out of us, thee can afford some better clothing. What about Gwenna and Hugh. Thee can now cloth them better."

"My Lord! What is wrong? These clothes still serve me well. Besides, it is summer. My children run around like wild animals hardly wearing anything at this time of year."

"What did thee do with our two coins?"

"I gave my coins to Lady Saran as a wedding gift."

"Thee did not."

"I did but she would not take them. Said the shooting was gift enough. She did say she would hold them safely for me until the need for them came upon me."

"Well, thee have a house now. Thee will need furnishings, things," Haralde prodded him."

"I will trade for that. I have never owned silver coins in my life. If my Lord will leave off, I will hold onto them for awhile, just for the feeling it gives me. I know! I know!" begged off Rhys. "They will have to be spent in time."

Haralde and Rhys poured themselves a third cup of joy and they touched with Riennes.

Riennes stood up, farted, and then sat down, still nursing his second cup of wine. "You know Riennes, Owain said something to me, something about . . . ."

"Trading things," Riennes picked it up. "At the joining."

"Aye. I am also sure I heard the clink of a few pence. . . . I think we need to do something like that again. If we could just . . . ."

"Enough! Enough!" Riennes put his hands on the side of his head and rocked it from side to side. "Are thee never satisfied. Rhys. He wants more. Hide your coins."

The three chuckled, but a thought like a mouse began to gnaw at Haralde.

"I have seen Owain much about thee of late," mused Haralde. "I found him in your stall the other day stirring one of your stinking pots."

"Aye. It seems I have an acolyte," suggested Riennes. "He has shown much enthusiasm. He came to me after the saving of Leela from the river. Told me everyone was talking about it, the magic of it. He wants to know about healing. He is of a gentle nature, and seems to learn quickly the things I teach him."

"Tyne should have come with us," Rhys suggested. "He would have enjoyed the hunt, this."

"I think he still is in the clutches of mama," smiled Haralde. "Her needs as a woman still need fulfilling."

A mood change in Riennes prompted him to inquire: "Rhys. How many bowmen could thee assemble at a short call?"

"Let me think . . . about 12, maybe 15 if the need was serious."

"And Tyne, he now has in training about 10 who can fight from a horse," tallied Haralde. "Why do thee ask Ren?"

Riennes sat staring into his wine. "I do not know. 'S truth it is just a good thing to have a set number of our men ready in our minds."

Gwenna and Hugh came running into their company and ran up into their father's arms. There followed serving woman after serving woman with trencher wood plates of steaming eels, seasoned with herbs from the garden and loaves of bread with a local mild cheese.

"Aaah!" shouted Haralde. "Where have thee been all this eventide." The men got up and went and sat at the large family trestle table on the raised dais.

"Food! Food! We want food!"

The older women ordered the younger slave girls to file in a line and present each of the men with their servings at the table.

The fish was followed by some stew with beef and then small capons. At last came the baked fruit dessert.

Haralde roared his approval, and asked Riennes and Rhys: "Naught have any of thee seen such a thing so fine. Eh? Eh?"

He leaned over, touched a serving girl's ass, and said loud enough for all to hear. "Stay close. Later I may have other appetites thee can appease upstairs."

The girl ran off tittering.

Riennes leaned across the table. "Be careful Lord Haralde. The girl might take thee serious one of these days."

"One can only hope Lord Riennes, one can only hope." And Haralde leaned over with chunk of chicken. "Here Gwenna. Try a bit of this. It is as sweet as thee are little one."

chapter 13

A peace now threatened.

"**S**TAND DOWN! STAND down! STOP IT!"
The 'clanging' echo of broadswords banging off the walls of the bailey stopped all together. Haralde, with his broadsword halfway over his shoulder, stopped in mid-swing, while behind them both, Riennes stepped back from smashing at one of their fighting soldiers and looked over to see who barked the command.

Tyne stepped back, leaned on his sword and shook his head and all the while trying to get his breath back. He was out of puff.

Too much good food, and wine . . .and Saran, he thought.

"What ails thee Tyne?" asked Haralde.

Riennes walked over and stopped to look into the face of their stronghold commander sucking air. "Pray, what is wrong? Are thee bunged up?"

"I think it is age," suggested Haralde with a straight face. "I think father Tyne is getting too old for this."

"Or, with respect to our mama, I think Tyne of Cumraugh is mellowing, settling into the life a fat reeve," followed Riennes. "He has found life with a wife who pleases his every whim. Or maybe Crowfeeder is losing the struggle on the battlefield of the bed."

"Nay! Nay! Leave off you two. This is serious."

"I think he wants to go home," suggested Riennes.

"Listen. You have a lot to learn yet. You must needs know how to wield a broadsword in a battle field way," demanded their teacher.

Tyne as commander had ordered his men to learn to fight with broadswords and had suggested the two lords with big bladed weapons of their own would benefit from his instruction. Two weeks ago, he started morning practices for all. Swords were a scarce weapon in the two fiefs but a few spare were available in Haralde's armory.

They had done well, quickly picking up all the movements. He wanted first to strengthen their wrists and hands. He wanted to strengthen their upper torsos to take the powerful slamming of heavy iron. He had heard them complain some days after their first session of how their wrists and shoulders ached.

Tyne was a powerful fighter with a broadsword. He was short, muscular and a firebrand when he waded into an enemy phalanx. He knew how to scythe through a crowd.

"This is a smashing weapon," he reminded them again now. "You have to plant your two feet . . . ." and Tyne stamped his bare feet into the ground . . . . "to give you balance; to give you something solid to hit from. Bang, bang, bang you must come, strike first, fast, do not give the bastard a chance to recover, drive him back until he falls to the ground. You are two, big strong lads. You should be able to do it better than me."

They stood there, their torso's bare, all sweating lovely in the warm morning sun, as were their stronghold soldiers in training. It was grand exercise, but he wanted them somewhat experienced with the weapon and somewhat in shape at the same time.

All had done well over the two weeks, especially the two young masters. They got the rhythm down, accelerated the speed of the arching blade, and at the last session, they had got the measure of him and had started to make his arms ache.

Now, this morning, everything seemed to fall apart. Just as he got his rhythm going, they kept poking him in the face with their new big broadsword, the ones not rounded on the end but sharper pointed. The kept moving around him, making him move back off his feet. He was so busy shuffling around and trying to swing at them, that he was getting tired. The two kept crowding his right side, his sword arm, so he could not extend his arms fully in swinging at them. It was all too unsettling.

"Rush in. Plant your feet. Cut into them, and be prepared to deflect their answering swing back at you. None of this, pokee, pokee, thrust, thrust, thrust, shuffle, shuffle your feet."

Haralde wanted to make a jibe of the 'pokee, pokee' but did not want to appear disrespectful. Tyne had succeeded in doing what he set out to do; train them to be proficient with the heavy weapon. Each time he had left to go home, Haralde and Riennes had practiced some more with the big swords and even came up with a few different offensive and defensive variations of their own.

So he said: "We know all call thee Tyne Crowfeeder. Terrible are thee in battle. Thee feed the crows the eyes of your enemies. It is just that where we come from, we were taught to move quickly, slip a blade in and out before your enemy is even aware of it and move onto the next."

"My lord Haralde. There is no time nor room to do thus when you are amidst a crowd of shoving, pushing, smashing men all swinging at you, all jostling to smash your brains in," argued Tyne.

"Thank thee for that Master Tyne, but we think we will have time. A great sword master taught us how to bend time to our fighting needs," revealed Riennes.

"This I must see. Put it up please," Tyne instructed Riennes as he swung back to hit the young Norman. As he started to swing down, their soldier guard on the wall shouted: "Here comes the ale mistress."

He swung down but Riennes was not there. He turned to catch Riennes's back scurrying up a ladder to the catwalk. The young lord's quickness impressed him again.

Riennes hurried over to the wall and looked down. At the other side of the meadow, just coming out of the trees from Neury was Magda and Odim bumping along. In their cart were two small barrels of ale, her render to her lord's needs

Riennes leaned forward and put his chin between two spiked tops of the wooden wall and smiled. He wondered if he could make her smile again. She had been to the Longshield stronghold just once before and he felt he was winning to her, drawing her out with humour. She was softening into bemusement.

He jerked upright. A horseman, no two, came out of the woods and cantered towards her cart. By the looks of his big horse, the first looked to be of some wealth. Also, a warrior's bearing. The other was smaller, younger. He pulled the reins of a smaller horse behind. It was a paltry carrying packs. They were outfitted for travel.

The horsemen closed with Magda. They talked back and forth, then Odim stood up and pointed towards the fortress. The big horseman nodded and then all made their way towards them.

Then, a man broke out of the tree line along one high shoulder of the meadow behind them. He was running with a long stave in his hand. Rhys.

The soldier barked out the presence of all these coming towards the palisade.

The juxtaposition of all this, of all the elements, of the green of the meadow and the blue of the sky and the sweat on Riennes's lips, all at the same time, did not bode well. It was like a chess board, all the forces aligning.

He rubbed his side. A sharpness there annoyed him. He must have picked up a stitch from all the exercise.

He checked Magda and Odim again. The composure of the rider bespoke one image: chevalier.

He bounded down the ladder and spoke to Haralde and Tyne and to the others who still stood with swords in hand waiting upon his words.

"Magda and Odim are being accompanied by a Norman chevalier and a boy. Behind and above, Rhys is running towards us. Haralde! Something serious is afoot."

Haralde nodded his understanding, turned and handed the Irishman his heavy sword. "Master Tyne. I think we had better prepare ourselves."

"Yes Haralde." And Tyne rounded up his men, and they started pulling on jerkins. The soldiers raced for their spears and headed for the walls. Tyne started putting the swords in their scabbards.

Riennes ran up the narrow road to the bailey above and to his stall. He went into it and there was Owain grinding away with motor and pestle at some substance. Owain, the fourth son of a farm family somewhat related to Lady Saran, had a keen intellect, one that rebelled against the daily physical monotony of field labour.

"Young Owain. Go tend to your lord and receive his guests. Go," and he tapped the young farm boy lightly on the shoulder. Then Riennes stripped off his clothes, stepped under the aqueduct spigot and quickly washed away his stink.

He dried himself off, shrugged into his blue silk undershirt, pulled on a fine jerkin and slipped into trousers.

He quickly wrapped leather around his legs and fastened it to his belt over the shirt, slipped his feet into leather boots, grabbed his kandos and slung it over his back as he ran to the main gate.

He could see Saran's uncle Gwengarth shuffling quickly towards the same ground, as were the stronghold's carpenter, cooper and smithy.

He arrived just as the thumping of some barrels full of liquid and the squeak of a cart's wheels came through the gate. Behind loomed the horseman with strong leather trappings on his beast and a boy on a paltry pulling a smaller horse with back packs.. He wore patched clothes and a leather cap.

Haralde met them as they came in.

"Greetings Mistress Magda," grinned Haralde as Riennes intercepted the horse, and then made his way to the two on the seat.

"Good morning Magda, and of course, young Master Odim with the big smile on his face," grinned Riennes. "I see thee have brought us liquid sunshine again."

"Oh yes Lord Riennes. And this time we made it with sunshine. We smiled the whole time did we not mama?" he joked with Magda.

She lifted her eyes and the skin crinkled in the corner and there was the beginning of a smile. She nodded.

Then all turned curious to the strangers.

He was indeed a Norman horse warrior accompanied by a squire. His warhorse was of a size. He looked around, suspicious, cautious.

"Greetings sirrah!" Haralde addressed him in Norman French. "Thee are welcome here!"

Though puzzling over Haralde's foreign accent, relief came to the man's face. "Bon. Thank you sirrah. I am lost. I thought all here would speak Welsh only. And I cannot. And the first person I meet is this lovely lady with her son, and they greeted me in my tongue. I was much relieved."

"Will thee dismount, thee and your gillie there?"

"I will sirrah, with much thanks."

He swung down, a little moan from sore muscles escaped him. Haralde liked what he saw, a fair-haired, clean shaved handsome man a little older than they. The man had the courtesy to remain ahorse until he was invited.

He pulled off riding leather gloves, bowed and offered his hand as he said: "Alan, son of Flaad, a subject of Roger de Montgomeri, sirrah."

Haralde motioned questioningly to the lad still ahorse.

"This? This is my squire, ... come down!" The boy swung down, snatched off his cap. "This is Roloph."

Haralde stepped forward, bowed, shook hands with the Norman gentry and then stepped over to Roloph, who unused to attention, jumped forward, bobbed his head and shook hands.

"Owain, will thee take these horses to the stables, water and grain them . . . . do thee wish them stripped of their burden Sirrah Alan?"

Alan nodded, grateful for the question and the obvious hospitality he was offered.

"Do so Owain. Get some of the other boys, wipe the horses down, and then take them to the smith to check their hooves. Then leave them in quiet."

"They do look travel weary. Right away my lord."

"Gwengarth. Take Roloph into your hospitality, feed him, and if I am not mistaken, find him a soft pallet afterward. He looks done in."

He motioned Sirrah Alan towards the others. "This is Tyne, commander of our fortress and reeve of Neury and Wym." Tyne offered his hand. Sirrah Alan hesitated, and then shook it, apprising the man of Hibernia the whole time.

"Sirrah Alan, this lady whom thee spoke to is Mistress Magda of Neury whose timing with her refreshing ale amazes us all." Magda bowed slightly, then smiled, then dropped her gaze downward. Sirrah Alan bowed, then raised his eyes to her beauty. "And the young lad beside her who thee talked with is her treasure, and ours, her son Odim."

Odim stood, bowed, offered his hand, which Alan again hesitated to accept, but then did and that pleased Odim. It was obvious the Norman was not used to all this familiarity with the common.

"And may I introduce my brother, a countryman of yours, Lord Riennes de Montford, Lord of Wym."

Sir Alan jumped forward with a smile of relief on his face and shook hands. "You! My Lord de Montford! You are who I seek."

"Thee honor me Sirrah Alan," greeted Riennes in smoother Norman, and Sir Alan was at once at his ease. "Yea, though, what would thee have of me that brought thee all this way?"

"I have been sent to find you. And some Saxon thegn with loyalties the Earl of Cheshire requires." Alan whirled around and pointed to Haralde. "That is you!"

"Aye. Lord Haralde Longshield, Lord of Neury and Brekin. Welcome to my house." And the two shook hands.

"And I have others on my list. They must be neighbours of yours."

Haralde and Riennes chuckled at the relief that crossed Alan's face.

"Magda, Odim. Would thee take your cart up? I think a drink of your ale would spread much comfort in Sirrah Alan's innards."

"A fine idea," interjected Riennes who vaulted up onto the seat, shoved Odim over closer to his mother, took the reins and clicked their small horse forward. He glanced over at Magda, she smiled and nodded her head down. Odim looked from one to the other and grinned. As the wagon passed, Haralde reached in, unlatched, flipped the back down, jumped up, sat on the gate and invited Alan to do the same.

He shouted to Tyne. "Rhys is coming. Both of thee come up when he gets here." Tyne saluted, then made for the wall.

The cart left the common and trundled up the narrow road. Just before they turned towards a side door of the stone bastion, Haralde stepped off followed by the Norman, and the two skipped up the stone steps and through the double doors into the family hall. Sir Alan eyed the strange weapon on Haralde's back. He hesitated just for a moment to gaze with admiration out over the meadow and the alpine vista seen from this high point, then followed his host in.

"Get us a basin of warm water, towels, and five drinking cups," Haralde signaled to his senior matron of the kitchen who was waiting for her lord's instruction.

The matron hustled back, put the basin on the family table and bowed to Alan as she handed the towel to him. Sir Alan spread his arms wide holding the towel with a puzzled look on his face.

"Take your vest off sirrah and wash the dust from your face and hands and thee will feel so much better. I will return in a moment."

Alan did so, and Haralde heard a splash and the "aaaah!" come from his weary guest.

In the kitchen, Riennes had rumbled in the two kegs through a side door. Riennes heaved one up and carried it under his arm.

Haralde pulled the wooden spigot out of Magda's last contribution, and he turned to her. "Remain here Magda, but leave us not. I suspect something serious is about to befall us and we men need to talk. And I needs talk to thee before thee return home."

"Aye my lord. We will do that," she answered, this time not dropping her eyes before her lord. A relationship of master and servant had now formed, and no more.

"Thank thee. And everyone, get some food into this boy and his mother. In fact, get something together. Our guest will need sustenance."

Haralde and Riennes then headed back into the hall. There was no pit fire as it was too hot now so the women stirred the coals on an outside hearth and there prepared hot food.

The Norman visitor had his vest off. His undershirt was of fine linen the color of an oak nut. He wiped his hands and his face. His hair was tousled. Yea, though there was a smile on his face.

"I have not done that in a long while. I forgot how refreshing that is."

"It pleases us that thee are," smiled Riennes, who thumped the keg onto the table and wedged it secure. Haralde drove the spigot into it just as a slave matron came in with a tray of cups.

Haralde poured their cups, presented the first to Alan, and both he and Riennes stood and hesitated while their guest sipped his first.

"Oh! Say!" And he slowly slurped it all down.

Haralde drank deep his cup, refilled all, and they drank again.

"Aaah. That wench, she is talented in so many ways," smacked Alan as he slammed down his cup.

"That wench, she is her lord's ale maker, much treasured by him and much loved in our villages," commented Riennes as he slowly picked up the cup, filled it, and then handed it back. He gave his fellow Norman a somewhat cautious warning look.

Alan was no fool. "Forgive me my lords. I bespoke myself. I should have known. She was gracious to me and my squire. I will express my appreciation for her help, and my admiration for her ale—making skills. She is indeed admirable as I should have seen."

They sat down, Haralde and Riennes hungry for news from the outside. They waited expectantly over the purpose of Sir Alan's hard ride here.

"I am amazed sir."

"Oh! Of what?" asked Haralde, himself a little more cautious about his guest.

"Way back up here. Lost in these mountains. And I find this . . . ." he passed his hands around the room . . . . "a fine mountain redoubt. Though somewhat rough, it is very impressive, as is your hospitality. I thought this was only the land of the mad, backward Welsh, and I mean no insult by that."

"I am both Welsh and Saxon and proud of both," Haralde said quietly.

"Good for you." Alan barked out a little laughter. "I loved that ugly, tormented mountain god on your great door who greeted me when I came in. There is a story there, I know. Would that I had time to remain a guest in your great hall and to hear all your stories," he said.

The matron came in with a tray of bread, cheese and cold capon. "There is some stew heating up master," she bobbed.

Haralde nodded, offered his guest the food. Sir Alan sliced cheese with his dirk and folded a piece of bread around the fowl. He got up wolfed some of it down and walked over to the wall where the great sword gleamed. The blade was lightly oiled. He saw the words newly carved into the limestone: HONOUR, DUTY, SERVICE.

He saw order in this household, cleanliness, deference by the kitchen slaves and the people around their lord. He liked what he saw in this big man. He glanced over to Riennes and wondered what a de Montford of the powerful family of Normandy was doing up in these mountains.

However, time was running out for him.

He waited for the matron to bring in a steaming bowl of stew. He wolfed down spoonfuls of it and made sounds of appreciation. When she left, he tipped the remainder of the bowl down his gullet, wiped his mouth and nodded his appreciation to the two.

"Listen. I must away soon. Sent I was to order you to gather yourselves up immediately and to travel to Chester. All subjects are to attend Lord Gerbod, Earl of Cheshire. My Lord Roger is to be appointed Earl of Shropshire by the king. This whole border area of Mercia along the Welsh

March has been given over to powerful Norman viscomtes and barons by William. William fitzOsbern, newly name Earl of Herefordshire, now is slashing through Wales just south of us.

"Immediately?" asked Haralde.

"Immediately."

A noise came up the stairs of the front verandah and Rhys and Tyne hurried through the open door. Rhys was dusty with travel.

"Sirrah Alan. Rhys of Gwent, our forester and a fine hunter of deer at times," introduced Haralde.

As they were separate across the room. Sir Alan simply made a bow and Rhys returned it.

"What is it Rhys?" asked Riennes as he sensed the bowman's urgency.

Rhys looked to Riennes, then Haralde, then at Sir Alan across the room.

"Go ahead Rhys. We all need to hear," ordered Haralde.

"A runner has come in from Wym. A large party of Welsh raiders slipped down through the woods east of us. They surprised some of our people. Another large band came over the mountain and through the pass of Brekin. They passed north of us here last night. My lords. They are heavily armed and moving east.

Haralde and Riennes stood up. "Did they hurt anyone?"

"No. Munch's message was that they ignored everyone and simply passed through the farmlands. They stole not a thing. They do not want to be noticed. The one party left Wym from the Roman road, and cut east towards Shropshire.

Riennes turned to Sir Alan. "Where is Earl Gerbod?"

"When I left two days ago, in Shrewsbury, his party was to travel slowly to Chester."

Riennes was rubbing his side again. Haralde noticed it. "I like this not Harry. Do thee remember Arwel?" reminded Riennes.

"Aye. He told us he would pass through our lands. He said there was a strong Norman presence coming," recounted Haralde.

"He hinted his prince wanted to deal with it," went on Riennes. "Bleddyn wants to be king here. I think this is very serious."

"Aye," agreed Haralde. Tyne, Riennes, Rhys and Haralde seemed to gather as conspirators around the table. "Tyne. Gather up all your men and go into the tower and brings weapons out," said Haralde, pulling at keys from a hook on the wall and giving them to the Irishman. "Take food for a week. Two are to be left here to guard. Put all in Magda's cart and take her and Odim to Saran. Where are your children Rhys?" "With Saran." "Warn Lady Saran of what thee have heard here, and tell her to keep Gwenna and Hugh there, that we may be away for a time. Then take her and Odim down to Neury where we will meet with you."

Riennes hurried towards the kitchen area. "I will tell Magda of what is to happen."

"And tell the kitchen to start packing food for us, for a week," Haralde shouted after him. "Rhys, how many bowman can thee gather up in short notice?"

"You mean to take our people with you?"

"Yes!"

"Fight they will to defend their lords and their families. But this, I do not know if they want to be part of an army?"

"It is an order from me and Riennes," growled Haralde. "Remind them of their oath of loyalty. Tell them I intend to attack a Welsh raiding party before they attack us here. Now, how many can thee assemble quickly?"

"Three here. Then I will with Tyne to Lady Saran, then to Neury to gather more. I recommend we then to Wym, overnight there while I gather more. It will be 20 ready for you my lord."

"Tell each they will be away with us for awhile, and to prepare themselves accordingly. Tell them their skills will be used to defend us, not to be thrown against an armed force. And tell Gwengarth to pull out our big drays, put horses in the traces, and to ready our own war horses."

Rhys nodded. "It would seem you have planned for this day."

"Nay. It was my brother's doings. Now, away with thee all. We must make haste."

Haralde turned to Alan as Tyne and Rhys dashed away. "It would seem I must deny thee any more of my hospitality and chuck thee back upon your horse. Thee will not have time to go gather others for Earl Gerbod. My neighbours sirrah are all Welsh, and would have your head if thee showed your Norman face before their hearths."

"Then, stay with you I will. You suspect they are after Gerbod?"

"Riennes thinks so. He has a way of being right about such things."

Haralde grabbed his bowl of stew and wolfed it down. He motioned to Alan to enjoy the same of the remaining bowls, that this might be the last good food they will have in a while."

"Now sirrah. I recommend thee go upstairs to my room and lay thyself down for some sleep. I will show thee where. Thee will need it as thee must ride again for the remainder of the day. I must away to do the things I must."

Odim ran towards Riennes who swung him up and plunked him down on the seat of the cart.

"Are you going to leave us?

"Yes. I must away for awhile."

"Is it a bad place. I heard Lord Haralde tell mama you may have to kill people?"

"It is a bad place but I hope I do not have to do anything like that."

"Is Lord Haralde your brother? I have heard you both call each other that, but mama says you are not, not really."

"Yes Odim. We are truly brothers, not by having the same mama but by having the same soul, the same love for each other. I think thee can understand that. We have saved each other's lives many times."

"Yes," was all Odim replied. He was satisfied with that answer. Then: "Will you die?"

Riennes did not know how to answer that truthfully.

"I think all we are doing is just going for a ride to meet a very important man. He is a good man who holds the safety of all of us. We just want to make sure he too is safe."

"Odim. You must not ask Lord Riennes so many questions," said Magda to her son as she came out the side door and down to the cart. "He has many things to do."

She looked right at him as she said it. He quite lost himself in the depths of her black eyes. She looked at him in soft. She looked at him as if she wanted to be with him. He almost melted before her. Such was her presence that she was reaching out to him even from behind her reserve.

She held her hand up and he took it. He assisted her up, but halfway up she stopped and complained "Ooh!"

"What is it Magda. Did I hurt thee somehow?"

Still standing half up, she turned and looked down at him. She rubbed her side. It hurt.

"Do not go." The words came out flat, cold.

"I must. I am a king's man. Our Earl is the king here. Without a king, we could have blood on the land again. Do thee want that?"

"You can not go there. There will be killing. You are a healer, a quiet man. You saved Odim's little girl from the river death. Now, you wish to go to a place of murder and slaughter."

Riennes pleaded with her with his eyes, his body posture.

"Know you that there is no thin place over a battle field. It is a hard way to die."

"I must do this Magda. I do not wish to, but I must."

She beheld him with her eyes, to remember this moment. Then, she would talk no more. She got in, snapped reins in her hand and the two pulled away for the road down to the common.

"Magda. Tyne will escort thee to Lady Saran's house," he yelled after her.

Magda held the reins tight and saw Tyne mount up as she approached him. Each bump in the road seemed to sharpen the pain in her side. She lowered her head, and began to cry.

"Mama. What is wrong?" pleaded Odim.

"Oh. It is naught my son. I just have a kink in my side. It will go away."

chapter 13

War, wretched bloody war.

SIRRAH ALAN TURNED around in his saddle and looked down the line of the company he found himself in, and shook his head in disappointment.

Behind on horse was the Irishman, mounted soldiers behind with lances, a dray with a priest on its bench, another cart with a young man aboard, and a line of farmers and their sons running behind. Some of the older farmers rode in another dray. All carried staves or poles. He quickly saw they were bloody big bows.

He shook his head and turned to Riennes beside him. "Lord Riennes? These vassals of yours. You will throw these farmers against armed Welsh raiders?"

"It is my wish not," answered Riennes, looking around at the Berwyn Mountains they were passing through. "However, what else can we do Sirrah Alan? We are Earl Gerbod's poorest fiefdom. We have no money or resources to equip regular fighting men. We manage our horse fighters there, where a few months ago they were only five."

Alan understood. By their dress, he could see their poverty. Riennes and Haralde wore threadbare clothing, ragged at times. Some had patches sewn over rips. Why did he get the feeling they did their own sewing?

"Ragged they may look to thee Sirrah Alan, but they have been blooded in a skirmish against a shield line just months ago," informed Haralde riding on the other side of Riennes. "They are deadly with those poles as thee call them. They could part your hair across the distance of a hide field without touching your scalp."

Alan shook his head again, greatly in doubt. In fact, he thought the two young lords allowed too much familiarity to taint their station as masters over this rabble. He was surprised last night when the two had bedded down with this common band around their fire. Even though they invited him to do the same, he was rather put out when Riennes and Haralde did not join him at his fire, a position he maintained through the night.

It was not that he was a high and haughty noble man. Rather, he was his father's third and last son and therefore unable to inherit any of the family estate in Normandy. There the peasantry did what their masters ordered, and woe betide any of those whose lips spoke disrespect or whose minds thought better of their low station in life.

Primogeniture, the civil custom of the first-born inheriting all the family estate, meant all other male issue had to leave and go afield to find his own lands and wealth. So, Alan joined the army of the bastard Duke of Normandy in his sea invasion of Britannia.

Thus did he acquire lands and manors in Shropshire, and thus did he apply his strict Norman authority upon his hapless Saxon peasantry.

This, this was just not the way for an overlord to conduct himself. Yet, grudgingly, Alan had to admit these peasants gave freely of their loyalty to their masters to a degree, well, it almost made him envious.

Riennes had a strong sense of his Norman self-importance. Yet, Alan wore not an overbearing cloak about him. Alan was comfortable with it. He shifted it to suit the company he was with.

Haralde slowed down and let the two Normans chatter comfortable in their Norman tongue.

"Do not be long Harry," Riennes suggested as Haralde dropped back.

Haralde murmured encouraging words to Tyne as he passed; something about the saddle would do wonders for the lard on his ass, and then called to each of his soldiers by name as they passed.

He fell in beside Monk Godfroi on the dray bench and trotted a way with him.

"Godfroi. There was a day thee and ox fought over those reins thee hold so easily now. Think thee of renouncing your vows? I have need of a good drover."

"Get thee behind me, my lord," Godfroi smiled, indeed, enjoying an easy ride on a worn road through the mountains. "You should not tempt a holy man thus."

Haralde chuckled. "I do wonder why thee insisted on joining us. Our fate may be that very terrible thing that sickens thee."

"I hope not. I am grateful you allowed me to come. I hope to stand with you and support you when you petition our Lord Gerbod for our chapel in Neury we agreed on."

"Ah! Thus is all made clear to me now. It is good to have thee along to remind me. It might have slipped my mind," said Haralde as he pulled away and dropped back, mumbling to himself: "Agreed on indeed."

At the back of a dray sat Munch and another older farmer. Munch was working on a number of bow strings.

"Master Munch. Thee should not be here. This could be hot work. Your sons should have come in your place."

"It is an old dog for a rough road, my lord. Wear out the old one's first, Polcher always says," joked Munch. "No. Best my brother keeps my sons on the land from morn 'till night. I hate hoeing."

Haralde let the line pass some more and fell in with Owain on the bench of Magda's cart.

"Thee be well lad?"

"Yes my lord, though I seem to be a bit tipsy from the fumes of Magda's ale. I think her sunshine is stained deep within the wood there," he indicated with a jerk of his thumb to the back of her cart. Haralde had taken it from her at the last moment and piled it high with supplies, including many bundles of arrows.

Haralde turned his mount and moved quickly back to the head of the line. They were coming out of the Berwyn Mountains. As he understood it, the borderland between Cheshire and Shropshire would open to them, an area of infertile soils, heaths, mosses and meres.

A kind of distant commotion softly touched the edge of Haralde's hearing. He dug his heels into his black mount ribs.

Ahead, he could see Riennes waving back at him. Beyond, was Rhys running towards them from where he was scouting ahead. Beyond the shoulders of the opening mountain pass Haralde could see an opening plain.

"Trumpets, my lord!" puffed Rhys as he ran up. "Suddenly, trumpets, men yelling. I hear men roaring and beating a rage on shields. Many shields. A battle is being joined immediately in the opening of this pass."

"Did thee see anything?"

"I thought I saw a few men running from the heights down into the opening ahead," said Rhys.

Riennes stood upright and looked towards the noise. Then: "Harry! It is an ambush! And I fear the worse for Earl Gerbod."

Haralde whirled and yelled down the line. "To arms! To arms! Prepare yourselves."

He, Riennes and Alan then charged back down to Godfroi in the dray. They dismounted, pulled the back cover off and started pulling out their mail, their cuirasses, their helmets and broadswords.

Back along the line staves were arched into bows. Men pulled on hard leather chest coverings and some tied leather hats on their heads. They dashed to gather around Owain's cart and the large supply of arrows. Quivers hung from their sides they stuffed with arrows. They would follow behind the cart to be close to their arrows in whatever direction their lord ordered.

The soldiers pulled on padded wool hacquetons, then leather vests over that. They tied on leather helmets. Tyne pulled on a leather vest imbedded with bars of iron. A fierce mountain boar's face roared out from the chest. His powerful muscled arms were free, protected at the wrist and forearms by leather chaps covered in mail. On his head he clapped an iron helmet with a nasal guard.

Alan had left his mail back at his estate, but he too strapped on leather fighting gear. He strapped on boots. His eyes peered through two slits where his helmet came over his face to his nose.

Haralde helped Riennes with his mail. When Riennes rubbed his side, Haralde asked: "What is wrong?" "Nay, just apprehension. I felt it earlier. I should have warned us sooner," answered Riennes, who then helped his brother into his fighting gear.

In a moment, they lifted onto horses, and all galloped to the front, then followed Rhys who was running ahead of them barefoot.

They rode just over the lip where the full roar of battle hit them. Rhys ducked down, then made his way to one side out upon a knoll, where he signaled his lords to join him.

It was a scene from hell. It was Riennes's worst fears.

It was not a raiding band, but almost a full army. They moved, shields before them, a forest of spears over them, in rank after rank in a rectangle, They thundered out a deep "Uuuhh! Uuuhh! Uuuhhh!" stamping bare or sandaled feet under them as they moved, the ground almost shaking from their beat and rhythm. Some of them had painted blue, red and black faces. In the front, young boys blew on horns. The whole image was to terrify, strike fear into their victims.

"It is a Welsh teulu," whispered Rhys.

"More than that my lords, I see a large band of Norsemen amongst them," warned Tyne. "I think we be looking at a combined Welsh and Hiberno-Scandinavian army. I make it almost two hundred. A small but dangerous ambushing army."

"Look there!" Rhys pointed out. "Some I see are wearing heavy Saxon byrnies. See how they go down all the way to their knees. That much chain mail has to be heavy. They must be in command. And those riding in the midst, they are uchelwyr, the Welsh leaders."

"I wonder if Arwel is out there with his prince. Maybe Bleddyn himself is ahorse under one of those helmets," pondered Riennes.

"This is not a raiding expedition. This is an organized power. This has been planned for some time," concluded Haralde.

The mass moved towards their enemy up on a high hill before them. Norman chevaliers were there on horses. Thirty of them presented a solid line of mail and cowled helmets. They had pennons and flags on their lances, and eagles, dragons, and beasts of all kind emblazoned on tunics over their chain mail.

Another 20 horse fighters were out front of them, hacking with swords at Welsh skirmishers who fought to push and bunch the Normans against the hill 'till the coming army overwhelmed them. A few arrows stuck out from some of the Normans and their mounts.

Five armored warriors ahorse sat behind them all, bedecked in rich trappings. One man sat tall, surrounded by four magnificent fighting men on horses. Behind them were fires, four-wheeled carts and some linen shelters stretched over poles parallel with the ground. They had been caught in ambush in their camp.

"The tall one. I guess Earl Gerbod, our overlord and King William's confidant," observed Riennes. "And they are trapped."

Alan, standing back, leaned on his broadsword and observed the unfolding spectacle casually. "That army. A hammer that will smash our lord earl and his men like bugs against the anvil of that mountain side."

Haralde stood back and rubbed his chin. All the elements were before him. All he had to do was pull them together into a stratagem. Come on! Think! Think! Thee have been thus before.

He glanced at Riennes whose eyes were centered upon his. They nodded together very slightly.

"We will charge them," Haralde decided finally. "We will make them stop, stand, and break up their intent. They have Earl Gerbod in their eye and will be intent upon their blood kill and the booty up on that hill. It is all we have."

"Yes," contributed Riennes. "Confusion. How many times has victory turned on that in a skirmish."

"What will happen if we charge? Tyne?"

"The army will change its form. It will turn and form a shield wall, maybe a long line, maybe a double line."

"And if we charge?"

"Oh! My lord! With my paltry few?" Tyne protested in disbelief.

"No. With our stronger many, me, Riennes and Sirrah Alan."

"My lord, understand. They will lock shields and forbid us to enter. We cannot get through. In fact, they will pull us down off our horses and cut us up."

Haralde nodded. A stratagem was forming. He had seen thus before.

"Then we must cut a hole in that shield line." He called Rhys to him. The two got their heads together. They glanced at the ever-changing battle conditions before them. Haralde pointed to a little hillock overlooking the battleground, one the Welsh-Norse army was marching past at that moment.

Then Rhys: "Aye my lord. We can do that."

Rhys turned, and looked at Tyne, Riennes and Alan. "May God guide us this day." He moved off quickly.

Haralde gathered his strength around him. "We have no time now. We will charge down this hill and make ourselves known. If they form a shield line, we will have stopped them in their forward intent. We will feint at a point on the end, to make it difficult for their others to run behind and form a second wall. We will lower lances as if to engage. Then at the last moment, we will change direction. Thee will follow me as if I am going to attack another point in the line. Rhys and our bowmen will pour in arrows upon their exposed shoulders. We will turn and follow the arrows in. If Rhys and our bowman have opened up an avenue, we will pour in and fight our way to our lord."

Alan barked a protest: "Lord Haralde. You expect me to risk my life on the silliness that is your band of commoners? And archers. How cowardly! How treacherous! How weak a weapon to wage war you have."

"No sirrah. I expect nothing of thee but your very best. If thee cannot, then leave. And as thee ride away, our band of churls and villeins will pick up your faint heart and bear some of it in their courageous efforts in a very short moment," Haralde admonished him aloud for all to hear.

Alan's face reddened. He made a motion towards Haralde, raising his sword slightly, then stopped, fumed, then turned and made for his horse. He mounted indignant.

Haralde turned to his brother and his corp of soldiers. "Prepare to mount!"

He walked over to his brother. They touched each other on the chest. In the Eastern custom, Haralde embraced and kissed Riennes on each cheek. "We have been here before," whispered Haralde. "It is not the end of our road. We have a way to go yet together. We have faced this before, and I too hurt at the time. Do not let the pain in your side determine the final outcome."

Riennes put his arm around his brother's neck, and kissed him on each cheek. He whispered:" "My dear. Whatever happens, we have been as one."

"Do not say that!" Haralde scolded.

"Always we have spoken our minds. Always we have been honest together," Riennes replied.

They mounted. Each faced their own thoughts, their own mortality. Haralde accepted a heavy lance from Tyne, and Riennes one from Oswald.

"If one falls and the other survives, give all our love over to our mama," said Riennes to Tyne.

"Damnation lad. You tell her. You will not fall this day," shouted Tyne, his eyes bright with the expectation of action. "It will be that bunch out there that will fall."

Haralde stood straight upright in his stirrups, lifted his lance, and shouted for everyone to hear. "BY THE GRACE OF GOD AND FOR KING WILLIAM, WE FIGHT THIS DAY FOR OUR NEURY AND WYM!"

A fighting shout went up from all the company. Below, Rhys and his band of farmer bowmen echoed their battle cry as they moved into position on the little raised knoll.

The shout launched Haralde, Riennes, Tyne, his soldiers and Sir Alan who raised his sword and yelled his battle cry.

Down they streamed, heading for the rough meadow where even now their presence had been heard and the Welsh, Norse and Norse fighters were turning about to face the battle charge they heard behind them. Caught by surprise, the rear half of the phalanx scrambled to form a shield line. The rest of the rebel host slowed in their forward movement, somewhat in confusion.

They came out onto the flat meadow. Now the fear in their guts left. Now, all was just instinct and physical awareness. The power of the horse beneath them and the weight of lance in hand roused a blood lust.

Riennes slid in beside and just behind Haralde. No pain now in his side. No fear now, just cold, steady, calculating awareness of his enemies. Now Tyne slid in beside and behind Riennes, Oswald up behind Haralde, Alan beside and behind Oswald, and the others formed likewise, until they were a thundering wedge aimed at the end of the enemy's forming line and just in front of Rhys and his archers.

A shout went up from the line in front, and they could hear the rebels banging and locking their shields together. Beyond, a shout went up from the chevaliers on the hill behind the enemy. The Normans had spotted the little company bearing down.

"RIENNES! NOW!" shouted Haralde, who dropped and leveled his lance at the wall before them. Riennes followed, and all behind did the same. The wall seemed to come at them. A few arrows came whistling up from behind the wall, but passed well behind them.

"RIENNES! TURN!" shouted Haralde, who lifted his lance, as did Riennes. Riennes's arm pointed to the left and the whole wedge followed perfectly; lances up, horses reined back and forced around.

They charged down the line of the shields. Surprised by the manoeuvre, those behind shields stopped yelling and watched with wide eyes as they passed. At the planned point of impact, the shield line broke open. Some stepped out in surprise. More came out and stood. All turned to follow, the shield line opening in gaps.

Rhys saw it immediately. It was as Haralde predicted. He stood up to reveal himself. His neighbors and his friends, all in a straight line stood up. No one needed an order. Bows arched, men loosed, notched, loosed again, notched and loosed and the motion became automatic.

In somewhat surprise, they saw their arrows climb into the air as a dark cloud of their own making. They had never seen this before. They had never known they could do this. They never realized the potential force and destruction they possessed.

Within a minute, each archer had released four, six, even eight arrows, and those shafts swarmed upwards in a host to fall upon the men standing exposed out in the open, some with shields resting on the ground. As they got the feel of their weapons and the range, the swarms became darker, the number of ash arrows raining down on the enemy even greater.

The men on the wall started falling, dropping their shields. The archers heard them grunt, and fall, and shout, and scream. A whole section of the wall was falling apart, strewn with bodies. And still more fell. Some of the ash shafts passed through shields and into the bearers. Most of the archers were killing men for the first time, and they did not care.

Owain, moved his cart gently into the midst of them. The archers ran over as they ran out of arrows, grabbed a bunch and stepped back into the line. Their blood was up.

And thus did the blood lust overcome the gentle Owain. He jumped down with his own bow, even though he swore to himself he would not. He ran and stepped in beside Rhys.

He shouted: FURTHER NOW! HIT THE ARMY NOW!"

Rhys glanced over his shoulder at Owain, and then looked to where Owain was gesturing. He nodded, yelled to his men, lifted his bow higher, and by example showed them where they were to shoot next. They did immediately.

And the next arrow storm fell upon the interior ranks of the invading army. Constant practice over the years was telling. They were sharp. Their deadly accuracy made most arrows count. Rhys started forward, leading his host of their little knoll to advance and shoot more directly into the collapsing shield wall.

It was time to turn about. Haralde had heard shouts of pain and confusion behind them. He yelled at Riennes who put his arm up and then pointed to their left. They wheeled together and kept formation as they headed back.

The roar in his ear told him the line they had just passed had broken and the enemy was running to form a second line where they were headed.

Yea, but it was too late for the enemy to close it. They were too slow to react. Haralde and his fighting horse saw the sky filled with arrows and heard the cries of downed men and saw the rank torn open, bodies lying askew out from the shield line. Arrows stuck out everywhere, in men's chests, in their faces, in their legs, through their shields, and all over the ground, growing like a crop of new spring flowers.

They turned, down came the lances and they plunged into a hole, an avenue through the ranks of the enemy. They hit a second mass of men still trying to lock shields. The shock of his horsemen en mass, all of them with their power and momentum, smashed men down. Each of them drove their spears through shields, through men, through bodies, shook the flesh off the cross pieces of their lances, and lined up the next man, the next shield.

"My lord look at that," nodded the mailed hood of one of the chevaliers.

Robert de Rhuddlan looked to where his armed companion pointed. He nodded, astonished.

"They are either fools, or very brilliant in their attack. Either way Raegnar, they are dead men if we do not reach them quickly."

Lord Robert and his band of 20 Norman horse fighting men bedecked in mail had just come up over the rim of the pass to join up with Gerbod.

He had only a moment to watch with keen interest as Haralde, Riennes and their small band of lancers smashed through the shield wall.

Beyond that army, he saw the other Normans up against a sharp slope of the mountain behind. He knew who they were and knew he had no choice but to charge if he was to save his overlord.

He ordered his chevaliers to ready themselves. Metal helmets were quickly tied on over mail coifs and cinched under chins.

A band of foot soldiers ran past them and headed down to support them in the fight.

They had been riding hard for days to answer the call of Earl Gerbod. This powerful member of the king's inner circle demanded all his undertenant subjects meet him and escort him in triumph into the port city of Chester, seat of the massive holdings of Cheshire.

King William had made the Fleming earl the sole lay holder of the Palatine shire. He was at this moment a Marcher Lord of the Welsh border and more important, now one of the most powerful nobles in Wales and Britannia. William had given Gerbod as Count Palantine in Cheshire unlimited powers for his to hold by the strength of his sword as the king held his kingdom by the strength of his crown.

Sir Robert now was a vassal of this Palatine prince. He was to have large estates and holdings northeast of Chester along the Wirral coast, including the stronghold of Rhuddlan, which he would re-build into a powerful redoubt.

"WE GO NOW!" he shouted at Raegnar, his professional hired sword, as he did to his other companions.

Men shouted, screamed and cursed at Haralde and Riennes as they rushed in to engage the horsemen, to crowd them to a halt.

Haralde and Riennes had lost their lances in some bodies. They both armed their horn bows and from a leather quiver at their knees began to loose a deadly stream of the bamboo arrows. They stood up, leaned forward in their stirrups and released, and released and released, clearing a way before them. Their deadly rain of missiles dropped bodies in front of them over which their squealing mounts jumped.

Yet, they knew the outcome. Running out of arrows, and with arrows and spears coming at them, they knew they must dismount. The Welsh and fighting men of the north were deadly spearmen. Up high ahorse, they now became a target for those deadly shafts.

It was all familiar. They acted in concert, like brothers, like the experienced fighting men they were. From the memories of tribal fighting in the deserts and in the armies of the Ger Khan, their royal master and ruler of the 10 walled cities of the Kush, both knew they must amongst their enemy afoot, lose themselves in the melee and fight just one or two at time. Whatever advantage there was in fighting in the midst of their enemy, where enemy numbers were not a factor because the horde got in the way of the horde, they took it. They dropped smoothly from their horses and hoped their inexperienced companions would do the same.

They had been trained to fight with both hands. With a longsword in one and their deadly kandos in the other, they strode up to meet the first wave, the first onslaught of screaming madness.

Haralde heard Riennes yell. Riennes heard Haralde yell his battle cry. Then both heard Tyne roar his battle rage beside them. They formed a fighting wheel, which Tyne understood and dropped into. They went round to the right, pushing against any sword arms. Tyne now understood in the moment before his anger took hold the final exercise with the broadsword back at the stronghold. Do not plant the feet. They moved around, taking the thrusts of spears and axes at them, but presenting a new adversary before their enemies each time. In the beginning, Tyne roared as he fought to protect the backs of his lords. Then slowly, he was turned to fight a frontal advance, then he was at the side, then he was protecting their backs. Beside him suddenly was Sir Alan, being taught the same lesson in the heat of madness, flailing, cutting down his enemies.

Then, there were some of Tyne soldiers thrusting with their spears, not all, but some.

The enemy crowded in, bumped each other, lost their footing, or their aim as they were about to launch a spear, or an arrow, or crash in with an axe. No one could gain an advantage on anyone. It was a free-for-all, death-to-all mass of madmen.

As the Irish and Norse fighters flooded into this that they were not familiar with, they were cut down when they tried to come in behind. A buzz in the air dropped them. A deadly hail of missiles cut them down, would not let them sneak in behind.

Haralde and Riennes fought as they knew how, in a way, in a style their enemies knew not. Deadly warriors, they knew there was safety in the madness of many. Such it was, such had they known before. Many thrust spears out from behind shields. Most were simple spears where the iron was not attached far up the shaft. Each young man deflected the sharp points with their broadswords, then their kandos sliced through the wood behind the spear points; a thrust, a cut, and the butchery of fingers, hands and arms flew into the air. Opening up a thrusting arm was familiar to them. A scream, a fall, and a wall of downed spearmen got in the way of the shield man behind. The line behind fell over the crumpled pile of downed bodies in front. Haralde and Riennes and Tyne created this battle mess. Those behind stumbled, fell forward over the bodies in front and exposed necks. Such were an instinctual offering to the steel kandos. A head separated from a body, blood pumped red into the morning sunshine. The head rolled under feet. Men in front rolled on the dead head offering and fell again. The advantage of the short, sharp, curved kandos dominated in such a crowd. It was a place for the kandos, as Haralde and Riennes had learned in many battles.

Whatever Riennes held decent as a man, he abandon it now. He moved so fast in his devastation of flesh before him that any philosophy of life was gone. He entered the physical state of madness. Thrust, cut, slash, blood, yelling; do anything to survive. Haralde beside was entering that same state, only it was a yellow funk of heated madness. Tyne now the scything mad Irishman did the same. This time his madness did not lead him to the same crazed state as lord Haralde's. Maybe it was the sensibility of his love for the woman Saran that kept him on an even fighting plane. That civility kept him even, a part of the Haralde and Riennes fighting unit.

In the heat of battle, he thought of only one thing: protect the backs of his lords.

Alan's lungs screamed for air. Yet, he stood shoulder to shoulder with Tyne, swinging two-handed into the mass, guarding the flank of the Irishman. Around him, five of Tyne's soldiers still standing protected Alan and Tyne. It was hard to fight on instinct and to understand what they were doing was working; yet it was.

The roaring, raging, mad Welsh and Vikings almost climbed over each other to get at such easy prey. Before them was dead meat, and yet each was an interference to the other, a bother, a bump, an impediment to a clean, cut swing at this insolent enemy. It was Haralde and Riennes and Tyne and Alan and the soldiers of an alpine thegn who had set the battle tempo. What a frightening, deadly world it was. And yet they continued to prevail over the mass of madness screaming to get at them.

Alan was the first to go down.

His helmet was struck from his head by a flying axe. Then, in quick succession, something hard thudded into his face. He dropped. A missile, a stone flung from a sling by a young Irish youth, brought him down. He and the stone fell together. He crashed to the ground, breaking his nose. He passed out. He was left behind as the fighting wheel of his comrades moved forward.

A Viking rushed over to him, heaved up a broadsword and it went flipping away free into the air. The blond-bearded man, his faced contorted into that of a beast, staggered for a moment, confused over the arrow that had hammered into his chest. His legs would not work. His eyes slid up behind his eyelids and he fell on top of Alan. Another crowded in with a mighty ax, heaved it overhead, then gagged on an arrow terribly embedded into his mouth.

The man lowered the ax, trying to reach up to grasp the choking shaft. Another arrow hammered into his chest. He slowly sank down onto his knees. He leaned back, and stared skyward to his war gods with a look of frustration on his face. By nightfall, rigor mortis would lock him into that position.

Unbeknownst, that youth had opened a hole in the fighting wheel. Now there was a slight weakness, an exposure into one flank of that fighting unit. Such was war. One failure and the tide changed.

Now there was one less slashing sword. The mass of men started to crowd in behind. Tyne fought them off, then as the wheel turned, Haralde presented himself, and ground out a tough stalemate, then it was Riennes's turn. Then that swearing, blood-screaming mass fell down. Arrows felled them at an intended rate. The dead dropped in many numbers and formed a defensive wall of death behind them. Behind, the bowmen of Neury and Wym slowly advanced forward in the salvation of their lords.

At the fore, the enemy could not match the speed of Haralde and Rienne's fighting abilities. Each fought in a world of slow motion, of anticipating every enemy's angry intent against them. Both fought and walked through this time they controlled. It was all so frighteningly familiar. They anticipated every move of every anger before them. Yet, they were starting to tire.

Too many.

In the yellow funk of hysteria that had seized Haralde, his courage started to fail. They all were in trouble, and he knew it. They were not going to survive this. He had led his brother into this end, this finality. It would soon be over. They were about to be overwhelmed.

He moved action closer to Riennes, to be with him in the end, to go down together. Something hit his left hand and the longsword fell away from him. He flung up his arm as he saw an axe come down on him, stepped to one side, took the crashing axe handle on his forearm and heard the bone crack. He slashed back with the kandos in his good hand and felt flesh.

"RIENNES! INSHALLAH!" he shouted, to die with the name of that beloved loyal brother with his final breath of life.

Only, the terrible horror of the mask of Death that was the roaring mob in front, suddenly turned away from him.

It came to a sudden end as some fighting does. All around them, standing as they did in the hell of battle, the pushing, the shouting and their imminent death suddenly let them go, and wandered away to somewhere else. The push of their enemies suddenly let up. It melted away. Men were running away from them everywhere. Haralde fell forward onto his knees with the sudden release of that pressure.

Heavy horsemen thundered pass on each side of them one after another with lances down, burying spear points into the backs of the fleeing enemy host. The horde ran, thinner in ranks now, making for broken ground, for the forests on the hillside, for the rocks, to get away from the swift Normans on horses.

Their group, back to back, suddenly stood alone, weapons still at the ready, but now not needed.

One fleeing Welsh bowman turned, let loose an arrow at a charging horseman. It rang off his helmet and deflected into the Neury and Wym knot of fighting men.

Riennes gave out a little "Uh!" At first he felt nothing. His lungs pumped for air. He still held his kandoes double-handed. He dropped his head in deep fatigue and swallowed to moisten his dry mouth.

All around him were bodies, some dead, some alive. Some were screaming, holding onto horribly severed hands or limbs. Some were wailing, other crying out for a mother or loved one. Some were rolling on the ground, some were half-sitting, some were standing in the stance of the defeated.

Haralde stood up, feet apart, holding his deadly kandos up high. His left arm hung down listlessly. He still swung at some non-existent foe.

For his efforts, a little whine of pain would escape him. When a Norman horseman thundered by, he took a half-hearted swipe at him.

To Riennes, his brother was a magnificent sight, his helmet knocked askew; the very image of a strong, savage, fighting man at the height of his young male power. Haralde had done it again, carried them successfully through a terrible carnage. They were safe.

Men were running and riding everywhere. Smoke and dust drifted down across the battlefield from the Norman camp. Behind, Riennes could hear Tyne heaving and pumping air into his lungs to gather himself. Behind him he could hear some of their soldiers heaving and spitting and gagging. They were almost all here, together.

Then, the sky did not seem right to Riennes. The images about him soured, began to blur. He did not feel right. Then, he felt a foreign presence inside his body, an invasive bother, as if a sudden cold night wind under a warm blanket.

He turned to call to someone, and his hand struck the war arrow sticking out his side. The pain was so great it collapsed his legs. He fell to his knees and almost passed out. The face of Tyne filled his failing vision. It was a face staring above him down a narrow well.

"Lord Riennes! Are you alright? . . . .oh!" he heard Tyne come up short as he saw the wooden stem sticking out of Riennes's side. "Lord Haralde! HARALDE!"

"Get him here Tyne, please?"

Tyne got up and ran over to Haralde. He ducked as Haralde half swung at him and whined. Tyne, who knew what he was looking at, seized Haralde's shoulders and shook him.

Haralde yelled with pain. It doused his fighting flame. He allowed himself to be led over.

He arrived. He looked down upon the face of his brother, now pale white as the blood drained from his face. Haralde's eyes then focused on a sight he had ever dreaded.

Haralde looked down in the direction Tyne's eyes indicated, and gasped. Gently, he put hands on both sides of Riennes's face, pulled it to him and cradled it.

Riennes looked up at him with hurt eyes. "Is it bad?"

"No, no! If it were, thee would not be able to ask that."

"Get my bag," he whispered, his voice somewhat muffled against Haralde's chain mail chest.

Alan awoke, groaned and tried to roll over. He could not. Someone was on top of him. He moaned when he pushed the body off.

He looked at the sky for a moment, and then jerked up when he realized what had happened, and groaned again. His head was splitting. He had a deep gash across his forehead that would not stop bleeding.

He looked around. Dead and half-alive bodies were piled around him. An enemy half lay on his leg, dead from a white goose-feather. Another man kneeled beside him, looking skyward over an arrow in his face. Another pointed into his chest.

A shadow blocked out his sun. He looked up and Rhys quickly came into focus. Rhys put a foot on the chest of the man at Alan's foot and ripped out his arrow. He did the same to the kneeling man but did not pull the one out of the dead man's mouth. He just did not like the looks of it.

"You!" groaned Alan. "You saved me?"

"Where are Lord Haralde and Lord Riennes? Where is Tyne?"

"Further behind me," groaned Alan. "The last I saw them." Alan was trying to stop the bleeding.

Rhys leaned down and examined it. "It is not serious. You be fine by and by." He turned and signaled to someone behind him.

A cart bumped over bodies and came up and Owain looked at Alan. His instinct was to go to the Norman's assistance, but Rhys ordered him not.

"There!" he shouted to the boy when he spotted the three he sought.

The cart rolled up to the three bent men. The smell of blood and death was as a pall of smoke upon the battlefield.

Owain took in the gathering of his lords and saw the seriousness of it immediately. He jumped into the back of the cart. He grabbed some bags. He leaped over and dropped to Riennes's side.

"My lord! My lord!" he whispered gently.

"Owain. Leave that here with us." Riennes nodded towards Tyne. The Irishman's right cheek was slashed open, his back teeth showing inside the flaps of the wound. He bled from many gashes and small cuts, some serious that needed sewing. Riennes looked to his beloved brother and suspected Haralde's left arm was broken

"Owain. That smoke. Go to that camp. Get a pot or dish of hot water. Bring back hot coals or a torch. If they have wine, steal it."

When Owain hesitated, wanting to help Riennes, Riennes ordered him to go again. The lad hustled off.

"Harry?"

"Yes my dear?"

"Gather wood. Right here. Make a fire. Quickly. Tyne. Help him. Hurry!"

When they left, Riennes turned to Rhys. "I needs lean on thee a little?"

"A lot Riennes. A lot if you wish." Rhys laid his bow beside them, he put his arm around his lord, and the bowman took his head and nestled it under his chin.

They sat that way a moment as Tyne came running with an armful of wood. Haralde came shuffling behind his reeve with one armful.

"Look!" Rhys whispered.

A man in a black cloak to his sandals and his face hidden in a black cowl prowled through the smoke drifting across the field of the half living, half-dead.

He was a Spectre of dread it seemed, hobbling along on a staff, looking down at the bodies. Then what he did next, changed everything.

The man laid down his pole, kneeled, pulled a man upright, reached into his cloak and began to administer to the wounded man. They saw him wash away blood from the man's face, bind a wound in his scalp, arrange a sling around an arm, then lifted him to his feet. The man half staggered from the effort, almost falling away from the stranger.

Then two armed Normans going through the field, stabbing at men half alive, gathering arms and pulling off clothing, hustled over to them. One drew back his sword and thrust it into the wounded man who screamed and fell crashing to the ground.

"Get out of here! Do not try the evil eye on us," and the second Norman kicked the cloaked figure down onto the ground away from them, then fell looting upon the man they had just killed.

One of the Normans saw Rhys and Riennes and headed in their direction. Haralde arrived, rattled wood from his good arm onto the ground and staggered over to intercept them.

He drew his kandos and shouted: "Aaah! Get you bastards!"

The two Norman scavengers growled back but turned and walked in another direction across the killing field.

Haralde leaned down, gave the cloaked figure his hand, and hauled him up upright. Then he turned and hustled back to Riennes.

Owain came jogging back to them with an iron pot in one hand and a firebrand in another. Haralde took it and plunged it into the pile of wood, and it flared up.

Owain dropped to his knees and from a pack pulled out a wineskin and a bag of drinking water. He nestled the pot onto the fire and poured in water. Riennes had taught him to do so.

Haralde, bedraggled, tired, leaned on Rhys. "Our people. They are hurt?"

"No my lord," answered Rhys. "They be whole. They are full of victory. They wish to know of you."

"Go. Take care of our people. Feed them. And see if any of our soldiers made it. Gather up all our things and bring them closer when thee can. We will not move from here."

"Yes Lord Haralde. And I will bring back whatever I can that may comfort you and our Lord Riennes." Rhys glanced once at Riennes, then slipped away.

"Come here Owain. Open my bag and get out our sewing needles," whispered Riennes.

Owain did so. "Pass the needle through the flame Owain. Then, attend to Tyne's cheek. It must be closed carefully."

"Aye my Lord."

"NO! No! My lord. These are scratches. Owain. Attend to Lord Riennes. He is the seriously injured here."

"Sit down Tyne. Do not waste my time. Just sew up the serious cuts. Wash the others lightly down with hot water," ordered Riennes.

Haralde leaned over. "Ren. Please. Let us attend to thee now, immediately. Thee bleed."

"In one moment. Harry! Give me your arm."

"No!"

"I am going to need thee in a moment, whole. Let me feel it."

Haralde would not comply, so Riennes leaned over, and the movement made him yell out in pain.

Haralde quickly complied.

"Aahh. There is swelling in one place, but no break. Cracked yes. Do thee see that dead tree over there with the bark on the ground around it."

"Yes."

"Go get the bark."

Haralde shook his head no.

"Then I will."

"Damn thee Ren. I will not leave thee."

"I will," grunted Owain who got up. Tyne's cheek had been closed. Tyne was now washing down all his own wounds. "Go lad. Before he passes out."

Owain ran over and brought back four pieces. Haralde was ordered to strip off his mail. He did so. He was wearing his green silk. His muscled arm ran with blood and sweat from its day of slaughtering. There were cut wounds, stab punctures down his chest, all minor.

Under Riennes's instructions, Owain ran his hands over the swelling that now was turning blue-red. The lad slipped two pieces of bark around the bottom of the swelling and the other two around the top, then cinched it all in tight with leather thongs he cut off from a body lying beside them.

"It is not broken through," judged Owain.

Riennes nodded his head in some satisfaction.

A Norse fighter who had been staggering in the distance, wailing and shrieking, saw Owain binding up Haralde and staggered over.

He came to them, arm straight out, his hand hanging half severed from his wrist, blood pumping out. He cried out. "Help! Help! Please. Be merciful! Help me!"

"By my gods!" Tyne shouted out in anger and frustration and rose to shove the man away.

But Riennes stopped him. "Seize him Tyne!"

"What!" Tyne whirled around.

"Seize him Tyne. Hold his arm out," Riennes whispered hoarsely.

"For the love of God Riennes. Look to yourself."

"Do it Tyne! Hurry!"

The Irishman grabbed the crying man, roughly whirled him around and seized his arm out stiff.

"Harry!" And he whispered into his brother's ear. "Do not delay. He is losing blood fast!"

Suddenly, he moved so very fast. Haralde's kandos rang out across the clearing, flashed silver in the sun, and severed the dangling hand from the arm.

"Owain. The fire torch. Take it and put the flame to the stump. Sear it lad!"

Without hesitation, Owain jumped to the fire, walked up to the man, turned his face away, and scorched the stump. The man shrieked, passed out and fell to the ground.

"Tyne. Put a leather tourniquet around his arm, tighten it and let it loose ever so often. If Owain has done it well, the bleeding should stop."

He turned to Owain. "Go into our bag. Remember that poultice plant I showed you? Throw it in the warm water there, then slap it on the end of his stump and bind him up."

While Owain obeyed, Haralde started pulling up Riennes's chain mail coat. Riennes cried out as Haralde pulled one side over his head. The coat then hung down one side and they could not get it away. It was pinned to Riennes's side by the arrow. It had pierced the links, then entered the body.

"Oh God Ren. What do I do?"

Riennes, his voice more faint, asked: "Is it bleeding much? Is it in deep?"

"It bleeds, but not much. How deep is deep?"

Owain and Tyne came over and huddle around. "Gently seize it around the feathers Owain," suggested Riennes. Riennes trusted Owain. He had learned the lad had a gentle touch. The youth was patient.

Owain looked up into the men's faces around him. He should not be the one. He should assist only. He licked his lips and reached up and gently closed his fingers on the end of the arrow. It seemed solid.

"Do nothing yet lad," a voice said softly behind them. They turned and looked up.

The dark, cowled figure they had watched a moment ago loomed over them. His face was hidden in the shadow of his hood.

The man leaned down and looked at the entry wound. He sniffed it, then walked around, bent and looked at it from a different angle. Finally: "It has entered him somewhat at a steep angle. The arrowhead is down there, maybe buried where all the soft innards are. If it is buried deep in that soft place where all our belly works, then there is much danger."

Haralde, unable to be Riennes's salvation, felt totally helpless and useless before this overwhelming injury to his brother. "Who are thee?" he demanded of this apparition.

"A healer, like this brother here!"

"Brother?" questioned Haralde.

"Yes my son," said the Spectre, who then threw back his cowl.

Instead of a dreadful visage, they looked upon the warm face of an old but smiling man. Old yes, but his face was that of an elf, of a munchkin.

He was one of those old men whose face retained its youth. His skin was smooth. He had a small round ball of a nose. His cheeks were round, and glowed in health. More than anything, benevolence glowed from his blue eyes. It was the kind of face that made one smile when one looked upon it.

To the three men in this dreary hell of a place with their comrade mortally wounded, it was like the sun come out again.

"Tell me son? What do you feel inside?" he asked Riennes.

"It is like a hot coal. It sits in one place in my side."

"Here?" asked the old man touching one side above his hip "and not here?" he went on, touching Riennes's belly. "No. The first."

He turned to Owain. "Lad, bring me his bag there. Is it of herbs and unguents?" Owain pulled the bag over "Yes. And we have another of apothecaries he uses to fight the flux and what he calls gangrene."

The old man's eyes arched up at the mention of that word. "Fetch it."

Owain hurried back. Haralde, ever watchful, asked: "What do thee know of such things?"

The old man ignored him. As he turned earthen jar after earthen jar over and examined the contents of both bags, he asked a question of Riennes.

"Why did you help that man, and your companions, with you so seriously injured yourself?"

Riennes, his eyes now half closed, starting to feel the shock of his wound creeping over him, whispered: "Because they asked for help. Because they all needed help. I had to give it while I could."

"And that is important to you?"

"Yes."

"Why?"

"I am here on this field because others have helped me, my brother. I am alive. I can do no other."

The old man pulled out the half disc with the thin, keen sharp blade which Riennes used sometimes for shaving, sometimes cutting into wounds. Also, out came a pair of tweezers and a small stem with an open cylinder made of gold attached on the end. The old man knew he was looking at something quite unusual.

"Hmmmn. You use these?"

Riennes nodded.

"You are more than a leech. I have heard of the likes of you. Listen, and see if you agree. The danger here is if the tines of the arrow's broad head are big, and if they are embedded into your soft innards. If they are, and we pull on it, it may tear away the important parts if your innards, and the damage that results may be serious. If not, and the tip of the head is in the fleshy part of your side only, we may be able to extract it safely. Does that seem right to you?"

"Yes. The cylinder, slide it down the arrow shaft into the wound and seat the arrowhead inside it. Then pull the arrow out slowly through it."

"I understand. I am going to use this cutting tool of yours to first open your wound a bit. There might be a lot of blood then. Lad! Go get as many bindings of rags or linen or what have you. Soak them in that pot of hot water. What is this? Wine? When I ask you, pull the bindings from the hot water, and soak them in this wine."

"Aye. I will."

"Brother. When I open up the wound, I am going to slide my fingers down the shaft and see if I can feel the arrowhead. Who are you?"

"His brother," answered Haralde.

The old man looked at the black hair of Riennes and the yellow hair of Haralde, and smiled. "Yes. Then you are the one. Come around here," he ordered.

Haralde moved around behind Riennes. As the stranger directed, he sat down and shuffled in behind Riennes until his legs were on both sides of his brother's legs.

"Now lean him back and hold him firmly in your arms."

"You Irish, hold this earthen jar. When I tell you, pour the powder from it over my hands. Then I will ask you to pour some in the lid and hand it to me. I plan to blow much of it into the wound."

"I will. Who are you?"

"My name is Ambrosius. I am but a simple servant of God."

All of them looked at each other, and gladly felt more hopeful.

Then he turned to Riennes. "Healer, as you know, this will hurt in the beginning."

"Yes. I know. Owain?"

"Yes my lord?"

"Pass the cutting blade directly through the fire there a couple of times. Then the cylinder. Then give them back to this servant of God," instructed Riennes, suddenly fearful of what was about to happen.

"This water, just sip it and moisten your dry mouth." Riennes did so and sighed his gratitude. He leaned back against his brother and whispered: "Harry. This is not going to work, not this way. I am in growing pain. If I thrash around when he cuts, I will endanger my chances. I need your help."

"What can I do?"

"Harry. The brown vial. I need to go away from here. I need to enter the dream of nightmares."

"No Ren. That is too dangerous. Thee told me that, remember?"

"It was not for thee Harry. Hurry. Time is against me."

"What does he say?" asked Ambrosius.

Harry took a deep breath, then: "He wishes to use a dangerous liquid; one that will detach him from the pain of cutting. He came across Chinois writings from many years ago that directed how the sick and wounded can sleep and not feel pain while a healer cuts into the body to correct injuries."

"This is not possible. Pain is an ever part of life. Such is God's will. Such would be a cursed thing, a compact with the devil," admonished Ambrosius. Then: "He has done this?"

"It is dangerous. He has tried it three times. It puts a body into a deep dream of horrible nightmares. He tells me it is the body rebelling. Yet, one feels no cutting. Three times he had used it, one on a little girl who was trampled by war chariots. She died. The second time was on a farmer who was tortured by barbarians. He died. Both screamed of monsters in their heads."

"Who was the third?"

Haralde looked deep into the Christian healer's eyes. "Me!"

"Did you feel pain?"

"No. I remember only the nightmares."

"Thus, you survived."

"Yes. He told me he found a way to dilute the potency of the oil of strong mandrake plant, opium, bhang and a drop from the gland of a sea creature that can kill with a sting."

Riennes stirred. "Owain. There is a brown vial in my bag and some cotton rags. Boil water. Drop the rags in. Add what is left of the vial into the water. Harry, when he is finished, lay the rags over my face and let me breath deep. Harry. Hold my hand."

Owain looked to Harry for direction but Ambrosius interrupted. "Do it lad. We are pressed here."

Owain followed his lord's direction, pulled the wet cotton out of the hot pot with a stick and Haralde applied it over the face of his brother.

"How long?"asked Brosius. "I know not," answered Haralde, his head down and his cheek against his brother's.

The smoke drifted across the killing ground, the yelling ceased and Normans yelled across the scene of their finds on the dead bodies.

Then, Haralde lifted his head. "He is gone. He has released from us. I feel it."

Ambrosius grabbed a dirk from Tyne's knife scabbard and leaned into Riennes. He put the blade against the young man's lips. The blade fogged.

"He is not gone completely. Let us hurry."

The cowled one accepted the disc from Owain and without hesitating cut a slit into his side and pushed it down the shaft as far as it was safe to do so. Blood spurted and some gore bubbled out.

Riennes moaned.

"Good. Now roll him over more. He is not in a good position this way."

Haralde rolled Riennes gently over. Riennes started whimpering.

"Pour the powder over my hand Irish," ordered Ambrosius.

Tyne did so quickly. The old man then pinched his thumb and his forefinger and slid them down the shaft. His pinching fingers disappeared into the wound. He dropped his head and looked to the ground, as if to improve the sensitivity of his fingers.

There was quiet for a moment, then: "I can feel the broadhead. It is not buried." He grasped the cylinder, slipped it down the shaft and positioned it into the wound and around the arrowhead. "Where's the boy?"

"Right here sirrah."

"Grasp the arrow by its feathers. That is right. You have a good touch. Now gently, very gently twist it back and forth, in a wiggle motion."

Owain complied, slowly and deftly.

"Keep twisting lightly, but now pull softly. I have covered the tines inside the cylinder to protect against any tearing. I think only the sharp arrowhead tip itself touches his innards. Yes. That is good. Slowly . . . . slowly!"

The shaft slowly came up, up. Ambrosius grasped the cylinder as it exited the wound. He eased it out slowly and then the arrowhead appeared in a gob of red.

"Irish. The lid of the cup. Bless you." He leaned into the wound and blew the green powder in. "Now lad, sow him up." Owain was there instantly. "Bind him up. Do you have anything to make a poultice to add to this?"

"Yes sirrah. I have it ready in the hot water."

"Excellent lad."

Ambrosius applied the poultice, and then all assisted in wrapping Riennes.

Haralde held him. Reaction of the whole day began to set in. Tears began to slide from his eyes and into Riennes's hair.

They all sat quiet for a moment, listening to the dramas of other injuries, of other miracles of life, and of deaths across the battlefield. They watched as wounded men rose up from the ground, crying. They were cut down by Norman horse fighters patrolling the battlefield.

Then, Ambrosius rose and walked over to the hot water, splashed some on his hands and wrung them clean. He dropped the cutting blade and the tweezers in.

"I have naught seen anything like this in all my healing ways. My lord? Your brother has set me on another path, another way of healing. Why did he ask you to put the cutting blade to the flames?" Ambrosius asked of Owain. Owain explained Riennes believed it avoided festering of wounds. His frustration, said Owain, was that he did not know how it did this. "Ah. I will remember that. I have learned something. Can I have some of that in the brown vial?"

"Alas, that was the last of it. It now is empty," answered Owain.

Tyne came to him to thank him. "Bless you old man."

"Only God can do that. But I will ask Him to bless you all. You, all of you, are an exceptional band of brothers. I have not seen your kind ever here. Those are superb men there. Where did they come from?"

Tyne scratched his head. "We have been together such a short time. We have not had time to hear all their stories yet."

"If you find out, I would know it if you please. Those two. A very unusual bond," smiled Ambrosius. "Now I must go."

"Where will you go?" asked Tyne.

"I seek that which they have already learned. They come from a place that holds great knowledge. Would that I could discover it."

"Where did you come from?"

"From nearby." He drew his cowl over his head and his face disappeared into the shadow of it. He picked up his staff and trudged out into the moaning field of the living and the dead.

Tyne watched him go. Then he turned to Owain. "Let us put a backboard rest behind Haralde. See, he nods. He needs to sleep, but he will not let Lord Riennes go. Let us cover them up and keep them warm. Then let us stretch a cover over them from your cart. And then maybe you can close up the rest of me with your gut."

Owain turned away, but turned back and smiled when Tyne jokingly warned him: "And this time, no using the needle with the hooks on it. That last time hurt."

And as the day turned over, they worked around, set up camp, and from time to time, watched the cowled figure of God's servant out on the field move from body to body.

CHAPTER 15

A man's honour depends on where he draws the line;
Some out far, some in close.

THE FLEMISH LORD Gerbod walked across the field of the defeated, taking in everything. He was accompanied by a band of young fighting men, all shinning in their polished chain, all chattering away, all boasting of their recent exploits, their brave charge against a larger army than theirs.

"Here! Here, and again here my lord," explained Lord Robert Rhuddlan. "You can see where they opened up the line with archers. Look at these arrows. They are long, heavy. Here, and here. They have gone through even heavy shields."

"Yes! Yes!" agreed Gerbod who was anxious to be away. He had agreed on this tour of the field of battle only because Robert felt it was important for him to see something. The earl greatly respected the opinion of this young outstanding fighting chevalier.

Robert had been given over to him to be his vassal by King William who valued this young man very highly.

The king knew Lord Robert went back a way in Britannia. Robert had been a squire in the Saxon and Norman court of old King Edward. The young man had been trained there, had been dabbed by the saintly monarch and had quickly established his reputation in hinterland battles around Britannia.

Recognized as an expert in fighting small scale skirmishes, Robert had been chosen to lead a band of like young chevaliers into the western frontier of the March. This fresh young fighter had a way of gathering like men around him, ones who held a deep loyalty to him.

He was not only from his stronghold in Rhuddlan to launch forays into northern Wales and bring these most rebellious of all the Welsh under control, but also to be a buffer against Vikings out of Hibernia and the Scandinavians who in the past had sailed up the Dee Estuary, raided Chester and down into the hinterland, even east into the old Saxon kingdom of Mercia.

The king and his inner council had realized their tenuous hold on their newly conquered Britannia was most weak here in this northern corner of the country.

"After the way was swept clear for them, here is where they dismounted and clashed with the whole rear of the Welsh army," described Sirrah Robert. "Look at the pathway they cut into the ranks. Look at the bodies. Most are mutilated. Hands cut off this way and that. Spears cut. Axe handles cut. All made useless. Just a small band of men. We watched them from up there, dismount and begin to hack their way towards you."

"Uhhhh, yes. A remarkable effort." Earl Gerbod was a battle-experienced nobleman. His eyes began to take in what Robert was trying to explain.

"Not only remarkable my Lord, but courageous. It was a most singular exploit. And the use of their archers. I have seen these bows before but not used in this way. Deadly. I would that I had them in my household," said Robert.

"And all this they did was directed towards fighting up to me, to free me from the ambuscade?"

"Yes my Lord. They threw all caution aside. I do not know how they managed to get this far before we arrived in behind and afforded them relief. I would say it was an act of pure loyalty."

Gerbod nodded his head and looked all around. He looked at the stiff corpse of a man on his knees leaning rock stiff back on his legs, looking with empty eye sockets to the sky. Everywhere crows hopped about.

He indicated to his corp of men to remain put while he and Robert walked on in private conversation.

"And you recommend I should reward them?" asked Walter.

"If it meets with your wishes, yes," suggested the young noble. "You want to bind such men, such loyalty to you in this troublesome holding of yours. You will need all such fighting men as you can get."

One thing Gerbod demanded and loved was unwavering loyalty. "You know who they are of course?"

"No my lord. What means you?"

"They were presented to court earlier this year. They are, or were, ambassadors from a foreign interest, expressing support to the cause of our William. They told us an incredible story. One is a Norman, a de Montford. The other is a lowly thegn. I do not know who he really is. Obviously he has proved to be loyal to us."

"I am not privy to their background, my lord. I was away fighting in the north at the time."

"Talk to Gilbert de Montford the next time you see him. He is related to this young man. Powerful family."

The two fighting men walked a short distance, and then Gerbod turned. "I agree. Arrange it. But do it soon. I must away from here and move to the coast and Chester."

"Rider coming," yelled one of their young company. "Messenger!"

A young man rode into their company and presented a sealed linen envelope to one of the chevaliers. He trotted over and caught up with them. "He says he has ridden most of the night from Shrewsbury. It has the royal seal on it."

The Earl took it, walked a distance from Robert, tore the seal and read. He looked up after awhile and gazed into the sky very pensive.

Then, he turned and walked back. "Arrange it for tonight. There is trouble back across the canalem. Revolt is afoot in the Low Lands. My estate, my lands are threatened. It looks like I will not see my Chester this time. I must return. I have the king's permission. Yes. We will do this tonight. Do we have a holy monk amongst us?"

"Yes my Lord. We found one hiding under his cart on a road as we swept in here. He was praying. His prayers, it seems, were answered."

"Thus prepare him. Where are they in all this?"

"Up ahead my lord. By those two carts with the weather cover stretched across between them. I should tell you my lord that one of them was injured," informed Sir Robert. "Maybe mortally."

"Let us walk then to them. Bring the horses. Is it not a fine day Robert!"

They walked through the field of naked dead men, stripped of all their dignity by the victors. Gerbod's mind drifted back to the Battle of Hastings, and the same stripping of the dead.

They came upon the two drays. A third, a four-wheeled engine, had been driven into place. It was of his own. The gesture had been made on the recommendation of Lord Rhuddlan. He had created a central camp feel, with an open fire in the middle.

Gerbod ducked under the over cover. After all, thought the earl, we now all are comrades in arms and we protect our own. Such was this singular principle of war enhanced by the militaire Norman.

The earl and Robert found themselves standing within ranks of commoners, men of the soil, farmers, servii. It was a goodly number, standing, leaning on staves. They snatched off Phrygian caps, bobbed their heads, and moved back away to make room for their station. They moved away and crowded into the corners of the fly over them all.

Gerbod and his company felt pressed by the common. Their numbers were greater than he was used to in a conflict.

"Who are all these?" demanded the earl. "The same that laid waste to all that you saw today, my lord." answered Robert. As a man from the continent, Gerbod could not quite appreciate this rabble. Yet, as a fighting man, his sharp eye took them in.

They were all here out of respect. He bobbed his head back to them as fighters and for the respect they showed their own lords. He liked that.

"Who are you?" demanded the earl. A tall, straight-limbed man snatched off his cap in front of him. "Rhys my lord. A free man from Gwent, loyal to my Lord Haralde and Riennes." He did not bow, he did not give deference. He but stood his ground.

Lord Gerbod smiled. "I mark you as a good man, Rhys of Gwent." He signaled he wanted to look at Rhys's stave. Rhys, anticipating the lord earl's interest, bent the stave and hooked string to its bone nock on the end.

The earl took it, and attempted to draw it. It resisted. "My God this is impossible. How do you draw this in battle?"

"It is not a matter of strength my lord. It is a matter of strict practice," answered Rhys. "You are a stout-looking man. Give me a day and I could have you heave a stave to your satisfaction."

Gerbod barked a laugh. He liked the bowman's impertinence. He moved on towards the centre where he saw a man on the ground holding another. Was his comrade dead in his arms? The earl prepared himself as he approached.

The earl recognized Haralde who sat close to the fire and did not rise. His arms were around a man stretched out and covered in front of him. "Forgive me my lord. I cannot rise. The comrade who is my brother lies within my arms."

The earl moved forward. He was comfortable in the midst of this military roughness. "Are you both not my vassals? Does one of you owe me, I think it was some 30 silver coins, if I remember quite."

"Twenty my lord. Yes. It is I. And it is here. My obligation I shall deliver partially onto thee before this night is out."

"Aaah! A man of his vow. I like that. And how does our comrade do?" asked the overlord as he moved around to better a look at the two former ambassadors.

Riennes opened his eyes weakly: "Forgive me my lord for not rising. I seem to have such a thorn in my side."

Gerbod roared. He loved such rough company. "I understand. I too have a number of thorns in my side these days. We all have had quite a day. And how is your pain today." The overlord spent a time to hear the story of a Riennes down, but not giving up.

Riennes had been lifted gently by his subjects and carried gingerly up to the Norman camp. The fly covers had been removed. The central fire had been expanded. The sky was open to a wonder of stars and fire sparks rose to join those lights.

It was a fairly warm night for a pass up in the Welsh mountains. A large company of men gathered around the flare of this big fire pit.

Wealthy men they were in riches. Young bloods in hooded mail links murmured to each other. There were servants, young squires, a baker, a weapons maker, a clothier and a butcher, all avoiding brushing up against a bunch of peasant farmers back in the shadows. With the peasants was a disdainful Celtic monk. These unsingular men of lower status and rough clouts grinned, bumped each other, scratched at their balls, and sipped their own ale.

They were witness to something in all of the good green earth they were told they would never be privy to; a gathering of all the stations of privilege in their present life.

A seneschal of Gerbod's was handed a parchment package of written material by Godfroi earlier in the day. When he reported to his master that a religious representative of abbot Lanfranc was in the company of these men, Gerbod requested Godfroi present the religious emphasis in the evening ceremonies.

Monk Godfroi stepped into the light as instructed, scriptures in hand. He held it up and spoke in Latin to impress the assembly. Then, wisely, he addressed them in Norman. Rhys and a few others could be heard muttering in the background, translating for his fellows.

"Oh mighty God. Blessed is thy name within this sinful company. We gather to name three of yours to special company. By your grace, we confirm by a royal proclamation from the glory of King William, a blessing upon three of his lowly servants. This day, the king's reward of Chevalier upon lords Riennes de Montford, Haralde Longshield and their reeve, Tyne of Cumraugh. May they continue in the admiration of our William, to serve him, and the wishes of his kingdom."

Lord Gerbod stepped forward, looked out upon his company, and his realm. It was not often that he faced such a diverse mixed band of loyalists. For a lowlander, he too felt a special occurrence unfolding here in this high alpine realm. He was not comfortable with such a mix, but he had no time to debate it. He must away soon. He would sort it all out in his mind later, he convinced himself.

Tyne, called Crowfeeder by his mates, stepped forward and kneeled onto the ground. In all of his wildest imaginations, Tyne knew he never expected to be in such a ceremony.

"Tyne, reeve of Neury and Wym, and good servant to me and your king. I name you to the order of Chevalier under your good King William. From this moment on, you are a steiurhrd of the realm."

The lord took up Tyne's sword driven into the ground before him. It was an old sword, the sword of an old housecarl to King Edward.

He dabbed Tyne on the top of his head. Tyne bobbed his loyalty, then scuttled backwards

The earl then stepped forward to where the two men were on the ground, one kneeling and the other beside him, propped up by a back board, much brighter in his face.

Two short swords of foreign nature were driven into the ground at their feet. A seneschal came out and pulled up the two blades, and presented the handles to the earl

He examined them carefully. They were short and curved and the handles had small circular guards. They were light, balanced, and the blades very sharp. Even after their slaughtering work of the other day, they seemed no worse for wear.

Toad spitters, the earl remembered. A suggestion of less than a manly weapon. Gerbod now knew that was wrong.

The royal appraised these two and now looked favorably upon them as fighting men and the value they represented to him.

"Oh good and loyal servants. Wounded as you are, you have earned the good grace of your king. You cannot step forward to earn his blessings. So, he steps forward to you to acknowledge your loyalty to him."

The earl stepped to them, dabbed them on their heads with their own blades, drove the metal back into the ground and stepped back.

"I name you both to the order of Chevalier. From this moment, you are my champions subject to the king's wishes. You will doubt not. And for your act of constant faith, you will be rewarded."

A roar went up from the whole room, led by the farmer rabble in the back.

Then, out of the shadows behind, a cowled man stumped forward and leaning on a staff, said in a strong voice that seized the attention of all.

Godfroi stepped forward as if to protest, but stopped as the man's strong voice captured the assembled.

He shouted: *"Sylwch holl o chwi yma y dau rhyfelwyr bonheddig hyn. Sylwent holl y safonau anrhydedd y dau cnihtau hyn."*

"Who is that who would interrupt our lord?" asked a young noble.

Rhys stepped forward and dared to whisper an explanation. "That is Ambrosious sirrah. In these mountains, he is known as a wandering Celtic Christian monk. The Welsh call him *myrddin*.

"What means that?" demanded the youth.

"It means merlin, sirrah. He is a holy man who roams lost in these mountains. He lives lonely in a cell in an old broken abbey called Holywell. The local people say he works day and night to seek out and discover God's mystery of life."

"Paaah!" spit out the young man in disdain. He went on his own to seek out another drink.

chapter 16

The road begins again,
And God or the devil walks with whomever a traveler chooses.

OUNDED, BEATEN, HURTING inside and out, they set off for home.

All of his herbs, apothecaries and unguents were exhausted. Riennes would look for certain plants to make poultices along the way, certain vines to bind wounds, certain trees to sleep under at night, those that would soothe fevers and pains.

He would rely again on the forest to provide.

"And it will," he mused aloud.

"What say you my lord?" asked Tyne.

Riennes lay on a soft pallet in the dray behind Godfroi up on the seat. Tyne was beside him to insure he was not thrown about, to watch carefully in case a rough ride opened stitches.

"I said it is a fine day to be on a long road again," smiled Riennes. "Aaaah!," he then cried out as they went over a bump. "If I just did not have this sharpness in my side."

"Sorry my lord," said Godfroi above him. The good monk had apologized many times during the morning's bumpy ride home.

"Aaah!" Riennes would cry out each time a bump hurt his stitches, or Tyne would beat him to it with an "Oooh!" from his cuts and bruises.

"By the Ger's oaths, I swear good monk Godfroi thee are picking out every deep hole in this road. Aaah!"

"It is not me my lord. It is this cursed machine."

Machine or not, Owain sitting close to Riennes had reservations. He watched his mentor. It was not the cart machine that bothered him. It was the dark look on Riennes's face and in his eyes that disturbed him.

They stifled their complaining when they heard Haralde groaning atop his warhorse up ahead. His arm was wrapped in sticks bound by leather thongs to hold steady his broken forearm. Rhys trotted ahead of him as point man.

They rode that way all morning, yearning for home and the comfort of a bed.

Stopping at midday for food and some relief from the pains, Riennes fell asleep. When he awoke, he said: "I have been casting my mind back. That old man who cut me and mumbled over us? I did not have a chance to thank him. I mark him with deep healing abilities, unlike anything I have observed here. He saved me. Who was he really?"

"He was a Celtic monk of an old monastic order I do not think exists anymore. And he should have no licence to spread God's words anymore," Godfroi criticized. "He should not have been allowed to speak outside of our tongue when your overlord bestowed such of his favour upon you three."

Haralde who was slumbering beside Riennes, awoke. He groaned and holding his bound arm, inquired: "I could not understand him. What was that he was saying?"

Rhys who was stretched out under a tree beside them with his bow across his knees, got up, walked over and leaned into the dray.

"The best that I can remember: 'Mark all you here these two gentle warriors. May all take up the gracious code of these two cnihts', or something like that. I talked to him right after. He said you held within you something greater than the brutal code of chevaliers. He said you showed mercy and bore a gentleness about you. He said only true warriors have that."

"He called Haralde, Tyne and I cnihts."

"What means that?" Haralde asked.

"It means, 'knights'."

Along the Huron Road,
Bruce County,
ON., Canada,
Copyright by John Wright, 2010.

ḎARALḎE GLOSSARY

canalem – the English channel.

clerwr – a troubadour, a jongleur, juggler, minstral.

chevalier – a high borne Norman warrior whose status is confirmed by ritual.

cuirasse – a leather fighting vest.

hacquetons – padded jackets to keep out the cold, and which could act as light armour, being able to absorb blows by swords.

hallmote – a lord and peasant council to settle civic matters that touched upon a lord's interest.

housecarl – a king's champion warrior under the old Saxon regime.

myrdin – a merlin with mystic powers.

commote – a Welsh area, somewhat like the English manor, under the control of a chieftain.

Cymru – medieval Wales.

destrier – heavy hocked, heavy bodied war horse.

motte and bailey – Normans built strongholds on a motte, a mound either natural or artificial. The bailey was a donjon or keep built on the motte surrounded by walls.

ulchelwyr – Welsh men of high noble status.

toft – the front yard of a serf's hovel bound by fencing or ditches to contain small agricultural animals.

wica – witch, priestess.

leech – a Saxon administer of bleeding, applier of leeches and dispenser of potions.

bonheddig – a Welsh man free of obligations, whose will determines who he wishes to support.

BIBLIOGRApђy

The Adventure of English. Bragg, Melvyn. Hodden and Stroughton Publishers. (2003). Brisih Library. ISBN: 0-340-82991-5.

Anglo-Saxon Thegn AD 449-1066. Harrison, Mark. Osprey Publishing (1993). ISBN: 1-85532- 349-4.

The Archaelology of Medieval London. Christopher, Thomas. Sutton Publishing Ltd. (2002). ISBN: 0-7509-2718-6.

The Beginning of English Society. Whitelock, Dorothy. Penguin Books. (1952).

Circle of Stones. Waldo, Anna Lee. St. Martin's Press. (1999). ISBN: 0-312-19843-4.

Encyclopedia of Medical Plants. First Published by Dorling Kindersley in Great Britain. (1996). ISBN: 0-7513-1209 – 6.

English and Norman Government and Lordship in the Welsh Borders, 1039-1087. Abstract of D. Phil. thesis submitted by Lewis, C. P. Merton College. Oxford 1985.

A History of God. The 4,000 Year Quest of Judaism, Christianity and Islam. Armstrong, Karen. Random House Inc. (1993). ISBN:) 0-345-38456.3

Lanfranc of Bec. Gibson, Margaret. Oxford University Press (1978). ISBN 0-19-822462-1.

Life in a Medieval Village. Geis, Frances and Joseph. Harper Collins, New York (1990) ISBN: 0 06 016215 5

London. Rutherford, Edward. The Ballantine Publishing Group. (1997). ISBN: 0-449-00263-2.

Longbow a Social and Military History. Hardy, Robert. Haynes Publishing, Great Britain, (1976). ISBN: 1-85260-412 3.

The Middle Sea. Norwich, John Julius. Chatto and Windus, Random House, London. (2006). ISBN: 0-7011-7608-3.

The Norman Conquest. Higham, N. J. Sutton Publishing Ltd. (1998). ISBN: 0-7509-1953-1.

Paradise. Eberhart, Dikkon. Stemmer House Inc. (1983). ISBN: 0-916144-52-6.

Saxon and Norman London. Clark, John. Board of Governors of the Museum of London. (1989). ISBN: 0-11-290458-0.

Spices. A History of a Temptation. Turner, Jack. Harper Collins, London (2005). ISBN 0.00 655173 . 4.

Timeline. Crichton, Michael. Ballantine Publishing (1999). ISBN: 0-345-4176-3

When Was Wales. Williams, Gwyn A. Penguin Books. (1985).

Vikings. Magnusson, Magnus. British Broadcasting Corp. (1980). ISBN: 0-370—30272-9.

1066. The Year of the Conquest. Howarth, David. Barnes and Noble Inc. (1993). ISBN: 0-88029-014-5.

1066. The Year of the Three Battles. McLynn, Frank. Pimlico Publishers (1999). ISBN: 0-7126-6672-9.

BIOGRAPHY

WHEN 9/11 STRUCK, John Wright was a retired newspaperman of 30 years experience with no wish to write a book. A week after the twin tower tragedy, he awoke with a novel in him. Thus The Healer.

Born in Owen Sound, Ontario, Canada, John has been writing all his adult life. A graduate of Ryerson's College journalism program, he has been a reporter, editor, columnist, magazine, travel and outdoor writer. He has won several provincial awards and one national Canadian writing award.

He finished his career as an outdoor writer with a focus on environmental issues.

An outdoorsman, hiker, camper, sailor and cruising skipper of his own 35-foot sailer, he has rolled many of those outdoor experiences into his journal writings. When the first tracings of the plot for The Healer began to excite his mind, he hiked and traveled through The March, the border country between Wales and England, and found rich medieval history in a Shrewsbury library in an account of Norman invasion and Welsh resistance. The Healer and another novel, Knight Haralde, were born.

Today, he lives with his wife Elaine on Canada's Bruce Peninsula on the shores of Lake Huron.

Made in the USA
Charleston, SC
13 January 2011